DRACO

BOOK TWO OF THE STARDUST SERIES

AUTUMN REED

JULIA CLARKE

BUSINESS MODE

MY STOMACH CHURNED as I followed Theo through down-town San Jose. As we neared the Zenith office, I persistently reminded myself that I was excited to have my first job. Yet I was a bundle of nerves, my heart pounding in anticipation. *Was this how students felt on the first day of school?* Home-schooled by my dad since the age of six, I really couldn't say.

Until a few weeks ago, my life in the Sierra Nevada mountains had been extremely isolated. And most of my time since arriving, *involuntarily*, at Knox and Theo's loft had been spent in Santa Cruz. Ahead of schedule for my first day, Theo grabbed a cappuccino before giving me a brief walking tour of downtown San Jose.

This was my first encounter with a large city, and I marveled at the movement, the scale, the noise. Tall build-ings in various designs created a unique skyline with the mountains as their backdrop. Cars and bikes zoomed by while I attempted to avoid the people, dressed mostly in business clothes, crowding the sidewalks. And I had thought the University of California: Santa Cruz was full of people and activity; it seemed small in comparison to downtown San Jose.

I had always known there was a wider world out there beyond my reach. But seeing it now, I was only beginning to grasp how large it actually was. While I craved the tranquility of nature, I felt invigorated by the rush of the city.

The sight of Theo in his slim gray slacks and button-down shirt, complete with a herringbone vest and skinny tie, made me smile. Despite the professional feel of the ensemble, his signature style still dominated. I felt myself relax ever so slightly, reassured by his presence and the knowledge that I already had friends at the office. More than friends, really, although I wasn't quite sure what to call them.

Liam, Knox, Ethan, Chase, Theo, and Jackson had been amazingly good to me, and even though their entrance into my life was abrupt, I was incredibly grateful for all six of them. In addition to providing me with food, clothes, and a place to stay, they constantly went out of their way to make my unique situation better, easier. The only thing missing was my dad.

It had been two weeks since my eighteenth birthday. Two weeks since our house was destroyed. Two weeks since my dad vanished, pursued by men somehow connected to the client that hired the guys to find my dad in the first place.

I had so many unanswered questions. But, for the moment, my only real option was to earn money so I could go to San Francisco and access the safe deposit box my dad had prepared in case of an emergency. Realizing that no amount of worrying about my dad's current whereabouts would help me with my new job, I forced myself to focus on the present.

Theo smiled at me as we approached a large, multi-storied glass building. The design of the building was sleek and modern while still retaining a traditional feel. Although Theo's smile was reassuring, the building was imposing and even a little intimidating.

He opened the enormous glass door for me, gesturing inside. "Welcome to Zenith."

Considering my obsession with astronomy, I figured it was a good sign that my new employer was named after an astronomical term. But when we walked past an official-looking security guard in the lobby, my uncertainty increased.

What are you doing, Haley? I didn't have any job experience or even a high school diploma, but I now had a job. While Jackson knew all of that, and it didn't seem to phase him, I still feared that someone at Zenith would unmask me as a fraud.

As Theo and I crossed the lobby, light streamed in through the enormous glass windows. Since it was later in the morning, the lobby was quiet apart from background music playing over the speakers and heels clicking randomly against the tile floor. With a few large sofas and pieces of art placed throughout, it almost felt more like a modern art gallery than an office building. At the row of elevators, signs indicated the names and locations of tenants —law firms, consulting businesses, and of course, Zenith.

Riding the elevator to the fourth floor, Theo faced me and gently held my hands in his own. "Don't worry, Haley; everyone will love you. And besides," his eyes quickly scanned me from head to toe, "you look fabulous." He grinned.

I smiled sheepishly. "Thanks to you."

After spending most of the weekend at Jackson's uncle's

house, I hadn't even had time to think about work clothes. Fortunately, Theo—ever prepared and always shopping— had planned ahead. He came to my room on Sunday with an array of work-appropriate clothes.

I didn't feel the part of a young working professional, but at least I looked it in my black slacks, white ruffled tank, and coral cardigan paired with matching accessories. I had even opted to wear my long, wavy hair clipped half up to look more sophisticated. Exiting the elevator on the fourth floor, I hoped it would be enough.

I took a deep breath as we walked toward the opaque door with "Zenith" etched upon it. Theo greeted the security guard by name before swiping a card to gain access. While he held the door open for me, I got my first glimpse of the Zenith office.

I was pleased to find that my fears of stained carpet in a strip mall were completely unfounded. Even with my limited knowledge of office buildings, I was impressed by the tall ceilings, seemingly endless glass windows, and sleek, modern furniture and art.

Theo quickly introduced me to the receptionist before leading me to one of the conference rooms with a large table surrounded by chairs. Theo assured me that Jackson would arrive any moment, but as I watched him walk away, any sense of calm I had evaporated.

Sitting back in the plush leather office chair, I attempted to relax. I fiddled with the strap on my purse and wished I had thought to bring a book. At least then I would have something to occupy my scattered thoughts while waiting for Jackson to show up. I'd only been in the conference room for six minutes, but seconds were ticking by like minutes.

A few people passed by, peering in at me curiously.

Only a wall of glass separated me from the hall, making me feel a bit like a bird in a cage. As unsettled as Jackson tended to make me, I mentally urged him to hurry up, because my nerves were out of control. *Get it together, Haley. You can do this.*

Just when I was about to hop out of my chair and start pacing, I saw the elevator doors slide open, and out stepped Jackson and Knox. As they strode toward me, I couldn't help but take note of their differences. They both walked with a sense of purpose, but Jackson's gait appeared effortlessly confident while Knox's reminded me more of a studied march. Jackson seemed at ease, smiling slightly while he spoke, but Knox looked intense as he frowned and ran a hand through his blond locks. I wondered what their conversation was about but knew better than to expect them to share.

Entering the room, Jackson placed a folder on the table and sat in the chair directly across from me. "Good morning, Haley. Welcome to Zenith." Not surprisingly, his tone was polite but professional. After Friday's playfulness, he was clearly back in business mode.

"Thank you. The office is lovely."

Knox sat down next to Jackson. "Don't get used to it. Your cubicle won't be this fancy," he said, eyeing the sleek furnishings.

Jackson rolled his eyes. "Ignore him. The cubicles are perfectly fine. I doubt you'll have any complaints."

I shook my head slightly, "I'm sure it will be great. And, thank you once again for getting me this job. I really do appreciate it."

"It was no problem. Would you like something to drink before we get started? This will probably take a while."

Jackson started to pour coffee into a mug displaying the

Zenith logo, but Knox interrupted. "Don't bother. Haley is superior to us lesser mortals; she doesn't drink coffee."

Jackson raised one eyebrow. "Oh, so you're one of those." He continued pouring, "I'll go ahead and give this to you then," he said, looking at Knox. "We all know you're a bear in the morning even after a couple cups of coffee."

Knox growled as he grabbed a glass of water and plopped it down in front of me. "Here you go. Now, let's get on with this. I don't want to be stuck in this stupid glass box all day."

I laughed. Clearly I wasn't the only one who found this room disconcerting.

Jackson straightened up and opened the folder. He quickly went over the contents, then had me sign several pages that he described as general employment paperwork. He had already filled in all of my information, and I noticed that a few details were made up; I wasn't surprised considering the circumstances.

When there was only one remaining document to go over, Jackson's demeanor became particularly solemn. Staring at his strikingly handsome face, I got lost in his deep blue eyes for a few moments before forcing myself to snap out of it.

"Out of everything we tell you today, this is by far the most important."

He paused, so I nodded my understanding.

"Above everything else, Zenith demands complete confidentiality from its employees. That means that anything you see, hear, or work on in any capacity stays inside this building. Furthermore, do not discuss any matters with other Zenith employees unless you are specifically assigned to work together on that particular matter."

He passed me the document, and I quickly glanced over it, slightly disturbed by all of the legal jargon. "This is a fairly standard non-disclosure agreement, but you should read it and let me know if you have any questions."

After reading through the document, I could sum it up in one sentence: Other than stating that I worked at Zenith, a private security company, everything else about my job was off limits. Considering how accustomed I was to keeping things to myself, I wasn't worried about following the rules. But, it did make me curious; why all the secrecy?

I signed the document and returned it to Jackson. He added it to his folder before leaning back and crossing his arms over his chest. "Now to the hard part of the confidentiality discussion."

"Okay . . ." *What does that mean?*

"I need to ensure that you understand that just because you're now working at Zenith doesn't mean you will be privy to information regarding my team's assignments. Since you spend so much time with the team outside of work, you will inevitably find out about certain details that you wouldn't otherwise. But, the guys all know and have been reminded that they are not to share information with you about their assignments unless previously approved. I know it sounds harsh, but it has nothing to do with you personally. This is just how we operate."

I let his words sink in. It took me a few moments; then I grasped what he was really saying. The guys always have and always would keep secrets from me. It was difficult to hear because I wanted them to trust me and accept me as one of their own. But, the truth was, I wasn't one of them. I wasn't a part of their team, and I wouldn't be treated as such no matter how close I got to them. The knowledge stung, but deep down I understood. They were professionals, and they wouldn't break the rules just for me.

Deciding I might as well pose the question while we were on topic, I asked, "I'm not disagreeing with anything you've said. But, why such an emphasis on secrecy? What exactly is it that you do?"

For the first time in a while, Knox jumped into the conversation. "Don't think about it as secrecy. It's really about protecting our clients' privacy. It doesn't matter if we're providing security for a diplomat, celebrity, or a sixteen-year-old with protective parents. Every client is treated equally; they are all entitled to privacy. And, our reputation for keeping things confidential is one of the reasons why Zenith is one of the most successful private security firms in the country."

Jackson smiled, "I couldn't have said it better myself. And to answer your question about what we do, it's really a matter of what *don't* we do. We work a lot of events—swanky parties, high-profile weddings, that sort of thing. Sometimes we work as traditional security guards for clients who are in town on a short-term basis. Really, any scenario where you can imagine private security, someone at Zenith has probably done it."

Celebrities? I had a sudden flash of the guys providing up close and personal security for Taylor Swift and her Victoria's Secret model best friend. Why would they have any interest in me when they were used to hanging out with celebrities? I mentally smacked my palm to my head. *Stop it, Haley. You're being ridiculous.*

Trying to lighten the mood a little, I said, "So what you're telling me is that your life is basically the real-life version of *The Bodyguard*? Hopefully without the getting shot part, though."

Knox chuckled while Jackson just shook his head and said, "It's typically not that exciting, but we do get to meet some really interesting people.

Now that we've gotten that discussion out of the way, we need to talk to you about your backstory. I'll let Knox take over since he and Theo were the ones to come up with it."

Knox sat up and playfully stretched his arms above his head like he was getting ready for a hardcore workout. His muscles bunched beneath his fitted Henley, and I had to force myself to look away when his shirt rode up enough to provide a glimpse of his taut stomach.

"Since I've learned from experience that deciding things for you doesn't go over so well, let me start off by saying that this is our suggested backstory for you. We can tweak it, if necessary." He paused as if waiting for my agreement.

"Okay."

"I hate that you have to deceive people about your background, but you really don't have a choice. You can't tell people where you came from or the real reason you're here. And, your tie to our team will undoubtedly be obvious since you will be arriving and leaving with us every day. We don't want to hide it, so we are going to work with it.

You probably won't be surprised to hear that out of all of us, Theo is the most popular. My brother somehow manages to meet people and make friends everywhere he goes. So our best solution is for you to say that you are friends with Theo, and he helped you get this job.

You want to be as vague as possible when answering questions, but try to have some answers figured out before you start meeting people. Say that you recently moved to the area, and if prodded, you can say that we are renting you a room at our place for now.

The biggest issue is where you grew up. We don't want to make it too far off the truth; have you ever been to Reno?"

I started at his sudden change in subject. "Yes, my dad has taken me a few times just for the day."

"Okay, good. My suggestion is that you say you're from the Reno area. It's a big enough city that you could easily stay anonymous. Again, be vague, but you should do some research on Reno in case someone forces a more detailed conversation. Stick to your home-schooling story if schools come up, because you don't want to chance someone looking you up in an old yearbook or something. What do you think?"

My stomach knotted. Thanks to my dad's instructions over the years, I was practiced at evading certain questions. He always said that the best way to avoid giving away too much was to provide a general response, and then turn the question around since most people would rather talk about themselves anyway. But, I had never been in a position where I had to actually lie about my life. I knew that I didn't have a choice, but the situation made me uneasy.

"I think that I am really uncomfortable having to lie to people about my background, but I know it's necessary. And I'm fine with the backstory."

Jackson replied, "Good. You should probably take notes about what you tell people to keep your story consistent."

"Agreed, but where should I put the notes? I can't exactly carry around a notebook and jot it down every time I say something new."

Jackson's lips tipped into a slight grin. "No, that's why we have these newfangled things called smart phones." He pulled a cell phone out of his pocket and slid it across the table to me. "Here you go."

I peered at it curiously, recognizing it as the newest version of the iPhone. Considering all I had ever used was an old-fashioned flip phone, it looked intimidatingly sleek and high-tech. "This is for me?"

"Yes, consider it a perk of the job. I have already created an ongoing shared calendar that I will update with your work schedule as well as the protection schedule. Your pass-code is currently 7591, but feel free to change it to whatever you like."

I cringed at his mention of protection, the term the guys used for what would better be described as "babysitting Haley." Picking up the deceptively light phone, I turned it over to inspect the slim case. It was midnight blue with a white and silver glitter stars pattern. In small gold letters at the bottom were the words "Kate Spade New York" with a tiny spade emblem. Confused, I looked back up to Jackson. *How did he know?*

Knox cleared his throat. "Theo picked out the case."

I smiled to myself. Theo always seemed to know exactly what I wanted even before I did.

Flipping the phone back over, I pressed on the circular button like I had seen the guys do with their own phones and punched in the code. Scrolling through the apps, I was instantly overwhelmed with all the new technology.

Jackson must have noticed my wide-eyed amazement. "Don't worry, it's very user friendly. You can ask any of the guys to help you figure it out. All of our contact information is already loaded, so you can get ahold of us by either phone or text. And you can use the Notes app to keep track of your background story. Any questions?"

Knowing I wouldn't be able to articulate an intelligent

question at that point, I replied, "Not right now. Thank you for the phone."

"You're welcome. I think we're done for now; Knox will show you to your desk and introduce you to Melissa who will be showing you around. Call or text if you need anything."

And with that, he was gone.

2

INTRODUCTIONS

Knox led me down a hallway on the fifth floor toward my assigned workspace. Anxious about meeting Melissa, I bit my lip, hoping my nervousness wasn't too obvious. After spending most of the morning with Jackson and Knox, I had almost forgotten that I would actually have to interact with other people today.

Knox slowed his pace and spoke to me in a hushed voice. "Don't forget; if you need anything, you can text or call us." I nodded, and he looked me directly in the eye. "Seriously, Haley. Anything."

We finally stopped at a cubicle, and Knox leaned his head in. "Hey, Melissa. I'd like to introduce our new temporary office assistant, Haley."

A bright voice, muffled behind the fabric walls of the cubicle, responded, "Sure!"

A petite blonde emerged and extended a slender hand to shake my own. Even in her ridiculously tall pumps, she was a few inches shorter than me and, I was guessing, a year or two older. Her beautiful golden hair grazed her collarbone, offsetting her pale blue-gray eyes and fair skin.

I had no clue what she was really like, but I was thankful she at least appeared friendly. And I couldn't help but admire her sense of style. Despite being a classic girl myself, I loved her look—a gray pencil skirt, patterned shirt and shoes, and chunky jewelry. Somehow she managed to pair it all together without it looking crazy.

After Knox walked off, Melissa smiled. "Why don't we start with a tour? Zenith covers three floors. You saw the fourth, which is mostly public space for client meetings. This floor is where most of the work gets done; clients never see this space."

Passing a row of cubicles and open workspaces, I could see what she meant. The fifth floor retained the modern design of its counterpart on four, but there was more movement, more workers buzzing about. Employees sat or stood at their desks, focused on their computer screens or talking on the phone. Phones rang, people chatted, and printers ran off copies, providing the usual soundtrack of office work.

Occasionally Melissa introduced me to employees or explained their role in the company, but mostly she made small talk about where to park or the best restaurants in the area for lunch. When she asked questions about my life—if I had lived in Santa Cruz long and if I was a student at UCSC—I kept my answers short. Fortunately, just as my dad had always advised, all I really needed to do was ask open-ended questions. Melissa was more than willing to do most of the talking.

As we walked around the fifth floor, Melissa pointed out various offices, break rooms, and storage. Everything seemed extremely well-ordered and organized. She explained that the large offices lining the perimeter were shared by each team of five to ten members; name plates by each door listed "Team Falcon" and "Team Jaguar," among others. Most of the doors were closed, but since the walls and doors were made of opaque glass, the entire floor was bathed in natural light.

Melissa was likeable with her easy friendliness and bubbly nature. I learned that she was from the area and lived with roommates at a house they rented just outside San Jose. She was expressive and inquisitive, and apart from her slightly annoying habit of overusing the word "like," I thought we were going to get along well.

In the elevator to the sixth floor, Melissa tilted her head and grinned mischievously. "So, Haley," she said, inspecting my right hand. "Did your boyfriend give you that amazing ring?" Her voice was playful, but I knew she expected an answer.

"Um, no. I don't have a boyfriend." Unsure what more to say, I just hoped that she didn't ask anything else about my ring or my single status. My complete lack of dating experience was unusual for a girl my age. I definitely didn't want to admit that I had never had a boyfriend and was still waiting for my first kiss.

Her face lit up. "Good, me neither. You should come clubbing with me and my girlfriends. You'd love it!"

I highly doubted the club scene would ever be for me, but it was nice to be invited. Fortunately, the elevator opened to the sixth floor, saving me from responding with more than a polite smile. Even if I wanted to, the guys wouldn't let me go clubbing without them. I was sure Theo would take me if I asked, but how would I possibly explain his presence? It's not like I could tell Melissa that I had to bring a non-date along because I was under constant surveillance.

The sixth floor had a similar layout to the fifth. Melissa explained that this floor was for higher-level employees and executives, such as the co-founder and San Jose Regional Director, Patrick Ross. And while most teams had an office on the fifth floor, a few of the more experienced teams were granted the privilege of an office on the sixth floor.

Finally arriving back at my cubicle, I sunk into the chair, feeling overwhelmed. Zenith had a lot more employees than I expected, and I had only met a handful of them. And the overall atmosphere was very businesslike and rather serious. Without Melissa's effervescent personality to distract me on the tour, I would have been completely intimidated by my surroundings.

I heard a buzzing noise like something was vibrating on my desk. Puzzled momentarily, it dawned on me that perhaps it was my new phone. I pulled it out of my purse and looked at the screen, inserting the passcode before I noticed a new message.

Theo: Hi, Supergirl! Hope you're having a great first day of work.

Smiling at his newest nickname for me, I debated how to respond. Maybe if I convinced Theo that everything was great, I could convince myself of the same.

Me: Thanks, Robin! So far, so good.

I hoped Theo wouldn't read too much into being the sidekick to Knox's Batman.

* * *

It was my third day at work this week, and I was getting into a comfortable groove. Between my new job and a fairly regular schedule at the loft, I was relieved to be settling into to my temporary life in Santa Cruz. After so many years spent mostly alone, I was surprised how smoothly things were going; I actually felt like I was fitting in.

Melissa had me working on older files, scanning them into the system and organizing the electronic copies. The work was mostly mindless and highly confidential. Technically, I wasn't supposed to read the documents apart from the client name and date for labeling purposes, but sometimes I just couldn't help myself. I needed to know more about Zenith and what they really did, and I needed to stay awake.

So far, everything seemed pretty above board. Most of the assignments were private security for corporate functions and wealthy clients I had never heard of. I kept hoping to find something juicy. Was it too much to ask for a wedding that got out of hand with guests escorted from the premises?

An alert popped up on my computer, reminding me to set up a conference room for an upcoming meeting. Melissa walked me through the process the day before, but this would be my first time to do so on my own. Thankfully it wasn't a difficult task, mainly following a checklist of requirements for that particular meeting.

After I finished setting out refreshments and making sure the digital projector was working properly, I looked over my checklist to make sure I completed all the tasks. Satisfied that everything was ready, I started toward the door just as a small group of people entered.

In the lead was an attractive man wearing a well-cut gray suit, pale blue collared shirt, and matching tie. His silver hair contrasted nicely with his tanned skin. And while he had the look of a distinguished gentleman, his skin was still smooth and mostly wrinkle free. He was definitely older than my dad but not by too many years.

He excused himself from the group and walked straight to me, holding out his hand. "Haley, it's nice to meet you.

I've heard so much about you." His face was kind and his bright blue eyes sincere.

Confused, I shook his hand and stared at him in surprise. He continued, "I'm Patrick Ross, the San Jose Regional Director. How have your first few days of work been?"

Patrick Ross knows who I am? I tried not to panic, wondering how much the guys had told him about me.

I finally snapped out of it and responded. "It's a pleasure to meet you, Mr. Ross. And the first few days have gone really well, thank you."

He smiled, surprising me with his apparent friendliness. "Good. I will let you get back to work. I'm sure we'll be seeing a lot more of each other."

I walked back to my desk, pondering the encounter with Mr. Ross. Considering how many employees were under his supervision, I wouldn't expect him to even know my name. I was only a temporary office assistant after all. When he said that we would see more of each other, did he just mean around the office?

Knowing my questions wouldn't be answered until I talked to one of the guys, I sat down at my desk and got back to work.

It was late afternoon, and I was making good progress on my stack of files when Ethan appeared in the entry to my cubicle. Surprised by his sudden arrival, I almost dropped the papers I was holding. The corner of his lip twisted up slightly, showing off his trademark smirk.

"How's it going, Haley?"

I placed the files on the desk and stood up, smoothing my pants. "Pretty good. Everyone's been very nice and the work is easy enough."

"Glad to hear it." He paused. "Maybe we can grab lunch next week?"

My heart leapt at the idea. "I'd like that."

Remembering my interaction with Mr. Ross, I said, "I met Patrick Ross earlier."

Ethan laughed, "Oh yeah? You know he's Jackson's uncle, right?"

"What?" The shock in my voice was obvious. "How could you guys not tell me that? I didn't even know he worked here!"

Ethan just shook his head, "I guess it never came up. Well, I better get back to work, but I'll see you later." He winked before walking off.

Less than a minute after Ethan left, Melissa popped her head in my cubicle, interrupting the tirade I was mentally screaming at each of the guys. Her eyes were wide as she whispered loudly. "You know Ethan?"

Startled by her urgent question, I nodded, unsure why it was a big deal. She entered my cubicle and sat on the empty file cabinet; I swung in my chair to face her.

She sat with her legs crossed and her finger on her chin. "Haley, I need details!"

My confusion must have been evident because she continued talking. "Unlike some of the other teams, Team Jaguar, Jackson's team, is totally antisocial. The guys are polite, but none of them will hang out with any of us outside the office. Or even inside the office, really. They're like seriously mysterious."

She uncrossed her legs and placed both palms on the file cabinet as she leaned forward, lowering her voice. "And don't think every girl in this office hasn't tried. They. Are. So. Hot."

Melissa paused, the wheels turning. "When Knox first

brought you over, I didn't think much of it. But now, Ethan stops by." Her voice was getting excited and slightly high-pitched despite the whisper.

I sat silently, shrugging my shoulders.

"Come on, Haley. Spill!"

As much as I liked Melissa, I knew I couldn't tell her the truth. Instead, I put my acting skills to the test, reciting the brief story I had rehearsed with Jackson and Knox. I kept it as short as possible, hoping she would buy my explanation. After I finished, I tried to gauge Melissa's reaction, surprised when she seemed excited for some reason.

She leaned in, her demeanor serious for once. "Haley, I have a confession to make."

I raised an eyebrow. "Okay."

"I have a huge crush on Chase." Her pale skin flushed slightly pink. "This may surprise you, but I'm really into the silent, studious type. And that dimple, OMG."

I instantly felt a twinge of jealousy at the thought of Chase with Melissa. Not that I had any right to. We were just friends; he was free to date anyone he wanted. And who wouldn't be attracted to Chase—or any of the guys, really—myself included. Distracted by these thoughts, Melissa's next statement caught me off guard.

Her voice pleading, "Haley, you have to set me up with Chase. Please, please help me!"

In that moment, I wanted to disappear. This whole making new friends thing was harder than it looked. *What am I supposed to say?*

3

HOT & COLD

My FEET FELT light as I walked through the lobby; I was looking forward to a relaxing, low-key evening with Chase and his favorite board games. It had been a few days since Melissa revealed her secret crush to me, and I pushed it to the back of my mind. I'd bring it up with him at some point but not tonight.

Rounding the corner, I was surprised to see Liam leaning against a large column, his arms crossed nonchalantly as he watched people coming and going. He looked as polished and professional as ever in his gray pinstripe three-piece suit, textured lavender shirt, and patterned tie with coordinating pocket square. I raised an eyebrow; I was almost positive that the calendar on my phone indicated Chase was my companion for the evening.

"Good afternoon, Haley. Due to a last-minute change of schedule, you will have the pleasure of my company this evening." He grinned, clearly pleased by the idea.

I tried to hide my hesitation. "Is Chase okay?"

Liam's smile was dazzling, but somehow it always made me feel like I was walking into a trap. "Chase is fine, he just got caught up with work. And *we* finally get an evening alone."

Alone. Alone with Liam. Alone with Liam all evening. I gulped and tried not to panic. Telling Chase about Melissa's crush seemed almost relaxing in comparison.

Liam held out a hand for my tote bag and said, "Allow me," before placing his other palm on the small of my back as he guided me through the lobby. Entering the parking garage, a car beeped and the lights flashed on a cobalt two-door sports car. Elegant, yet powerful, Liam's car made a statement.

I whistled, admiring the Audi's sleek lines. "So this is how you get all the girls. Now I see why."

Feigning offense, Liam gasped, "Don't listen to a word Knox says; the ladies flock to me because of my devastating good looks and charm." He smiled then, his white teeth gleaming. "The car is just a bonus."

I laughed, once again torn between amusement and annoyance at Liam's considerable ego. And yet, I couldn't necessarily fault his confidence. He had a natural charisma that, combined with his dashing good looks and sexy accent, likely attracted most females he came into contact with. I imagined any one of them would be envious of me getting to spend the evening alone with him.

But, I wasn't most girls; I was truly dreading the next few hours. It's not that I disliked Liam, but I didn't know him very well. And he made me uncomfortable. Really, really uncomfortable.

I slid into the leather seat before Liam closed the door and walked around to the driver's side. Smoothing my skirt, I glanced down at my outfit—a navy dress with a camel-colored pattern, camel blazer, and skinny belt and flats. I'd been pleased with how the outfit came together, reflecting a dressier version of my classic style, but somehow I always felt underdressed compared to Liam.

Liam pressed a button and the car fired up without him ever inserting a key into the ignition. The black leather interior and dashboard were minimalist and sleek; everything was digital or touchscreen. As we drove out of the parking garage and onto the street, I felt like I was hovering just above the ground.

"Seriously. This car is incredible, and it's even my favorite color. I think it may be a sign that you should let me drive it sometime," I teased.

Stopped at a red light, Liam turned to face me. His eyes swept my face and body in a way that I was quickly coming to expect from him.

With a mischievous smile, he said, "How about this. You wear a bikini the next time we go swimming, and I'll let you drive my car."

My mouth dropped open in shock, and I felt heat instantly flood my face. "Did you really just say that? That is so insulting!"

Liam breezily turned back to face the road and laughed. "What? Is it so wrong to appreciate a beautiful girl?"

When I continued to silently glare at him, he sighed. "Do you even know how to drive? I must be off my trolley to even consider saying yes."

"Wait, what? Off your trolley?" Distracted by what I assumed was ridiculous British slang, I was able to ignore my anger for the moment.

"Yes, off my trolley. You know, crazy."

"Well, I would have to be off *my* trolley to agree to your proposition." Crossing my arms over my chest, I said, "I didn't want to drive your car anyway." Frustrated by my own childishness, I leaned back against the headrest and focused on the passing palm trees. Why did I let him get to me?

"Haley, don't be mad. I was just playing with you." Liam's voice sounded sincere, and my frostiness started to melt just a little. But, before I could respond, he continued. "Of course, you would look bloody fantastic in a bikini." *And we're back to winter.*

In less than ten minutes we were pulling into another parking garage. We took the elevator to the twentieth floor— the top floor of the building—where Liam swiped a keycard. The elevator opened, revealing a small carpeted foyer leading to several sets of dark gray, almost black, double doors. After swiping the card for another scanner and inputting a code at condo "2020," he held one of the doors open. *These guys are really into their security systems.*

Stepping over the threshold, I almost gasped. The entry quickly opened into a large living room with soaring ceilings and windows that stretched for two stories. The view was stunning, the city just beginning to light up as the sun set behind the distant mountains.

I followed Liam toward the kitchen where he tossed his keys on the counter while loosening his tie. "Make yourself at home." *Ha, right.*

I tried not to gape at my surroundings; simple met opulent in a play of light and dark in furnishings, fabrics, materials, and lighting. Thanks to the layering of textures and different metals, it somehow managed to feel modern without being cold. I imagined it was all incredibly expensive and hesitated to touch anything.

"Wow, this apartment is quite posh," I said, adding a slight British accent on "posh."

Where did he get the money for this place? I didn't know anything about the San Jose real estate market, but this apartment was nothing less than impressive. Between the loft, Jackson's uncle's (who I now knew was also my boss, Patrick Ross) estate, and now Liam's apartment, I was starting to think that private security generated way more income than I ever expected.

Liam smoothed a lock of his dark brown hair, ensuring it was perfectly placed, and grinned. "It's not bad, huh? Just wait until you see the pool!"

Great . . . a pool. If he mentions the word bikini one more time, I might scream.

Liam led me up a flight of stairs before we emerged on the roof. At first I only saw wood decking and potted plants, but as we continued walking, the swimming pool came into view. It covered a large portion of the roof and stretched to the very edge of the building. Lounge chairs lined part of the patio, and lights beneath the water illuminated the rectangular pool, casting an inviting glow on the outdoor space.

I grinned, delighted by the unusual rooftop retreat. "This is amazing."

"You're welcome to use it any time you wish. It's mostly private and usually quiet since only the penthouse owners have access."

I stood gazing at the skyline and the illuminated pool before glancing up toward the sky. I had hoped to see stars, but with all the light pollution it was practically impossible. Feeling hungry, I looked toward the door. Following my line of vision, Liam headed that direction.

He spoke in a playful tone as he held open the door to the stairs. "Let's make dinner; I promise to behave." I wasn't sure he could even if he tried. He must have seen my raised eyebrows, doubting his ability to do so.

"Brilliant. I'm not that much of a wanker, am I?

I shrugged my shoulders and smiled, allowing him to imply my answer before snickering.

Back in the kitchen, Liam had kicked off his shoes and was tying a white apron around his waist. "Are you sure you wouldn't like an apron?"

I shook my head. "I'm fine, thanks."

He smiled. "Well at least remove your blazer and shoes." He paused. "Come on, I dare you."

After taking off my shoes and blazer, I faced him across the large marble island. He tapped at his phone briefly before music started playing through the space. The music was unusual, sung mostly in Portuguese, with a relaxing beat. Some of the songs had a slightly seductive rhythm, but mostly, they struck a nice balance between soothing and stimulating.

Liam's home was inviting, as was his manner, but I felt out of my depth. I hoped my discomfort wasn't completely obvious.

"What kind of food do you prefer, Haley?"

Trying to drum up a little enthusiasm, I replied, "Whatever you're preparing!" Considering he was kind enough to cook for me, I wasn't going to be picky.

He rolled his eyes dramatically. "How disappointing. I didn't take you for one of *those* girls who says whatever she thinks the other person wants to hear."

I could feel myself getting agitated, and I sighed heavily. "I'm not, Mr. Snap Judgment. I'm just not very particular, but Italian is my favorite."

Liam stood, wheels turning momentarily and then sprung into action. I caught a glimpse of his fridge and pantry as he grabbed supplies from each; both were extremely well organized, complete with glass containers and labels.

He pulled the cork out of a bottle of white wine. "Good. I hope you like chicken piccata with sautéed vegetables and linguine."

I twirled my hair. "That sounds delicious and complicated. Really, you don't have to go to any trouble for me."

"No trouble at all. Especially with such a lovely and feisty sous-chef."

He busied himself, washing zucchini and extracting pans from the cabinets. His beautiful cookware was in pristine condition. If I hadn't witnessed him use it, I probably wouldn't have believed he actually did. After melting a little butter, he added garlic to the pan, and my stomach growled.

Water boiled, the skillet sizzled, and music played softly in the background. Liam cooked without a recipe, moving gracefully through the kitchen, the large marble island between us and the gas stove at his back. Seeing Liam so relaxed in the kitchen made me start to question my assumptions about him. Maybe there was more to him than flirting, stylish suits, and an exotic car. I hated to admit it, but he was kind of adorable like this.

Sitting at a bar stool chopping zucchini, I felt myself relax slightly in his presence.

I shouldn't have said it, but I couldn't resist. "So, do you cook for all of your lady friends?"

His gray eyes twinkled with amusement. "Well, I wouldn't say *all* of them. Why, are you jealous?"

I rolled my eyes and turned back to chopping vegetables.

Liam walked over to me and took the knife out of my hand, setting it on the counter. Standing close enough to get a whiff of his cologne, he said, "Look, Haley. I'm starting to think we got off on the wrong foot." He twirled his ring a few times before continuing. "Yes, I date. And yes, that sometimes allows me to show off my skills in the kitchen. But it's not like I'm making breakfast for a new girl every morning."

Tongue-tied, I gaped at him in silence. *Why is he telling me this? Does he actually think I'm jealous?*

After a few moments, Liam returned to his task and I went back to chopping. Hoping to change the subject to something much safer, I asked, "Where did you learn to cook?"

He smiled. "Ina Garten."

"The Barefoot Contessa? I watch her on PBS, but I don't cook like a professional chef."

He laughed, the sound full and easy. "I have taken a few classes, but I'm by no means a professional. Most of what I know is from trial and error."

"Do you cook many traditional English foods?"

He pursed his lips. "Have you had many English foods?"

I shook my head. *Does he not realize I practically lived under a rock until a few weeks ago?*

"Apart from fish and chips, most *English* food is bloody awful."

With dinner ready, I grabbed our drinks and followed Liam to the table. He set down the plates before pulling out a chair for me. I was half surprised he didn't light candles as well. I admired the perfectly arranged meal; golden-brown chicken rested atop a stack of steaming linguine with vegetables scattered around the plate.

I took my first bite of chicken piccata and almost sighed aloud from the pleasure of it; lemon, garlic, and buttery flavors mixed together. Distracted by the delicious meal, I let my guard down ever so slightly. Maybe Liam and I did have the ability to coexist in relative peace, especially if the situation involved food.

"Okay, Haley, I think it's time we got to know each other better. I'll ask you a question and then you can ask me one."

Relative peace, ha. I clenched my fork, nervous about what type of questions Liam would ask. But, he didn't give me a chance to disagree and started in.

"I'll begin with an easy one. What's your favorite food?"

"Chicken parmigiana."

"Good. Now your turn."

"How long have you lived in the U.S.?"

"Since I was 14."

"Why did you—"

Liam cut me off with a tsk. "You have to save it for your next question. My turn. Will you let me teach you how to play tennis?"

"How do you know I don't already play?"

He chuckled, "Call it a hunch."

"Fine. I don't, but I would like to learn. So, yes. Why did you move to the U.S. when you were 14?"

"I came here to live with Uncle and Jax after my parents died."

My stomach immediately dropped. I couldn't imagine how awful it must have been to lose his parents and then move halfway around the world. It also explained why Jackson and Liam seemed more like brothers; they practically were.

"What is the craziest thing you've ever done?"

With a straight face, I responded, "I had dinner with a wealthy, quasi-British, gray-eyed playboy."

He grinned. "Oh, so you noticed my eyes, huh? I knew there must be something you liked about me."

I just laughed in response. *Is it possible that I am starting to find his charming flirtation endearing?*

"Why move here to live with Patrick and Jackson? Are you related?"

"No, but Uncle was very close to my dad and he accepted custody of me. Jax was already living with him by that point, so we became a not-so-big happy family. Although, the happy part took a while. Jax wasn't a big fan of me at first, something you two seem to have in common."

My cheeks heated. "What? I—"

Liam cut me off again. "Haley, don't bother trying to hide it. I know that you're not my biggest fan right now. But I'm persistent, and I *will* change your mind about me. I promise."

I trembled slightly at his certainty. The prudent part of me hoped he was wrong; I was likely better off keeping him at a distance. Liam was the kind of guy who saw too much, pushed too far. And I wasn't sure how long my defenses would stand up against his charming assaults.

4

PROGRESS

"I HAD a feeling I'd find you out here."

I started at the sound of Knox's gravelly voice. Closing my sketchbook, I turned to face him, dusk setting in.

"What can I say? As much as I love the loft, I miss being surrounded by nature. But this little patio garden reminds me of home; it's peaceful out here."

Surrounded by the brick walls of neighboring buildings, the garden felt like an oasis, a retreat. Small and intimate, the plants were carefully chosen for maximum impact—a mix of native trees, shrubs, and flowers. In the evening, subtle outdoor lighting made the place even more magical, and the smell of jasmine perfumed the air.

He sat down in the chair next to me. "I know what you mean. When Theo suggested it, I'm sure I scoffed a bit. But I have to admit that even I escape out here now and then." He held a finger in front of his lips, "Don't tell Theo I said so."

Laughing softly, I said, "No promises. I have to keep something to use against you."

"Oh yeah?" I found myself staring as Knox ran his

fingers through his hair. Not for the first time, I wondered what it would feel like to replace his fingers with my own. Were the strands as soft and silky as they appeared?

"Haley?"

I snapped my attention from my mini daydream back to Knox. "Yes?"

He studied me, a bemused expression on his face. "Never mind. Actually, the reason I came out here was to give you this." He handed me an envelope with the Zenith logo on the front.

I opened the envelope, surprised to find it filled with dollar bills in denominations of twenty and fifty.

"That is for your first week of work. We decided it would be best to pay you in cash for now since you're trying to stay off the radar. You can open a bank account later on, if you want."

Flipping through the bills, I pulled out several and held them out to Knox. "Here, consider this my first payment for the clothes and everything else you've bought me."

He folded his arms, refusing the money. "No way, Haley. I want you to save every penny of what you earn. I don't need your money; neither does Theo or any of the other guys. So don't even think of offering it to anyone else. Consider every purchase a gift, okay?"

Standing up, I paced a few steps before turning back to Knox. "No, not okay. I'm not your responsibility; I want to contribute."

Knox just sighed. "You do contribute. You help with the cooking and the dishes, and you pick up around the house. And you even keep Theo entertained. That's worth more than a little money spent, trust me."

I didn't agree, but I knew how stubborn Knox could be, and I wasn't going to win this argument tonight. "Ugh, fine.

But this conversation isn't over. I'll find a way to repay you eventually."

"Sure," he said, noncommittally. Standing up, he continued. "Now let me show you how to use the safe in your closet so you have some place to stash your cash."

Leading the way to my room, Knox stopped suddenly and pulled his wallet out of his back pocket. "Oh, yeah, I almost forgot. Here's the fake ID Jax made for you. Hopefully you won't need it, but we didn't want you walking around without some type of identification."

"Thanks." The ID looked remarkably professional. I posed for the picture over a week ago and hadn't really given it any thought since. But now, seeing my name and photo on an official-looking California driver's license, I felt relieved and yet, uneasy. I didn't even want to know how Jackson pulled this off.

After Knox taught me how to use the safe, he left to work in the garage. I placed the money in the safe and then reset the passcode, repeating it several times in my head to make sure I would remember it.

It was strange to think of the almost five hundred dollars sitting in the safe. I'd never had access to that much money at one time before. Of course, it helped that my job paid so well. I knew from browsing Help Wanted ads that either Zenith paid all their part-time administrative employees exceptionally well, or the guys made sure that my hourly rate was well-above average. Either way, I was grateful. After calculating the amount of money it would take to travel to San Francisco and live on my own for a while, I knew that every dollar counted. At this rate, I might be able to make the trip sooner than I expected.

That thought gave me a glimmer of comfort. In the back of my mind, I'd kept expecting Dad to show up with a smile on his face, assuring me that the last few weeks were just a simple misunderstanding. But the longer I went without contact, the more certain I was that the safe deposit box in San Francisco was my last remaining tie to him.

I felt like I was living my own personal catch-22. I had to stay off the grid in case someone other than my dad was looking for me. But staying hidden made it unlikely that even Dad would be able to track me down.

Knowing I didn't have any control over the situation with my dad at that moment, I transitioned to something that I could control. I needed to reach out to Jessica before she went crazy with worry. I didn't know what her mom had been told, but if nothing else, Jessica knew about the house fire and the disappearance of both me and Dad.

Thankful for the laptop that Theo loaned me, I created a new e-mail account and sent her a short message.

HEY JESS,

I'm sure you're worried about me. I can't tell you where I am right now, but I'm safe. I promise. Please don't tell anyone (even your mom) that you heard from me. I'll explain more later.

Love you and miss you,

Your Elena to my Caroline

P.S. I've quite possibly met the most attractive guys ever (they even rival the Salvatore brothers). You should be jealous.

AFTER HITTING SEND, I lay back on the bed. An overwhelming feeling of guilt and relief hit me at the same time. Guilt because I should have contacted Jessica at my first opportunity. Relief because just sending a message to someone from my old life felt like a tangible connection to that part of me. For once, it felt like the fact that I couldn't reach out and touch anything from the last eighteen years of my life didn't negate its existence.

I hoped that my references to *The Vampire Diaries*—Jessica's favorite show—would at least relieve some of Jessica's worry. Things couldn't be that bad if I took the time to mention the Salvatores. *Right?*

I heard a ding from the direction of my phone, diverting my attention.

Chase: Sorry to bail on you last night. Hope you had a nice dinner with Liam.

Me: Thanks! I'm still waiting for that Carcassonne rematch.

I smiled at the thought of the latest board game Chase had introduced me to.

Me: See you soon?

Chase: Hopefully this weekend. Have a good night.

Me: Thanks. You too.

I put my phone on vibrate and started getting ready for bed. Even though I had been receiving random texts from some of the guys for the past week and a half, it still felt strange. I was used to having one friend and talking to her face-to-face or through e-mail. One of these days, I might actually initiate a conversation by text, but I was still too insecure to do so. I didn't want to bother any of the guys with a text if it wasn't an emergency.

I climbed into bed and relished the feel of the soft sheets against my skin. As I stretched out, I was surprised by how tired I felt. Drifting off to sleep, the world became fuzzy in that gray area between waking and dreaming.

Jessica? What was she doing with Knox? And why was Chase playing Monopoly with the Salvatore brothers?

* * *

WORK the next day was dragging. I'd been stuck at my desk all morning, and I was practically falling asleep in my chair. So when Melissa popped her head into my cubicle, I sighed in relief. Even though she tended to talk my ear off, I was thankful for the distraction.

"Did you hear that Team Falcon got a new member?" Her excitement at sharing office gossip was obvious, her voice practically straining with glee. "It's all the buzz because Kara is their first female member, and everyone assumed they'd stay an all-male team; lucky girl. Falcon has the hottest guys after Team Jaguar, of course."

The information took me by surprise. I had noticed that most of the teams appeared to be just one gender or the other. "Is it strange for a female to join a male team?"

Melissa moved closer and leaned against my desk. "Well, not strange exactly. It's just that most teams stay either male or female. It's easier that way, less drama."

Knowing this was the perfect time to question Melissa more about the inner-workings at Zenith, I asked, "So how does the whole team system work exactly?"

"Well, I don't have the whole system memorized, and it's kind of complicated. But basically, teams can be created once at least three individuals get together and receive approval from the higher-ups to form a team. A team can be anywhere from three to ten people, but most of them stop at five to six members."

"So Zenith lets its employees control who joins what team? Why don't the directors just assign the teams?"

"I thought the same thing when I first started, but it makes sense once you observe how the teams really mesh together. Zenith likes to foster camaraderie among the team members. And from what I know, the directors believe that Zenith's team system sets it apart from similar private security companies. Plus, there's the whole youth development program."

"The what?"

Melissa looked surprised by my question. "You didn't know about that? It's totally cool. You should ask Theo to tell you about it. He knows way more since he and the rest of his team are all former participants."

I was interested and also a little annoyed by what Melissa told me. Sometimes it felt like I was pulling teeth to get personal information from the guys. Clearly the youth program was something they should have mentioned by now if Melissa assumed I knew all about it.

My phone buzzed quietly on my desk, alerting both me and Melissa of an incoming text message.

"Oooh, a text. Go ahead and check it, I don't mind."

Knowing I didn't have a good excuse not to, I punched in my code and checked the message, holding the phone out of Melissa's view.

Theo: In the 1600s, French noblemen used carousels to train for equestrian tournaments.

Me: Thanks for sharing?

Theo: You're welcome for sharing. No equestrian tournaments (for now), but we're going to the Boardwalk on Saturday, and I'm making you ride the carousel with me.

The Boardwalk? I'd heard it mentioned in passing, but I didn't know much about the small Santa Cruz amusement park. And who did Theo mean by "we"? Just the two of us? Or were more of the guys joining us?

Me: Sounds like fun.

I put the phone in my purse and turned back to Melissa. She tapped her foot impatiently, an expectant expression on her face. "So? Who was it? Was it a boy? Come on, Haley. Don't hold back."

I laughed at her barrage of questions. "It was just Theo checking in."

"Theo, huh?" Melissa's smile grew, her white teeth shining. "Just how close are you two?"

Suddenly feeling nervous, I laughed again. "Oh, we're just friends. He's really fun to hang out with."

"And he's totally hot with that retro meets tattoos meets seriously well-dressed vibe. I think you two would be adorable together. And then you and Theo could double date with me and Chase. If he ever notices my existence, that is."

Oh no. Please don't ask me again to set you up with Chase.

Melissa's office phone rang, saving me from further conversation about Theo and Chase. *Whew.*

"I need to get that. I have a copy job for you to do; I'll e-mail the details."

Relieved to escape from my cubicle and Melissa's nosiness, I immediately headed toward the copy room, knowing I could check the assignment on my phone. As I passed multiple offices occupied by teams, I couldn't help but wonder more about them. Melissa's explanation of team formation gave me a little insight, but I still had so many questions.

While at the cabin, Knox told me that he, Ethan, and Chase worked in private security and did private investigation on the side. Was private investigation part of their job at Zenith? And if so, did other teams work on similar assignments?

I'd read everything I could get my hands on about Zenith's mission, and nothing indicated that the company was involved in investigation as well as security. But why else would the team have been hired to track down my dad? There's no way that assignment could be qualified as private security. I knew I was missing information essential to piecing it all together. If all else failed, I could ask one of the guys. But I would rather discover the answers on my own; they didn't need to know how curious I really was.

Glancing at my phone, I started to open my work email when I saw that there were two new messages. I checked my personal account first, hoping to see a response from Jessica.

My Elena,

It's about time you got in touch! I was starting to think that you'd eloped to Vegas with a handsome stranger. But maybe you have . . . with one of the most attractive guys ever? I have to know more! The idea of you having a more exciting love life than me is altering my entire worldview.

Miss you too and I better hear from you again soon!

Your Caroline

Preoccupied with my thoughts and reading the assignment on my phone, I didn't watch where I was going. I almost collided head on with a girl a few inches taller than me with long blonde hair and impeccable makeup. She wore a tight patterned dress that was low cut and some of the tallest shoes I had ever seen. *How does she walk?*

"Excuse you. Watch where you're going!" Her voice was snotty, and I was immediately taken aback by her attitude.

"I'm so sorry."

"Who are *you*?"

"Haley."

"Well, Haley, obviously you're new around here, so I'll let you off with just a warning this time. Stay out of my way."

With that, she walked off, her heels clicking loudly on the floor. Although not every person I'd come in contact with at Zenith had been overly friendly, this was the first time someone was rude. *Did I just meet my first mean girl?*

5

STARRY NIGHT

I GLANCED OVER AT ETHAN, my heart beating a little faster at the sight of him. This would be my first time alone with him in weeks, and I felt like one of those glass globes that had been shaken, the snow fluttering throughout. My nervous excitement was to be expected; despite all that we had shared, there was still so much I didn't know about him.

"So what's the plan for tonight?"

Sitting behind the wheel of his white A6, Ethan focused on the road, cool and confident as we drove away from the Zenith office. Upbeat music played softly on the radio, interrupted only occasionally by commercials. I admired his business attire—khaki chinos, a blue and burnt-red gingham shirt in a large pattern, a brown belt and shoes, and of course, his trademark glasses. His chestnut hair was tousled as usual, and the light coming through the sunroof highlighted flecks of gold and auburn that I hadn't noticed before.

"Dinner and stargazing. You like Mexican food, right?"

I could hardly contain my excitement and grinned widely. "Sounds perfect!"

After we arrived at the restaurant, the hostess led us through the building past couples, students out for a nice meal, and professionals catching a drink at happy hour. It was Thursday, and I could almost sense the excitement and anticipation for the impending weekend. Wearing a dark gray chambray dress, coral cardigan, and flats, I was glad that my outfit transitioned nicely between work and play.

We were seated at one of a number of identical metal tables on the back patio. The small, round table barely accommodated our silverware and drinks, and it was nearly impossible to keep our legs from touching. Surrounded by brick walls, hanging plants lined the stair railing and upstairs balcony. From within the courtyard, the cloudless blue sky was awash with pastel colors.

"Two meals together in one week; I better back off before you try to run again." Ethan smirked.

I rolled my eyes playfully. Earlier in the week, Ethan, Theo, and I grabbed a quick lunch near the office. The last time Ethan and I had eaten this many meals together was at the cabin in the woods when I first met him.

"Don't worry, since I rarely see you at work, it shouldn't be an issue." I flipped the menu over. "You know, I've been wondering; how exactly does being a paramedic fit in with your private security job at Zenith?"

Ethan pushed up his glasses. "I'm the designated team medic, but really, it's more of a side interest. Sure, it helps me with my role sometimes, and the company definitely sees it as an asset, but mainly I'm just another security guard for events."

I nodded while Ethan sipped his drink. The tables around us were filling in, and I was grateful for our little table tucked away from the more crowded sections of the restaurant.

"Actually I need to log some hours. With how crazy things have been lately, I'm getting behind on my annual requirements." The guys always seemed busy, and I wondered if they ever truly took a break from work.

"What does that entail?"

I felt his leg brush against mine before resting there. *Is he purposely touching me or is it just easier than running the risk of kicking me again? Or does he not even realize he's doing it and thinks my leg is the table? Should I move?* I sincerely hoped my face didn't betray everything running through my mind.

"Basically volunteer for shifts riding on an ambulance and prove that I'm still competent to properly treat people en route to the hospital."

"That sounds intense. And you like it?"

He smiled and I could hear the enthusiasm in his voice. "I love it." He paused momentarily while the waiter set down our meals before leaving again. "Most calls are minor and routine, but some are incredibly interesting. It demands quick, on-the-spot decisions; someone's life is in your hands."

"What sparked your interest?"

He didn't answer immediately, and I wondered if he was preoccupied with his meal or debating the best response. "My mom developed a serious health issue. I found that I liked helping people, doing what I could to make them better, to ease their pain." His rich brown eyes held a look I hadn't seen before.

"You certainly took good care of me." I smiled reassuringly, afraid to ask about his mom's prognosis. "So why not be a full-time paramedic?"

"And not get to work with the guys?" He took a bite of his meal, swallowing before speaking again. "Besides, for a paramedic, the pay is low and burnout is high. No thanks; I'll stick to doing it on a volunteer basis."

We finished eating, and Ethan paid for dinner despite my offer to split the check. I wasn't surprised; no matter how many times I tried to contribute, the guys never let me pay for anything. An outsider might think this was a date, but I knew better.

All the guys were friendly, and the way several acted made me wonder if they were interested in me, but we were just friends. I kept reminding myself that was a good thing. I was only here temporarily and didn't need to complicate the situation.

By the time we left the restaurant, the sun had set and the sky was growing darker. We quickly drove through downtown, accelerating to enter 680 North. With the city to our left and the mountains to our right, I wondered how long it would take to get far enough away from all the light pollution. I hoped we weren't wasting our time driving to wherever it was we were going.

We exited the highway and headed east toward the mountains. The road narrowed to two lanes and became hilly as we approached a sign for a park with equestrian trails, picnic areas, and hiking paths. Just twenty minutes away from the city, I was surprised by how dark it had gotten and how remote it felt. Ethan pulled into a gravel parking lot before turning off the lights and switching off the ignition.

I shut the passenger door and looked around, noticing that there were only two other cars. "Have you been here before?"

Ethan grabbed a backpack from the trunk and slung it over his shoulder. "No; I searched online for the best stargazing spots in the area. People recommended going to one of the smaller valleys within the park, but I don't think we'll have to go too far."

"Sounds good. Can I carry anything?"

"I've got it." He glanced around, surveying the area. "Let's head that way."

As we walked across the parking lot, my eyes were still adjusting to the darkness when Ethan muttered a curse. I saw him fiddling with his phone and assumed he was trying to illuminate the path. Involuntarily, I reached out with my hand even though he was several feet away.

"No, don't . . ." Before I could stop him, his phone lit up. But instead of the harsh white light I expected, it cast a reddish glow on the ground beneath him.

Surprised, I said, "How did you do that?"

He chuckled, his warm baritone voice carrying through the air. "It's an astronomy flashlight app. You can add one to your phone too."

"Really? In a pinch, I usually just put red plastic wrap over my flashlight and secure it with a rubber band."

"Clever."

We walked side-by-side along a dirt path nestled between large trees. The temperature had dropped a few degrees, but the evening was pleasant. Every so often I glanced toward the sky, excited for the chance to spread out under the stars twinkling through the branches.

Apart from our conversation, the area was quiet, our only company the crickets chirping in the grass beside us. Occasionally we heard cars in the distance, but we had yet to pass anyone else.

"What have you been up to outside of work?" Ethan asked.

"The usual: drawing, running, reading."

"Read anything good lately?"

"Knox and Theo have quite the treasure trove of books. I've been on a classic adventure kick the past week with *Mutiny on the Bounty*, *The Count of Monte Cristo*, and *Robinson Crusoe*."

"All excellent choices." He paused. "Wait, did you say the past week? You read all three of those in one week, worked several days, and did whatever else you've been up to?"

I laughed. "That's nothing; I once read all seven Harry Potter books in one week while still studying, eating, and sleeping as usual." The statement was out of my mouth before I could stop myself, and I cringed slightly at the admission. Ethan already knew my life had been mostly solitary, but now he would realize how much of a bookworm I really was.

"You should talk to Jackson; he's the only person I've met that might read as much as you do. Do you have a favorite book?"

I groaned. "That's such a hard question to answer. Do I pick a book that really stuck with me or a book I would read over and over." I was silent, considering. "Hmmm. If I had to choose one, I would pick . . . Argh. I really can't pick just one. Please don't make me." Ethan chuckled at my rambling response.

"How about you?"

"You might be surprised, but I would pick *Peter Pan*."

I didn't have a particular book in mind, but the story of a boy who refuses to grow up wasn't necessarily my first guess. Granted, the novel dealt with more serious, adult themes than the movie, but I was still surprised. Ethan intrigued me; the more I seemed to learn about him, the more I wanted to know.

We hadn't walked far when the trees opened to reveal a small valley that seemed almost too good to be true. We veered off the dirt path, the tall grass brushing against my shins as we walked further into the valley.

Ethan handed me his phone, and I held the astronomy flashlight to illuminate the ground and backpack. He removed a plaid flannel blanket and spread it on the grass before extracting a leather binocular case. After he sat on the blanket, legs crossed before him, I bent my knees until I was sitting on top of my folded legs.

Looking up at the sky, I could clearly see the Big Dipper, part of the Ursa Major constellation. I inhaled deeply, feeling a sense of calm and home flood over me.

Ethan pointed to the sky before handing me the binoculars. "That must be Virgo." I tried to stifle a laugh.

"So . . . not Virgo."

I shook my head. "No, actually it's Scorpius." I pointed at the sky, indicating where to look while I described the major features and outline before handing back the binoculars.

While Ethan peered through the binoculars, I angled myself to face the sky in the same direction as him. With my legs stretched out in front of me, I pressed my palms into the blanket behind me for support. Seated side-by-side in the same position, it became a sort of game—Ethan guessed the constellations like a child seeing shapes in the clouds, and then I explained what they actually were.

At some point, we leaned back on our elbows, simply admiring the sky. The ground was comfortable and the blanket soft; my hair hung behind me, brushing against the blanket. No more than a few feet apart from each other, there was a sort of magnetic tension in the air.

"Ethan . . ."

"Yeah?"

I hesitated, wondering if he would think my question was silly. "If you could have dinner with any person alive or dead, who would you choose?"

He was quiet before answering, "Bruce Lee."

"Why?"

"He's a badass, renowned for his physical fitness, fast reflexes, and dedication. Have you seen any of his movies?"

I shook my head, the ends of my wavy hair dusting the blanket.

His voice was incredulous. "What movies have you seen?"

I wanted to protest, but Ethan continued talking. "Add *The Big Boss* and *Way of the Dragon* to your list. Those are both mandatory, along with *Buffy the Vampire Slayer*—the TV show, not the movie."

I giggled at his serious demeanor. I had never heard Ethan speak with such enthusiasm, even about being a paramedic. "Okay. You obviously feel very strongly about this." I said in a mock-serious tone.

"I practice mixed martial arts; I wish I could have trained under Bruce Lee."

Ethan sat up and unzipped the backpack before digging around, clearly hunting for something. "What about you—who would you pick?"

I could hear a package rustling and smiled when he pulled out a package of Peanut Butter M&M's.

"Aside from the obvious answer of my mom . . . probably Leonardo da Vinci."

He tore off the end of the package before holding it out

to me and resuming his position, propped up on his elbows. *Was it just me or were we sitting a little closer now?*

I raised an eyebrow. "You're really going to share your precious Peanut Butter M&M's?"

"I think I can spare a few," he said dryly.

"Oh, just a few, huh?" I was taunting him, dangling the M&M's package in the air within his reach.

"Probably. I'm bad at sharing." He reached out to grab the M&M's, but I pulled them behind my back, keeping them just out of reach.

Ethan lifted on his side, his body hovering within inches of mine, yet never actually touching, before snatching the M&M's out of my hand. Considering all his muscle, I was surprised by how agile and quick he was. His face lingered close to mine, and I could see his eyes dancing behind his glasses.

"You're a tease, Haley." His voice was husky, and I felt lightheaded.

He returned to his elbows and popped a few M&M's in his mouth while I recovered from the intense moment.

"That was way too easy. Knox told me you knew how to defend yourself."

I looked over at Ethan. "I didn't realize you were threatening me," I said sarcastically. I was baffled; one minute it felt like he wanted to kiss me, and the next, he was talking about self-defense. *Did I miss something?*

"Never underestimate your opponent, especially when you're standing between him and his Peanut Butter M&M's." He smirked briefly before his expression turned more serious. "All joking aside, do you know self-defense? I know one of us is constantly with you, but just in case."

"Yes, but I could use some practice." I let my frustration

go; it was such a nice evening and there really was nothing to be upset about.

"I'll have Jackson schedule time for me to work with you."

I nodded. "Sounds good. But just beware," I turned my head to look at him, "you might be unleashing a dragon." I shot him a daring smile.

Ethan's eyes stared into mine, his rich voice slightly deeper than normal. "I fear we already have."

6

SANTA CRUZIN'

COASTING down the boardwalk on a beach cruiser with the wind blowing through my hair, the radiant sun cast a dreamlike quality over the scene. It was almost as if my daydream from when Chase first described Santa Cruz had come to life in Technicolor perfection. At the time, I never believed this moment would or even could happen. I resisted the urge to pinch myself to ensure that this beautiful Saturday afternoon was reality.

Theo and I meandered along the West Cliff Drive bike path with its breathtaking backdrop of ocean waves and dramatic cliffs. The scenery was so gorgeous I almost forgot to pay attention to where I was going, despite all the tourists and locals on the trail. In addition to a beach dotted with sunbathers, we rode past a surfing museum, historic lighthouse, and the Beach Boardwalk amusement park, not to mention large homes with beautiful gardens full of blooming flowers and succulents. The occasional skateboarder zoomed by, their presence practically ubiquitous in Santa Cruz.

As usual, Theo indicated points of interest and threw

out interesting tidbits about the area. He even spouted random facts about sea lions as we passed their rocky outcrop. His range and depth of knowledge always astounded and often amused me.

I couldn't imagine a more idyllic setting, and apart from a few anachronisms, it almost felt like we had stepped back in time. Theo's look—cuffed jeans, vintage T-shirt, funky sneakers, and retro sunglasses—only reinforced this idea. With his slicked back hair, freckles, and a few tattoos, he was obviously comfortable with the attention he drew.

After making the return trip, we turned in our rented bikes and walked toward the amusement park. When I saw Chase approaching from the opposite direction, I waved, excited that Theo's "we" included Chase. In his khaki cargo shorts, sneakers, T-shirt, and baseball cap, he couldn't have looked more different from Theo. And yet, I had no doubt that either one of them could have their pick of girls.

Chase gave me the one-armed hug that had become our standard greeting. "Having fun with Theo?"

I smiled, leaning into his shoulder and inhaling his familiar cedar scent. "Of course!"

Theo and Chase caught up on classes and campus news while we grabbed dinner. When we exited the shop to take our meal outside, Chase inclined his head toward Theo and I as we followed behind. "How's your training going, Theo?"

Theo nodded, finishing the bite of his corn dog before answering. "Pretty good. Thanks to Ethan's hard-core schedule, I should be ready to climb El Gigante by winter break."

It was no secret that Theo wanted to climb El Gigante, but the last time he mentioned it to Knox, the conversation hadn't gone so well. Since then, they both avoided discussing the topic; Theo was training as planned and trusting Knox would get over it while Knox silently hoped Theo would change his mind. They were both stubborn, and I honestly wasn't sure what the outcome would be.

I had just thrown away the packaging for my dinner when Theo grabbed my hand and pulled me after him, saying excitedly, "Come on, Haley. It's photo booth time!"

I rolled my eyes playfully, knowing that resistance was futile, and honestly, it sounded like fun. Theo ducked into the photo booth with Chase on his heels. I peeked my head in the curtained space realizing for the first time how tiny it was.

"Maybe I'll just stay out here." I played with the ends of my side braid.

"Don't be ridiculous. You can sit here." Theo patted his leg that rested next to Chase's. Before I could protest, Chase wrapped a broad arm around my waist and pulled me in. He quickly shut the purple velvet curtain while Theo fed cash into the payment slot.

Perched on their legs, I felt warm at the closeness and hoped I wasn't blushing as the digital screen appeared. I laughed at how ridiculous I looked in the preview, my head dominating the screen. I shifted, trying to scrunch down before leaning back to make my head even with theirs.

Theo exclaimed, "Say cheese!" But I wasn't sure I even had time to smile before the flash went off.

For the second photo, I saw the countdown on the screen. Theo, the artistic director, as always, said, "Let's try to get a nice one this time." I smiled, hoping at least one would turn out okay.

"Now make a silly face." I wasn't sure what else to do, so I crossed my eyes and stuck out my tongue.

"Last chance," Theo called. Fingers fluttered at my

waist as Chase and Theo tickled me. While I was laughing and squirming to face them, the flash went off.

The photos printed and Theo handed a strip to me and Chase. Our expressions progressed from unprepared to laughter and everything in between. Flanked by Theo and Chase, I still couldn't believe the girl smiling in the photos was me. Perhaps the evening was going to be even more fun than I anticipated.

Chase, Theo, and I tumbled out of the photo booth, laughing at our ridiculous expressions. As my eyes re-adjusted to the sunlight, I froze when I saw Jackson standing at the entrance to the Boardwalk.

My pulse quickened and I forced myself to act natural as Jackson strode toward us, confident as ever. In dark blue shorts, half-zip pullover, and boat shoes, his effortlessly casual look seemed almost too polished for an evening at an amusement park. I hated that his presence still intimidated me, but I hoped that my nerves would start to fade after spending more time with him.

"Here you go, Theo, as requested," he said, handing Theo a brown leather satchel.

Theo smiled, "Thanks. I really didn't want to haul this around while we were biking." He put the bag across one shoulder before pulling out a professional-looking camera. "Now I finally have an excuse to get a few shots of Haley. The photo booth pics, however awesome, don't count."

"What? Surely you can find a more interesting subject around here than me. And how did I not know that you're a photographer?"

As the four of us walked toward the park entrance, Theo messed with the camera settings. I didn't know enough about photography to understand his motions, but it was obvious that he was comfortable with a camera in his hands.

He moved close to me before quietly saying, "I'm not sure I could find a more interesting subject in all the world, so don't even consider denying my fun." His eyes twinkled, but his tone was serious. "And, I guess photography just hasn't come up; I have so many talents, it's difficult to keep track of them all," he said with a crooked grin.

He took a couple shots zoomed in on my face, and I instinctively looked away, embarrassed.

Entering the park, I didn't know where to look first. The sights and sounds were overwhelming and exciting; bright colors and lights dazzled all around, and the air was filled with screams of fright and delight as well as laughter. A number of sounds jockeyed for dominance—music playing over outdoor speakers, the rattle of rides, and arcade games to name a few. But the people were what really brought the park to life; children running around, game vendors calling out for competitors, and groups of teenagers out for a Saturday night of fun.

"In honor of Haley's adoration of all things astronomy, we're doing Space Race first." Theo tugged on my hand, pulling me after him for a moment, then dropping it.

"Space Race?"

Chase smiled, "Yeah, bumper cars. They're a lot of fun." He leaned in close, whispering, "If you want to team up, I bet we can take Theo down."

I bit back a smile before whispering back, "Okay, I'm in."

Apart from the neon-lit arena, the set-up was pretty much what I expected: goofy looking cars with a giant rubber donut racing around a dark concrete floor. I strapped into the car, feeling slightly cramped and looked over at

Chase. As the countdown began, we shared a knowing smile, ready to put our plan into action.

Theo immediately ran into my car and we laughed as we sprang back from the impact, my braid bouncing on my shoulder. Theo quickly sped off and bumped into a few other people on the opposite side of the space. Cheerful shouts and the sound of squeaking rubber rang through the air.

Fortunately, I managed to dodge other riders attempting to ram me. Meanwhile, Jackson was pursuing Chase and some other players. Chase caught my eye and we sped around in opposite directions, pursuing Theo; Theo was too busy to notice that we were closing in.

When Chase and I backed Theo into a corner, he feigned hurt. "Haley, you traitor. I can't believe you are siding with Chase over me." And then, moving so quickly that I never saw him coming, Theo maneuvered around us and shouted over his shoulder, "Guess he didn't tell you that I'm the superior driver!"

Chase sheepishly shrugged his shoulders. "It was worth a try."

Back outside, Theo pointed to a crazy-looking spinning roller coaster. "Let's ride Undertow next!"

My stomach dropped to my toes. "Um, I don't know, guys. Maybe I should try out a normal roller coaster before attempting that...thing."

Jackson stepped up next to me. "Theo, why don't you and Chase go ride Undertow. I'll take Haley on Sky Glider since it will get dark soon."

Chase and Theo agreed and headed toward the spinning coaster after making plans to meet back up.

As we stood in line for the Sky Glider, I observed the ride with equal parts excitement and trepidation. The ride itself looked perfect with its colorful seats and matching umbrellas floating high above the sidewalk, suspended from a cable. But the realization that I would have to sit so close to Jackson had my palms sweating. If I was with Theo or Chase, I wouldn't have thought much of it. But, as always, Jackson was a different story.

I felt my phone vibrate in my pocket and pulled it out, checking the text.

Knox: Hope you're enjoying yourself. Don't let the guys push you into riding anything you don't want to.

Smiling at Knox's protectiveness, I quickly responded.

Me: I won't. We did the bumper cars, and Jackson and I are getting ready to ride Sky Glider. I got out of riding Undertow.

Knox: Good. Have fun and be careful.

Me: Thanks.

Just as I shoved the phone back in my pocket, it was our turn. After Jackson and I took our seats, the attendant pulled down the safety bar, and we were off.

Jackson slid an arm around my back. "You're not afraid of heights, are you? I guess I should have asked before." He looked so concerned, I was certain my overall anxiety must have been plainly written across my face.

"No, I just haven't done anything like this before."

As we were lifted high into the air, I absorbed the gorgeous aerial view and started to relax. "Wow, this view is amazing." From our vantage point, with the sun about to set, Santa Cruz and the beach were bathed in soft light.

Jackson smiled, his eyes sparkling. "I'm glad you like it. I was hoping we'd get the timing right to ride just before sunset."

While he pointed out different landmarks, I found myself distracted by his proximity. Inhaling only made things worse, especially when I smelled his clean masculine scent. And those shiny black curls; he could drive a woman crazy. Before I knew it, we were descending. Clearly I was going to have to ride by myself next time if I wanted to fully appreciate the landscape.

When we met back up with Theo and Chase, they were animated from the excitement of the coaster. After convincing me to try something a little more adventurous than the Sky Glider, we rode the Haunted Castle, the carousel, Cave Train, and Pirate Ship. My initial anxiety had mostly subsided, and I found myself actually enjoying the adrenaline rush.

We had just stepped off of Cliff Hanger when Theo shot me a devilish grin. "So, Haley, you think you're ready? Can you handle . . ." he paused before holding out his arms to display, "the Giant Dipper?"

I gulped at the sight of the large wooden roller coaster looming overhead. In the back of my mind, I had wondered if, and when, one of the guys would suggest it.

I nodded. "I think so."

Chase looked concerned. "You don't have to, Haley. We can always wait out here while Jackson and Theo ride."

I smiled and shook my head. "No, it's okay. I want to."

But as we stood in line, I began to doubt my decision. Shifting slightly from foot to foot, I felt torn. I half-hoped the line would speed up so I could get it over with, and yet my stomach was in knots at the thought of riding the Giant Dipper.

While the guys talked, I tried to distract myself. Looking around, I noticed that there were a number of couples in line, hands intertwined or arms wrapped around each other's waists. Most looked like high school or college students out on a date, and I tried to subtly study them, their clothes, their interactions. I wondered what it would be like to be one of those girls, a cute guy holding my hand in line.

Before I could spend any more time dwelling on it, it was our turn. Jackson and Theo hopped into the first two seats with Chase and me right behind. As we pulled the safety bar down over our laps, I felt my heart racing. *Last chance*, I thought, staring straight ahead at the track stretched before us.

I felt a little panicky and was seriously reconsidering my decision when a warm hand clasped my own. I sighed in appreciation when I realized that Chase had placed his hand around mine and was smiling encouragingly. He squeezed my hand, silently asking if I was okay and assuring me that I would be.

I took a deep breath. *Here we go.* After emerging from a dark tunnel into the twilight of evening, we climbed the first hill; the gears clicked slowly in a seemingly endless progression as we climbed higher and higher. *How high is this hill? And how steep the drop?*

Pausing on the apex, I braced for the drop and squeezed Chase's hand harder as we plummeted to the bottom. I felt the air rush by and realized I was screaming. When we started climbing again, I was laughing. Relieved to have made it past that first hill, I thoroughly enjoyed the rush.

The rest of the ride was a blur as we twisted around corners, flew up and down hills, and whizzed through the white wooden passageways. When the car finally came to a halt, we were back where we started.

Exiting the turnstiles, Theo patted me on the back. "That wasn't too bad, was it?"

Feeling a powerful mix of adrenaline rush, elation, and relief, I grinned. "It was a blast!"

I could see the corner of Jackson's mouth rise slightly. "So you're a thrill-seeker after all."

With only thirty minutes until closing, we stopped at the games on our way to the exit. While Theo debated the best game to play, I felt my phone vibrate in my pocket. *Knox again?*

Liam: You better not be having too much fun without me.

Me: What if I am?

Liam: Good question, cheeky girl. I'll get back to you on that.

Liam: Send me a pic?

I got Theo to pose and then quickly took a photo and texted it to Liam.

Liam: No, send me a selfie.

Selfie? Should I know what that is? He must mean a picture of me.

Me: How do I do that?

Liam: You're so adorable. Never mind; I'll show you next time I see you.

I slid my phone in my pocket and stepped up to the counter next to Chase, Theo, and Jackson. Facing a wall of scary clowns, we each held onto our water guns and aimed at the target. When the attendant shouted, "Go!", water shot from the end.

Within a few minutes, the buzzer sounded, signaling a winner. The game attendant announced Jackson as the winner before Jackson selected a stuffed *Despicable Me* Minion as his prize.

Jackson held out the stuffed Minion. "For you, Miss Jones."

I shook my head. "You won it fair and square."

He offered it again. "I know, but I want you to have it."

I smiled and accepted the adorable Minion. If any of the other guys had done the same, I wouldn't have been surprised, but this was Jackson. Maybe he didn't dislike me as much as I thought.

The number of people in the park was dwindling, and I could sense that it was almost closing time. A voice announced over the loudspeaker, "The park is closing in ten minutes. Please proceed to the exit and visit again soon."

Chase said, "Come on, let's get ice cream at that spot on the boardwalk."

We exited the park, the bright candy-colored lights shining on the surface of the ocean. The breeze coming off the water was cool but pleasant as we walked along the lit pathway.

"What flavor are you going to get, Haley?" Chase asked.

"I don't know. I usually get mint chocolate chip, but maybe I'll try something new."

Theo chimed in. "Oh, you have to try something new. This place has great flavors, many of them quite original, like avocado."

"Yuck. Why would you ruin ice cream by adding avocado?" Jackson asked.

Theo immediately responded. "I don't know, I actually kind of liked it."

Chase laughed. "Of course you did, Theo. You like anything novel and unique." Theo made a face as if to disagree and then shrugged in good-natured resignation.

"What about you, Jackson?" I asked. "I know you're not getting avocado, so are you a vanilla person? Chocolate?"

He smirked. "Last time I had raspberry brownie. I'm really hoping they have that again."

"I've been dying to try the peanut butter chocolate covered pretzel, but I never seem to come on the right day.

Ethan raves about it." Chase said, holding the door open for me.

"Um, that sounds like a winner." I smiled.

The four of us savored our homemade ice cream out of fresh waffle cones as we headed back outside to sit on the edge of the boardwalk overlooking the ocean. We had each gotten a different flavor—blackberry sorbet for Jackson, cookies and cream for Chase, honey fig ricotta for Theo, and white chocolate raspberry for me.

Theo held out his cone, placing it inches from my face. "You have to try this; it's amazing."

After riding the Giant Dipper, trying an unusual ice cream flavor seemed like a piece of cake. I took a lick. The savory, sweet richness melted on my tongue, and I smiled at the delicious surprise.

With the waves crashing in the distance, I reflected on my day with a sense of awe. I couldn't have imagined a more perfect day. Now surrounded by Chase, Theo, and Jackson, it seemed almost too good to be true, the reality exceeding even my daydreams.

7

RUMORS & RIVALRY

I CHECKED the clock on my computer, shocked to find that it was almost noon on Friday. The week since my board-walk adventure had flown by, and none of the guys had mentioned any plans for this weekend yet. I tried to keep my expectations low; I knew we couldn't keep up that kind of pace every weekend, but I still hoped I would get to do something fun. There were still so many things in the area I wanted to see and do.

A box lit up in the bottom corner of my monitor, indicating an instant message. *I wonder who that could be from?* Melissa was the only person who sent me instant messages, and she was off today. If any of the guys wanted to contact me, they usually just texted me.

I saw the name "Tyler Mason" on the message box, and a face immediately came to mind. I met Tyler in the copy room earlier in the week, and we chatted for a few minutes. He seemed nice, but all I really knew about him was that he was a member of Team Falcon and considered Starbucks Frappuccinos a guilty pleasure.

When I read the message, I almost jolted out of my seat

in surprise. *He wants to meet me for lunch? What should I do?*

Deciding I didn't have a good reason to say no and didn't want to be rude, I agreed to meet him in the café downstairs in fifteen minutes. I tried not to panic as I contemplated an entire meal alone with someone who was virtually a stranger. Of course, considering the events of the past month, it shouldn't be a big deal; mere weeks ago Theo and Knox were complete strangers, and now I was living with them. My heart tried to tell me it was different with *my* guys, but I knew it was basically the same thing.

Entering the café, I wiped my hands on my slacks and tried to calm my nerves. Tyler was standing near the entrance and gave me a huge smile when he spotted me. Tall and handsome, with broad shoulders and ebony skin, he looked sharp in a blush pink button-down shirt and charcoal slacks. He could look imposing with his shaved head and goatee, but when he smiled, all I could see was kindness.

"Haley, thanks for coming; I'm glad you could make it on such short notice."

"Of course. It was kind of you to ask."

He laughed, "I don't think requesting the pleasure of your company makes me kind so much as selfish, but I'll take it."

Tyler led me through the line, selecting a large wrap for himself and providing pointers on the best dishes. He reached the cash register first, and by the time I arrived, he had already paid for both our lunches.

"How much do I owe you?"

"Nothing. Lunch is on me." He smiled. "Let's snag a table outside before they're all gone."

I didn't know what else to say, apart from thank you. I

felt just as awkward pushing the issue as I did about accepting the free lunch.

We grabbed one of the few empty tables on the outdoor patio. Surrounded by a waist-high metal fence and planter boxes, the patio bordered the sidewalk and provided a good vantage point for people watching. Shaded from the sun by a large canvas umbrella, we sat facing each other as we ate.

"So, Haley. Tell me about yourself."

Wanting to stall for a moment, I took a sip of ice water. This was the part of the conversation I had been dreading. Even though I shared part of my fake background with Melissa, the thought of lying still made me uneasy. Hopefully I could evade at least some of his questions.

"There's not that much to tell. I grew up near Reno and just recently moved to Santa Cruz. I like to read and I try to run almost every day. I'm boring, really. How about you?"

"I very much doubt that you're boring, but I'll let that go for now. I'm from the Bay Area and I grew up wanting to be a professional football player. When it became obvious I would never reach that level, I decided to attend Stanford and started working at Zenith part-time until I graduated last spring and joined Falcon."

"Wow, Stanford. What did you study?"

He smiled, his bright white teeth gleaming. "Believe it or not, I was a chemistry major."

I raised one eyebrow. "Okay, football player I believe. Chemist...not so much."

Tyler laughed, "I know, I know. I've heard it a million times. You know, not all science geeks wear pocket protectors."

Wanting to keep the conversation revolving around him, I asked, "So, how is it that you're working in private security instead of a chemistry-related job?"

"What can I say? I'm good at science, but it gets boring. And I enjoy what I do at Zenith too much to give that up."

His answer should have surprised me, but it sounded familiar. What was it with guys who seemed obviously overqualified for private security working at Zenith? Once again, I knew I was missing a vital piece of information. And while it often seemed possible (based on the ridiculous number of incredibly hot guys), I seriously doubted the missing link was that Zenith was secretly a male modeling agency.

"So I heard a rumor about you living with the Bennett brothers. Is that why you're working at Zenith?"

He heard a rumor? There were rumors going around about me?

"Yes. When Theo found out I was moving to the area, he offered me a room at his place and helped me get the job here."

Tyler cleared his throat, suddenly looking a little hesitant. "So are you and Theo . . ." he trailed off. When I didn't immediately respond, he continued, "An item?"

Surprised, I responded, "No, um, we're just friends."

Why was he asking me this? I hoped it was just curiosity and not . . . something else. He was attractive, but I had enough drama in my life at the moment, and I could never be honest with Tyler about who I really was.

He wiped his brow, his movements exaggerated. "Well, that is a relief. I didn't want to start a *West Side Story* situation in the office by asking you to lunch."

"What?" I'm sure my face betrayed my sincere confusion over his comment.

"It's not a big deal, but Team Falcon and Team Jaguar are considered rivals. It's mostly friendly competition, but several of the guys take it a little too seriously."

"Really? I had no idea."

"Yeah, it's mostly because our teams are generally the same age and experience level, so it's natural to have some competition between us. Everyone wants the good assignments."

Thankfully, he changed the subject to his favorite Bay Area haunts, and the rest of the lunch passed without further awkward conversation. As I made my way back to my desk, I had to admit that I enjoyed the lunch. Tyler was friendly and easy to talk to. Maybe I did have the ability to make a friend without extenuating circumstances involved.

* * *

A FEW HOURS LATER, I was lounging on the couch reading when Liam strolled in carrying a fancy glass bottle with a red satin bow tied around the neck. He looked dressed for a night out in his black slacks and crisp white fitted button-down shirt, open at the neck with the sleeves rolled up to his elbows. Despite how uncomfortable he often made me, I couldn't deny the slight uptick in my heartbeat at the mere sight of him.

"Ahhh, the lady of leisure." He smirked as I side-eyed him. My calendar for tonight listed Knox; since Knox hadn't mentioned anything specific, I was expecting a quiet evening in.

I reached for my phone. "Did the schedule change again?"

Several times within the past week, my schedule had changed without much notice. Babysitting me was probably a low priority for the guys, but every time I tried to ask about the change in plans, I received vague answers. I wasn't sure what was going on—work, family, girlfriends; all I could do was speculate.

"No, but I wish I could have you all to myself." His gray eyes danced.

"Is anyone else coming over?"

Before Liam could answer, Knox and Theo walked down the hallway from the garage with Chase following behind. They each set a large cardboard box on the kitchen counter, and I could hear glass rattling gently.

I closed my book and placed it on the couch before standing up. "What's going on?"

Theo smiled. "We're just having a little get together."

Based on the number of boxes seemingly filled with alcohol, it didn't look like a "little" get together.

Chase interjected. "We're having a stock-the-bar party for Theo's twenty-first birthday!" He gave me a one-arm hug before following Knox back down the hall to the garage. Liam went to the kitchen and started pulling items out of the fridge.

"A what?" I shook my head. "Wait. It's your birthday, and you're just now telling me? How was I supposed to get you a present if I didn't know?"

"Relax, Haley; it's not even my real birthday until Sunday." Theo pulled several bottles out of the box. "And besides, I don't need a present."

"Liam brought you a gift. You have to let me get you something. I want to."

He shook his head and continued setting up for the party. A few moments later, he said, "You know, now that I think about it, there is something you can give me."

"Yeah . . ." I tilted my head to the side, waiting.

"It's my birthday wish. And it would be cruel to deny me the one and only thing I really want for my twenty-first birthday." Theo grinned in such a way that I could tell he was up to something, and the possibilities made me nervous.

"Okay, Theo. What is it?"

"I want you to wear *the dress* to the party." He raised his eyebrows suggestively as he said "the dress."

Liam looked at me from behind Theo, confusion written on his face, but I knew that Theo was referring to the sapphire dress we bought on my first day in Santa Cruz. The one that made me look and feel fantastic but was considerably outside of my comfort zone.

I raised my eyebrow. "Won't I be a tad over-dressed?" I was ignoring Liam's attire for the moment; like Jackson, he was always on the dressy side.

Theo scoffed. "No. Trust me, Haley. You will be perfect. Have I ever steered you wrong?"

He had a point, but I still wasn't ready to agree. Distracted by Chase and Knox returning with a large stainless steel barrel, I realized I had more pressing questions. "So what is a stock-the-bar party anyway?"

Liam stuck his head out from behind the fridge. "Basically, guests bring a bottle of alcohol like this one," he held up the bottle with the red ribbon, "or an alcohol-related gift, like shot glasses, to contribute to Theo's home bar."

"I see. So exactly how many guests are we expecting?"

Knox set down the latest box on the counter and looked toward Theo. "You kept it to thirty, right?" *Thirty!*

Theo fluttered about, acting as if he hadn't heard. Knox spoke louder, almost growling. "Theo?"

Theo grinned sheepishly. "It may be a few more than thirty."

Knox glared at Theo. "How many?"

Theo turned toward the kitchen and muttered, "Somewhere around forty."

Forty. Forty people. A wave of dizziness hit me at the thought. Feeling a palm tracing large circles on my upper back, I turned my head to see Chase giving me an understanding smile. My panic eased slightly, calmed by his presence and his gentle touch.

Knox quickly glanced over the supplies. "We're going to need more cups, ice, and booze. I have time to run out, right?" He looked at Theo. "Or did you change the start time too?" Knox sounded annoyed, but we all knew he would do anything for Theo's birthday.

Theo grinned. "Still set for seven."

I glanced at the clock. S*even? That's only a little over an hour away.*

"Why don't you call Jackson and have him pick it up on the way?" Liam said.

Knox responded, "Jax is coming a little later because he's bringing Penny. I'll text Ethan; he should get here early anyway."

Penny? Who is Penny? Chase spoke, interrupting my attempt to envision Jackson's girlfriend, Penny. "Come on, Haley. Want to give me a hand?"

I nodded and followed Chase to the kitchen counter where we started removing bottles from the boxes. Theo combed through records while Liam prepared food and Knox worked on various tasks around the house.

With the dishwasher running and music playing in the background, I would have been relaxed were it not for the impending party. I struggled to stay calm, but I was getting more and more anxious the closer it got to seven. Still adjusting to meeting new people and forging friendships, the idea of taking on thirty plus strangers at once seemed completely overwhelming. I wished I could hide in my room all evening, but I knew Theo would never let me get away with that.

As I sliced lemons for the bar, I wondered how long they had been planning the party. Knowing Theo, he would have been preparing for a while.

"So . . . were you guys planning to tell me about the party at some point?"

Theo walked over and pulled me aside, speaking to me in a low voice. "I'm sorry I didn't tell you sooner, Haley. I just didn't want you to freak out about it. I want you to have a good time." His eyes were questioning, pleading.

Appreciating that Theo was just looking out for me, I nodded. I would have to put my limited acting skills to work tonight, because I wanted him to enjoy his party despite my anxiety. He gave me a quick hug, squeezing me with my arms pinned to my side, before returning to the record collection.

I went back to slicing while Liam took the lemons I had already cut and started placing them on a divided dish. "Isn't there something you would like to tell us, Haley?"

I furrowed my brow; I wasn't planning any parties that I knew of. And apart from my plan to go to San Francisco at some point (which I definitely wasn't going to tell them about), there were no real secrets I was currently keeping. *Do they know I e-mailed Jessica?*

Shrugging my shoulders, I asked, "Did you have something specific in mind?"

Liam leaned over the counter. "Perhaps your lunch date with Tyler." He winked.

My jaw dropped in surprise and embarrassment. I couldn't believe Liam already knew about my lunch with Tyler and that he referred to it as a date.

Knox interjected. "Wait, Haley, is this true?"

"Yes, but for your information, it wasn't a date." I could feel myself getting warm.

Liam smirked. "Oh ho ho, thou dost protest too much. He is totally interested in you."

Theo groaned. "Oh Haley, how could you? The Falcons are always trying to outdo us, but this is low, even for them."

I struggled to maintain my composure. "Are you saying that Tyler only asked me to lunch because of your little rivalry? And how do you even know about it, Liam? Were you spying on me?"

Theo just shook his head, looking apologetic, and Liam rolled his eyes. "Oh please. I saw the two of you eating at the sidewalk café. It certainly looked like a date to me."

Feeling more and more agitated, I briefly closed my eyes and inhaled deeply, but Liam wasn't ready to let the topic go. "Tell me one thing—did he pay for lunch?"

I raised an eyebrow. "Yes, but . . ."

Liam chuckled. "Nope. Case closed," he said in an annoyingly smug tone.

"I tried to pay. Besides, you guys buy me lunch or dinner all the time without it being a date." I looked around the room, hoping at least one of them would back me up.

Knox gave me a sympathetic look, and when he spoke, his tone was gentle. "Haley, the usual rules don't apply with us. You can't go around with other guys like you do with us." He paused as he shifted some boxes around. "Just be careful; things get complicated with office romances."

I sighed. I knew things were different with *my* guys, but I didn't like feeling attacked. Hoping to deflect their attention, I said, "Well, even if Tyler is romantically interested in me, I'm not the only one with an office admirer."

Liam waved a hand through the air. "I already know that Vanessa fancies me."

I grinned smugly and shook my head. "No, not you, Liam. Chase."

Chase looked up from his task, surprised but silent.

Theo walked closer to the kitchen. "Do tell, Haley. Been talking around the water cooler, have you?"

"No. Do we even have a water cooler?" I furrowed my brow as I shook my head. "Never mind." I wasn't really sure this was the right time or way to tell Chase, but it was too late to turn back now.

Knox, Theo, Chase, and Liam stared at me expectantly before I said, "Melissa likes Chase."

Liam looked slightly puzzled. "The chatty blonde who works next to you?"

Theo swatted Liam's back with the back of his hand and said, "Yes, dummy," before he turned toward me. "Haley, that's no secret; the whole office knows it."

"What?" I quickly looked toward Chase, wondering if he already knew about Melissa's crush. His embarrassed look and shrug of the shoulders confirmed that he did. *So much for helping Melissa with Chase*, I thought. He already seemed to know about her crush and either wasn't interested or hadn't yet made a move. I felt oddly relieved.

Suddenly, Theo said, "Holy knickerbockers, guests will be arriving in thirty minutes." As he walked toward the stairs, he said, "I'm going to get ready." He pointed a finger at me and grinned, "And you should too, Haley." Like it or not, apparently I was attending the party.

8

PARTY IN STYLE

I WALKED down the hall toward my bedroom, a sense of dread settling over me. It wasn't the typical reaction to attending a friend's birthday party, I knew. But considering this would be my first party of any type, I felt justified in my apprehension.

Plopping down on my bed, I evened my breathing and slowly counted to sixty. Once I was calmer, I attempted to evaluate the situation rationally. With so many people at the party, at least I had a chance of blending into the crowd. And, I would undoubtedly find one or more of the guys at my side most of the night. Maybe if I just showed up for an hour or so, I could disappear back to my bedroom without Theo noticing.

Aware that the party was starting any minute, I forced myself to get up and begin getting ready. Since I was wearing a revealing dress (well, revealing for me), I decided to leave my hair down. At least then my long hair would help cover some of my exposed skin. Thankful I hadn't put my hair up today, I added a little product to tame the flyaways and moved on.

Standing in front of the mirror, I scrutinized my reflection. I wondered if I should wear makeup to fit in with the other girls, but when it came to applying it, I was hopeless. Sifting through a bag of samples that Theo picked up for me, I wished that Jessica was here. Despite her frequent lectures on the subject, I'd never had the inclination to wear much makeup and didn't bother to learn the art of application.

Deciding that attempting it tonight would likely be disastrous, I gave up on the samples and stuck with my standards: mascara and berry-colored lip gloss. Pinching my cheeks Scarlett O'Hara-style, I laughed when my face took on a rosy glow. *I can't believe that actually works.*

After slipping on the sapphire blue dress Theo—with his adorable charm—manipulated me into wearing, I had to admit that it was a perfect fit. The fabric followed the contours of my waist without being tight, and the neckline—while lower than I was used to—showed off just enough cleavage to draw attention without looking immodest. The dress hit me mid-thigh, thankfully long enough that I wouldn't have to worry about flashing anyone.

I looked through my limited shoe collection and selected the cork wedges that Theo gave me as an off-the-crutches gift. Hopefully they would give the dress a slightly more casual appearance, since I didn't totally trust his word that I wouldn't be over-dressed.

While checking my completed outfit in the full-length mirror, I started noticing loud voices and laughter from down the hall and tried not to panic. Clearly the party was in full-swing; now I just needed to work up the courage to walk out there.

But, that was definitely easier said than done. I felt practically naked in this dress even though logically, I recognized that I was appropriately covered. My self-consciousness about the dress itself was nowhere near the level of anxiety I was experiencing just having to face so many new people at once.

Lost in my thoughts, I jumped when I heard a loud knock at my door followed by Theo's voice. "Haley, the party's started! You need to get your cute butt out here."

Knowing I wouldn't get away with hiding any longer, I slowly made my way to the door and forced a smile.

When I opened the door, Theo let out a slow whistle, his hazel-green eyes sparkling. "That dress is even better than I remember. You look stunning."

Pink filled my cheeks. "Thank you. You look great as well." Theo always looked nice, but tonight I could tell that he put extra effort into his appearance. His russet colored hair was freshly clean and perfectly swooped into his distinctly Theo, retro style. And his outfit was flawless from head to toe—golden brown wingtip oxfords; rolled dark-wash jeans; a subtly patterned shirt with vest, tie, and even a tie clip. All that was missing was a hat, but it would be a crime to mess up that hair.

Theo grinned. "Did you really expect anything less? Now let's get out there and get you a drink."

He tugged on my hand, pulling me out of the room. "I don't know, Theo. I've never tried alcohol before."

"I'm not going to force you, but if you decide you want one, I'll make you a delicious girly drink. You will barely even taste the alcohol."

We headed down the hall toward the living room and bumped into Ethan.

"Ethan, glad you're here. Thanks for picking up stuff at the last minute."

"No problem." Spotting me, his trademark smirk

appeared. His brown eyes seemed darker than usual as he slid them over my face then down my body. "My, my, Buffy. You clean up quite well." Heat instantly crawled up my neck. *Ugh. How many times would I blush tonight?*

He slung an arm around Theo's neck, whispering loud enough for me to hear. "I see what you meant about that being the *good* dress."

Theo snickered and tugged on my hand, pulling me down the hall. As we reached the entrance to the living area, my steps faltered. Even though it was clear not everyone had yet arrived, my first view of the crowded loft was still rather startling.

The loft was quickly filling in with people and most of them were already holding drinks. There was a buzz in the air as they circulated throughout the space and talked amongst each other. Some sat on the couches or at the table while others stood at the kitchen counter or grouped together. Music played in the background and the lights were dimmed.

We stepped into the room but quickly stopped, our progress thwarted by Knox. Looking at Theo, he said, "There you are. Your guests having been asking for you."

When Knox's attention swung to me, he groaned. "Theo, are you trying to kill me?" He threaded his fingers through his hair, the usually fluid motion jerky with agitation. "With her in that dress, I'll have to keep an even closer eye on her all night."

Ethan chuckled while Theo just grinned. "Chill out, big brother. Between the six of us watching over her, she'll be fine."

Knox grunted, "She better be," and then stalked to the kitchen. I stared after him in surprise. He almost seemed upset with me, and I wasn't really sure why. Surely my dress wasn't that big of a deal.

"Ignore him; you look perfect," Theo said as he led me by the hand through the crush of people; several stopped and gave him a hug or a pat on the back, and Theo briefly introduced me. I tried not to gawk at the guests as we passed by, but I was fascinated by their style, their vivacity. I tried to remain calm, reminding myself that I was blending in, apart from the obvious lack of tattoos.

Many of the guests were dressed like Theo, retro-flair with an edge; I loved the style—it was playful and flirty without being too suggestive. And Theo was right, I wasn't overdressed. But even with all the skin I was showing, I was still quite modest compared to some of the other girls. There was no shortage of short skirts, low tops, and skin-tight dresses that left little to the imagination.

We finally reached the bookshelves and I almost laughed aloud. The giant traveling trunk (the one I thought was a magician's chest) was actually a bar cart. With the hinged top open and front panels dropped, the glassware and decanters were on display, glimmering in the mirrored lid.

Scanning the bottles of liquor, I was shocked by the sheer number of options. It seemed like it would take months to taste them all and years to try different mixtures.

Theo started collecting bottles and other ingredients. "So, Haley. What do you think?" I could tell Theo was trying not to pressure me, but he seemed excited to make something for me.

Knowing Theo wouldn't steer me wrong, I relented with a smile. "I'll give it a try."

"Fantastic! I love mixing cocktails and trying to match

people with just the right drink. Since this is your first, you need something light and a little sweet."

I watched, fascinated, as he expertly poured, cut, squeezed, and shook the ingredients. Clearly he knew what he was doing. I should have been surprised considering he was just turning twenty-one, but somehow it seemed like a natural skill for Theo.

"Here you go. One mojito for the girl in blue." He presented the glass to me with no shortage of flourish.

I took a tentative sip. It was pleasantly effervescent, and the mixture of lime and mint was refreshing. If I hadn't actually seen him put the alcohol in it, I wouldn't have believed it had any.

"This is delicious. Thank you."

Theo's delighted expression made me smile. "You're welcome. I'm glad you like it. Just don't drink it too quickly."

While Theo worked on another cocktail, I took tiny sips of my drink and let my eyes wander over the room. Liam and Ethan were in the kitchen helping Knox, a group of eager-looking girls standing nearby. My eyes roved some more before catching sight of Chase with a small group of guests dressed in what appeared to be normal college student attire. Friends from school, perhaps?

I continued my perusal, but when I noticed Jackson leaning against a wall across the room, I froze. He was surrounded by people but staring straight at me, his gaze unwavering. I studied the girls in his vicinity, but none of them seemed to be there with him. Did he not bring Penny after all?

When he continued to watch me, confusion washed over me. Did he think I was going to get into trouble? Was he upset because I was drinking? Neither seemed likely.

Theo was only a couple of feet away from me, and if Knox hadn't objected to my drink, I didn't think Jackson would care.

I may have been imagining it, but something about the way he examined me was unexpected coming from Jackson. *Is it possible he's checking me out? Surely not . . . Just how quickly could alcohol take effect?* Perhaps the mojito was clouding my judgment, but I doubted it considering the miniscule amount I had consumed.

Theo finished at the bar and led me toward the couch, forcing me to break eye contact with Jackson. I took a seat on one end of the couch, but before Theo had a chance to join me, a female hand shot out to catch his arm and pull him into her group. Sending me an apologetic look, he joined the conversation and was talking and laughing within seconds.

When Theo shifted, I got my first view of the mysterious female who was still grasping Theo's arm. I wasn't sure what to call her style, but she looked like an edgy, modern-day pin-up girl. Her patterned halter top and high-waisted black pants clung like a second skin. And I was pretty sure her dramatic red lipstick perfectly matched her ridiculously-high red heels.

Surprisingly feminine tattoos were visible along both arms and over her collarbone. And most notably, her glossy black hair hung down her back in loose waves like a raven-haired Veronica Lake. With her bangs pinned away from her face in a large roll and a large white flower placed on the opposite side near the hairline, she was undeniably alluring.

I hated to admit it, but she looked like Theo's ideal match. Together, they were striking, glamorous even. I couldn't imagine Theo keeping the existence of a girlfriend from me, but I got the feeling that she was either a close friend or something more. She seemed right at home at the party, even greeting new guests and refilling food and drinks.

She constantly watched Theo and her face lit up every time he addressed her. I didn't notice Theo treating her any differently than the rest of his friends, but it was difficult to know for sure. What I did know was that watching them together made me uncomfortable. Out of all the guys, I was the closest to Theo since we spent so much time together at the loft. And seeing him in his world—with friends so different from me—was unsettling. In this picture, I was the one who conspicuously did not belong.

Something brushed against my leg, startling me out of my gloomy thoughts. I looked down to find a beautiful golden retriever sitting at my feet, patiently waiting for my attention.

"Well, hello there. Where did you come from?" I reached out with both hands to scratch behind the dog's ears and pet its soft coat. "You are so pretty and sweet, aren't you?" I cooed.

Busy fawning over the dog, I jumped at the sound of Jackson's voice right next to my ear. "Penny's not bothering you, is she?"

Penny? Then it hit me. *Oh my gosh, Penny is a dog.* I almost laughed out loud at my mistaken assumption about Jackson's girlfriend.

"Not at all, Penny is a perfect little lady. She's yours?"

Jackson joined me on the couch, sitting close enough that we were almost touching. "Yes, I rescued her as a puppy almost three years ago. She's the best."

My heart started beating wildly in my chest. As Jackson continued talking about Penny, his already handsome face transformed into something altogether magnificent. For the first time since I'd met him, he regarded me openly and warmly, his smile relaxed and genuine.

With all the people and the talking, it was getting warm. But my drink was refreshing and

after several more sips, I was more relaxed. I wasn't sure whether it was the energy in the room or maybe the mojito, but my body was tingling pleasantly.

"You should come running with us on the beach sometime. I've heard that you're quite the runner."

"Oh that's right, Knox told me you live by the beach. That must be amazing."

"It is. After living at Uncle's estate, I really loved the idea of a cozy bungalow. And, I can go surfing every day, which is a major bonus."

"Surfing, huh? I didn't take you for the adventurous type, Jackson."

His grin was slow. "Is that so? Well, you have a lot to learn about me, Haley."

I glanced down at my glass and realized it was half-empty. *Okay, this time I am blaming the mojito, because I could have sworn Jackson's tone of voice was suggestive. Must. Change. Subject.*

"I've never run in sand before, but I'd love to try."

"It does take some getting used to, but I'll make sure Penny goes easy on you at first."

I laughed, "I'm looking forward to it. Running by the ocean always looks so fun in movies and on TV. Plus, I would accept pretty much any excuse to go to the beach at this point. Although I've been to the boardwalk and seen the ocean, I've yet to visit a beach."

"Wow, the guys have been slacking. We will definitely have to remedy that soon."

"Hey, Haley," Knox suddenly interrupted. "How are you doing?"

I smiled up at him. "So far, so good."

Jackson stood. "I'm going to get another drink. You want anything, Haley?"

"No, I'm good, thanks."

Knox leaned against the edge of the couch right next to me. "Is your first party everything you expected?"

"I guess, although I hadn't given it much consideration. It's actually pretty tame so far."

Knox scoffed. "Oh, give it time. It's early yet."

As if to prove his point, glass shattered from the direction of the bar. Knox lifted one brow, "And that's my cue. Will you be alright by yourself for a minute?"

"Of course."

Out of the corner of my eye, I saw five girls lined up at the kitchen counter taking shots and sucking on lime wedges. *Did they just lick their hands?* I had an inkling Knox was right...this party was just getting started.

9

SPINNING

When I caught sight of Chase hanging out with the same group as earlier, I took a closer look. The group was a mix of guys and girls, and while Chase spoke occasionally, he definitely seemed to be doing more listening. Unlike most everyone else in the room, he was holding a bottle of water instead of a beer or cocktail. It didn't surprise me; Chase struck me as a rule-follower, and he was only nineteen.

Realizing I'd finally finished my drink, I decided to force my way through the maze of people to the kitchen for a glass of water. Before I'd made it more than a few steps, I was stopped by a guy around my age who reminded me a lot of Theo but with more tattoos and less freckles.

"Hello, there. We haven't been introduced. I'm Devin."

Suddenly feeling shy, I replied, "Nice to meet you. I'm Haley."

"Haley, you're friends with Theo? Why haven't I seen you around before?"

My throat closed up with nerves as it always did when I had to talk about myself with a stranger. "Oh, um, I just recently moved to town."

"Well then, where is our Santa Cruz hospitality? We can't let a pretty girl go thirsty, and I noticed you need a refill." Devin motioned to my empty glass.

He held a short glass with reddish-pink liquid and a lime wedge. "It's a vodka cranberry. I'm told girls love them," he said with a big smile.

Not wanting to appear rude, I accepted the drink, and he took my empty glass from my hands.

"Thank you."

I played with the straw, wondering what to say next. It wasn't that I felt the need to escape. In fact, I was surprised by how much I was enjoying myself. I was beginning to think that I had overreacted about this whole party thing. *Why had I thought it was so hard to talk to people?*

I started to take a sip of the drink when all of a sudden, a hard, muscular arm wrapped around my waist, and a hand plucked the drink from my hands. Inundated with a familiar masculine scent, I knew at once it was Knox.

He growled in my ear. "No accepting drinks from strangers, Haley."

Devin scowled at Knox. "What's your problem, dude?"

"My problem is that I don't know you. Come on, Haley, I'll get you another drink."

Knox put his hand on my lower back and directed me through the crowd. I looked back at Devin and shrugged my shoulders. There was no stopping Knox when he had his mind made up.

"You should probably just have another mojito. You don't want to mix liquors when you're not used to drinking. And seriously, Haley. Never take a drink from someone you don't know. Got it?" His forehead wrinkled with concern, and I had to hold in a laugh. He was so darn cute in overprotective mode.

"Yes, Knox. I got it."

He looked through ingredients on the bar, mumbling under his breath. *Does he even know how to make a mojito?*

Liam appeared, shooing Knox away from the bar. "Please do not tell you me you're trying to make Haley a drink." He faced me, flashing his brilliant smile. "What'll it be, love?"

"Oh, thank god," Knox muttered, before sending me a small grin and walking away.

"A mojito, please."

"Excellent choice."

As he gathered the ingredients, he gave me a long look. "I'm glad we finally get to spend time together. You're the belle of the ball with all the attention you're getting this evening."

I rolled my eyes. "I have no idea what you're talking about. I've basically just talked to Jackson, Knox, and Theo. Well, and Devin, but that was only for a minute."

Liam laughed. "You're so adorable. You have no idea how many guys have their eye on you, do you? Not that I can blame them. You look bloody sensational in that dress."

I blushed. Again.

A pretty blonde displaying a shocking amount of cleavage interrupted us, and I was almost grateful for the distraction. Almost.

"Hey, Liam," she practically purred as she leaned over the bar, showing off even more of her considerable assets. "You got something back there for me?"

Surprisingly, Liam barely spared her a glance before shooting a half-hearted grin. "Sorry, my bartending skills are reserved for Haley tonight."

She cut her eyes to me, assessing, before turning back to Liam. "Too bad," she said with a pout. "Come find me if you change your mind." She sauntered off, her hips swaying with exaggerated movement.

I snapped my jaw shut. "Wow, is that normal for you?"

Liam just shrugged. "I've told you. The ladies love me." Handing me the completed mojito, he changed the subject. "Why don't we try to finagle a quiet spot over there," he said, pointing to a couple of unoccupied chairs in the corner.

Once we were seated, he angled his chair so that our knees just barely brushed. "Do you have your phone?"

I very obviously looked down at my dress and then my hands that were only holding my drink. Sarcasm oozed out of my voice when I replied, "Yes, just let me retrieve it from my back pocket."

Liam ignored my tone. "That's okay, I'll show you on mine."

"Show me what?"

"How to take a selfie, of course. You need to be able to send me pictures of yourself . . . the less clothes the better."

I smacked him on the arm, and his responding grin was mischievous and ridiculously appealing. "Kidding, kidding."

Using his iPhone, he explained the steps for taking a selfie and then suggested we take a practice shot. Liam moved his chair next to mine, then with one arm outstretched and the other wrapped around my back, he held the phone out in front of us and snapped a photo. I stayed surprisingly calm despite being practically cheek to cheek with Liam.

When I saw the resulting photo, I had to admit that we looked really cute. With Liam in his white shirt and me in my sapphire dress, we could easily be taken for a couple out on the town.

"Don't worry, I'll text it to you. I'm sure you'll want to save it as your wallpaper."

"Geez, Liam. I almost forgot how conceited you are. Thanks for reminding me."

"You're welcome."

When Liam became suddenly quiet, I wondered at the shift in the atmosphere. Twirling his signet ring, he stared down at it like it held the answers to global warming. *What is going on with him?* Deciding to wait it out, I took a sip of my drink and smoothed out the wrinkles in my dress.

He finally spoke, and his words stunned me more than his silence had. "Haley, I wanted to ask you something." He paused, "Will you accompany me to a fundraising gala on Halloween? It's a work function, but there will be dancing, and you will get to wear an elaborate costume."

Shocked silent, I stared at him. Was he asking me out on a date? It sounded like it, but he also referred to the gala as a work function. Either way, I needed to give him an answer.

Saying the only thing I could think of, I responded, "I don't really know how to dance."

Liam smiled one of his dazzling smiles. "I'll take that as a yes. And don't worry about the dancing; I'm great at leading."

Still surprised by his question, I couldn't think of another excuse to refuse. *Was I really going to a dance? With Liam of all people?*

I sensed a presence nearby and looked up to see Jackson watching us. "Liam, can I speak with you?"

"Sure. Haley, you staying here?"

"Actually, I'm going to head to the restroom. Would you mind holding my drink?"

Reemerging from the hallway into the main living space, I was struck by the loft's dramatic transformation.

The lights were dimmer and the music louder. Full of people and noise, it was no longer my quiet escape, my home. *Whoa, did I really just call the loft my home?*

I didn't have long to dwell on it because Knox nearly ran me over, and he did not look happy. Used to seeing him in jeans and a T-shirt, I was struck again by how good he looked tonight. Sure, his business casual attire was nice (and I had yet to see him wear the suit I found in his closet the day I was snooping around the loft), but the black motorcycle boots, leather belt and bracelets, and black button-down shirt rolled to the elbows suited him to a T. His dark jeans hugged his muscular thighs without looking tight or trendy, and man, did his butt look good.

He passed by quickly, barely noticing me as he marched off. *Knox is kind of hot when he's angry; well, when he's not angry at me.* I smirked. *No, even then.*

Alone for the first time in a while, I took advantage of the opportunity to people watch once more. On closer inspection of the crowd, I noticed a shift since the last time I had looked around. Several couples had paired off, and Theo's raven-haired friend was selecting records to play and dancing around the coffee table.

I turned my head when I heard the chanting of, "Shot. Shot. Shot. Shot." A few seconds later, Theo and several of his friends quickly downed a small glass of liquor before loudly setting their glasses on the counter. Most of the food was now gone, picked over, and the kitchen was littered with an assortment of items, the normally clean counters cluttered.

When Theo spotted me looking at him, he called out to me. "Haley! Come over here," he said as he waved me over with an overly dramatic movement. He was even more enthusiastic and happy than normal, and I wondered just how much he'd had to drink.

I walked hesitantly over to Theo and his group, hoping they wouldn't try to make me take a shot. Theo smiled and extended a hand, palm upturned in invitation. I placed my hand in his before he raised my arm over my head and then spun me around to do a twirl before pulling me in close to his body. It was such a fluid, almost automatic motion, that it seemed natural.

With his arm wrapped around me, and the heady combination of his woodsy-citrus scent, I was speechless. I stood transfixed by his freckles, and with those fiery green eyes and russet hair, ugh, he could make a girl weak at the knees.

Theo grinned and squeezed me lightly. "You're so pretty, Haley," he said before giving me a quick peck on the cheek and releasing me. Stunned by the impromptu affection, my cheeks burned as I blinked rapidly.

Theo's friends called for another round of shots and fortunately, Liam reappeared with my drink. I felt pleasant, like I was floating, and there was a golden glow about the room; everyone seemed so happy.

Except for maybe Jackson. He hadn't looked pleased when he'd pulled Liam aside earlier. "Liam, what happened to Jackson? Everything okay?"

Liam stiffened so slightly that I wondered if I imagined it. "Nothing to worry about; just work stuff. He's over there with Chase," he said, pointing toward my favorite armchair.

I got a glimpse of Jackson in the chair with Penny at his feet, but my focus zeroed in on the leggy girl sitting on the arm of the chair, leaning in so that her chest was practically at his eye level. Fortunately, he was looking the other direction talking to Chase; otherwise he'd unquestionably get an eyeful. Her intent, no doubt. *What is up with the girls at this party? Or is it normal for every pretty girl to be so forward?*

"Earth to Haley!" Liam's voice broke through my internal speculation, and I quickly twisted my neck to look up at him; even with my cork wedges, he still towered over me. He glanced between my face then back to where Jackson was sitting. "You okay?'

"Fine. I'm just getting tired."

If he noticed my fib, he ignored it. "You know, you don't have to stay out here all night. The party will probably drag on for a few more hours. And we can't have our party virgin overdoing it." He smirked, and of course, I blushed at his use of "virgin." *I am so out of my league compared to the rest of the girls at this party.*

Once again proving my point at the opportune moment, a slim girl with magenta streaks in her blonde hair sauntered up to us, her sultry smile aimed at Liam. "Liam, right? We're starting a game soon, and I've heard you're quite the *player*." She very obviously skimmed her eyes over his body. "You up for it?"

His accent exaggerated, he responded, "Sorry, kitten. I'm getting ready to leave, but you have fun."

Without giving the girl a chance to respond, he tugged on my hand. "Come on, Haley. Walk me to the door." *Wow, did Liam actually blow off at least two beautiful girls tonight? He's not exactly proving his player status right now.*

"Are you sure you want to leave with your adoring harem so willing to shower you with attention?"

Liam chuckled, "I'm just one man; I can't please them all."

He stopped near the door and leaned in close. "You know, you owe me a dinner." He ran his fingers over a strand of my hair before resting his hand gently above my collarbone.

My breath hitched at the contact, and I heard the tremor in my voice. "I do?"

"Yes, it's your punishment for having too much fun without me last weekend."

"So you admit that having dinner with you is a punishment?"

Liam grinned before leaning in even closer and whispering in my ear, "Good night, gorgeous." Without a backward glance, he opened the front door and left.

REVELATIONS

I SLOWLY WALKED BACK to the party, and everything seemed louder, more chaotic. I surveyed the scene, noticing people arguing, dancing, singing. The party was definitely starting to get out of hand, and the initial golden glow of my mojito was wearing off. My glass was almost empty, and I was very relaxed but also a little drowsy.

Raucous laughter rose above the noise of the rest of the party. Turning toward the source, I saw a large group sitting on the couches playing some sort of game. The coffee table was covered with bottles and glasses, most of them empty. Cards with words like "arm" and "tribal design" were strewn across the surface and scattered on the floor.

The girl with magenta streaks in her hair leaned forward, her low-cut shirt flashing a black lace bra as a guy drew on her lower back with a marker. When I saw a box with the word "Ink'd: the Tattoo Guessing Game" it all made sense. I scanned the circle, embarrassed at the idea of the game as I noticed a number of players with suggestive tattoos drawn on various parts of their bodies.

When a guest moved, I saw Ethan sitting on the leather

sofa, arm outstretched, glass resting in his hand. A knot formed in the pit of my stomach when I realized that a brunette girl with medium-length hair and loose waves sat perched on his thighs. I couldn't see Ethan's face, but from the few glimpses I got of the girl's profile, she was certainly enjoying herself.

Their easy intimacy made me uncomfortable. *Does she really need to sit on his lap?* They weren't the only ones that looked cozy; glancing around, I saw a number of couples leaning close together, touching and even kissing. Since I was pretty sure Ethan arrived alone, perhaps he had just met up with her tonight. *Awesome.* I had successfully managed to make myself feel even worse about the situation. I rolled my eyes before turning away. *Whatever.*

My desire to be pleasant and talk with strangers was fading quickly. Unfortunately, the girl that had been buzzing around Theo all night walked up to me. Feeling slightly awkward about the peck and wondering what exactly their situation was, I braced myself for whatever conversation was coming.

"Haley, right? I'm Kenzi." I nodded and tried to smile.

"Your hair is so pretty. Are those highlights? I love the brown with red coming through when light shines on it."

"Thanks," I smiled, "just my natural color. Actually, I've been admiring your flawless makeup all night."

She grinned and looked downward, almost demurely, before speaking. "You seem so close to Theo; I'm surprised he's never mentioned you." She smiled as if she was being nice, but it was a little too forced, and I could read between the lines.

"We haven't known each other very long. But you know Theo; he's never met a stranger."

"That's true," she said as I saw her peer in Theo's direction. She sighed. "I just worry that his friendliness can sometimes give the wrong impression." I didn't like her tone, and I wasn't in the mood to play games.

"Really?" I smiled sweetly before continuing in a level voice. "Theo can be pretty vocal about his opinions. I should know—he tries to barge into my closet and select my clothes every morning." I had the satisfaction of watching her jaw drop as I turned to walk the other way. I bit my lip; I had just been catty for the first time in my life, and I didn't like the feeling.

My initial ideas about tonight were correct—partying wasn't for me, and I had stuck around longer than was perhaps wise. I was tired of the party and tired in general. Figuring I made enough of an appearance to satisfy Theo, and positive he wouldn't even notice my disappearance in his current state, I decided to sneak off to bed. I glanced around once more, shaking my head at the scene. *Definitely time for bed.*

Looking forward to stretching out beneath my clean sheets, I moved wordlessly through the crowd, trying not to attract notice or conversation. But as I walked toward the hallway to my bedroom, a sight on the upstairs walkway stopped me dead in my tracks. I did a double-take, hoping I wasn't really seeing Knox, but his broad shoulders and dirty blond hair were unmistakable.

With one arm on the banister, the other encircled the waist of a tall, curvy blonde in a short, tight dress. Their bodies were pressed together, his lips hovered close to the bombshell's ear as she leaned into him. The sight made me recoil like I'd taken a punch to the gut, and when I heard the girl giggle loudly, I forced myself to look away.

I didn't want to see any more and stalked off down the hallway to my room, more than ready for the night to be over. But when I twisted the handle, I found the door locked. Refusing to return to the party and frustrated that I couldn't even retreat to *my* room, I stomped out to the back patio, hoping it would at least be empty. All the while, I felt like I was going to explode.

Pacing around the patio, my cork wedges pounded the pavement beneath me as my dress swished dramatically about my thighs. *Sheesh, Haley. What did you expect—that you were living in a perfect little bubble with six super hot guys that only have eyes for you?*

If their assignment to find my dad hadn't gone so wrong, I would never even have met Ethan, Knox, Jackson, Liam, Theo, and Chase. I often thought about how they crashed into my life, but I failed to consider that I had also invaded theirs. Tonight's party made that abundantly clear; no matter how much I saw them as *my* guys, they weren't.

Sure, Liam had invited me to the fundraising gala, but that was a work function, so it didn't seem right to call it a date. And Theo kissed me on the cheek, but he was so tipsy by that point, he probably would have kissed the refrigerator and called it pretty. I had to remind myself that to them I was an obligation, and for me, this was a temporary stop on the road to finding my dad.

My mind spinning in circles, I flung my hair back from my face before extracting the remaining strands from my lipgloss. I sucked in a deep breath, releasing it with a loud sigh. What they did with other girls was really none of my business; I had no real claim on them, no right to be upset.

So why do I feel so betrayed? Why do I feel like such a fool?

For the first time, I let myself admit it, if only to myself —I wanted them to be *my* guys. But even if one of them showed interest and I allowed myself to choose just one, I knew the situation was too complicated and my time here too fleeting.

I closed my eyes and inhaled, surprised at just how upset I was getting. I knew all along that this was a temporary situation. And if I'd learned anything in the last month, things could change dramatically in an instant. Agonizing over what might be or couldn't be was useless; my best option was to live in the here and now.

Trying to compose my thoughts, I remained standing with my eyes closed for several moments. So caught up in my anger and frustration, I was completely unaware of my surroundings.

"Haley?" Startled, I opened my eyes to find Chase standing in front of me. "Are you okay?" His voice was tender, concern shining from his pale blue eyes as he reached out toward me but stopped just short of touching me.

I nodded. "Yeah, I'm fine. I just want to go to bed, but my door's locked."

"Knox locked it before the party so no one would go in there. If you have your keys, you should be able to get in."

"I didn't realize I would need them, so they're locked in my room."

"No worries," he said, extracting a set of keys from his pocket. "I can get us in."

As I followed Chase into the house, I felt a little better. In all the chaos, I knew I could count on him. He had rescued me from the fire, he understood what it was like to be shy, and he was always there with a reassuring look or touch when I needed it most.

Chase unlocked my bedroom door and let me in before switching on the bedside lamp. The party was still going strong, the loud music sporadically punctuated by outbursts of shouting or laughter.

"What a party," Chase said, shooting me a knowing look. He seemed as relieved as I was to be hiding in the bedroom.

"No joke." I was beyond tired, worn out by the events of the evening.

"With all shenanigans going on out there, I'd rather not leave you alone. People can be pretty stupid when they're drinking."

I nodded, thankful for the offer; I didn't want to be alone and Chase was protective, comforting. I stepped into the closet to slip on my star-pattern cotton shorts and matching scoop-neck T-shirt, and when I returned, Chase was slumped over in the leather chair, barely awake. "Why don't you grab a pair of Knox's pajamas and sleep here?"

"Knox isn't really the type to wear pajamas," Chase said.

"Oh." *Oh!* No wonder he was always dressed in the morning and never lounged in pajamas, even on weekends.

"But I have an overnight bag upstairs. I'll be back in a sec. Okay?"

When Chase returned, he went to the closet to change. He reemerged in athletic shorts and his olive undershirt; he looked so cute with his sleepy blue eyes and disheveled blond hair.

As he walked to the leather chair, I asked, "Where are you going?" Rubbing the back of his head, Chase looked at the chair then back at me.

"Don't be silly. We should just share the bed; it's not a big deal." *THIS IS SUCH A BIG DEAL.* Sure, I had shared a bed with Ethan, but I didn't initiate it; it just kind of happened. I had no idea where my sudden moxie came from, brazenly inviting Chase to sleep with me like it was an everyday occurrence.

As we pulled down the comforter on the bed, I yawned. "I can't believe I'm sleeping with you and I don't even know your last name." Hearing my words too late, I cringed. "Not *sleeping* with you." I laughed nervously, "just sleeping," I said, drawing out the last word. I sighed; I wasn't making this any better.

Chase focused on the sheets. "I knew what you meant. And it's Phillips. Sorry, I didn't realize I never told you."

Just as we were about to climb in bed, the door swung open. Knox stood in the frame—face flushed and eyes blazing, the only thing missing was steam coming out of his ears. He glared at Chase, making me wonder if Knox had automatically assumed that this situation was less innocent than it really was.

He quickly turned his focus on me. "Where the hell were you?" His gravelly voice boomed through the room loud and clear despite all the music and shouting in the background.

"I went outside for some air. What's the problem?" I was tired and really didn't want to fight, especially with Knox.

Knox charged toward me, pulling me into a fierce hug. He held me so tightly, my feet lifted off the ground, and I instinctively wrapped my arms around his neck. Burying my face into his muscular chest, I inhaled, scarcely believing what was happening. I couldn't see anything; I could only feel his strong arms around me and his heart beating rapidly beneath my ear.

He dipped his head close to mine and spoke in a tone that was barely audible. "I was worried about you."

I could have stayed like that forever, but the sound of

breaking glass shattered the brief moment of peace. Knox squeezed me gently before releasing me from his embrace. He seemed torn between staying and leaving.

"I better go before they destroy the loft." Knox rolled his eyes and closed the door on his way out, leaving me and Chase alone.

Relieved that the evening was finally over, and still on a high from Knox's hug, I sincerely hoped no one else would barge in. I switched off the light and got into bed next to Chase. We were inches apart, and I tried to stay calm and act normal, unsure what defined "normal" under the circumstances.

But his presence was calming, and before I knew it, I was quickly fading into sleep. Just as I was drifting off, I heard Chase whisper my name.

"Haley . . ."

"Yeah?" I managed to mutter.

"You looked really nice tonight."

With my eyes still closed, I smiled in the darkness. "Thanks, Chase . . . And thanks for always looking out for me."

11

READ BETWEEN THE LINES

AFTER THE CHAOS of Theo's birthday party and the subsequent clean up, I was almost relieved when Monday morning arrived. I fed another document into the scanner, grateful Melissa assigned me such a mindless task for the day. Fortunately, she was too preoccupied to demand a rehash of my weekend. And considering I had shared a bed with Chase on Friday night, I didn't know how I would act if she interrogated me about him again.

The entire office seemed on edge, and I suspected it was due in no small part to Kenneth James's visit. As one of the four regional directors, head of the Washington, D.C. office, and a co-founder of Zenith, he was one of the few people that ranked as highly as Patrick Ross. I wondered if these inter-office visits were a regular occurrence, but judging by the atmosphere, it certainly didn't seem like it.

Honestly, I didn't understand why everyone was so intimidated by Kenneth James. Sure, he was one of the most senior members of Zenith, but so was Patrick. And while I hadn't actually spoken to Mr. James, he didn't seem as scary as everyone made him out to be. He had a long, oval face with a dimple in his chin. He had to be about the same age as Patrick, but unlike Patrick with his silver hair and tanned skin, Kenneth had blond hair and pale skin. *Must spend more time inside in D.C.,* I thought.

By five o'clock, I was more than ready to escape, and according to my calendar, Jackson was meeting me in the lobby. I was a little nervous at the prospect of spending time alone with him, but thankfully, the schedule said he was simply giving me a ride to the loft. Exiting the elevator, I reminded myself that Jackson was just another guy. But when he glanced up from his phone, my good intentions shattered like glass. His smile, though slight, made my heart jump and my steps falter. *Sheesh, Haley. Get it together before you embarrass yourself.*

When he led me to a charcoal Jeep Wrangler Rubicon, I forced down a squeal. "Can you put the top down? This is the closest I've ever gotten to riding in a convertible," I said excitedly.

He looked pointedly at my long hair hanging halfway down my back. "Are you sure? You're not worried about messing up your hair?"

I laughed. "Not at all. Why? Are you embarrassed to be seen with me and my crazy windblown hair?"

"I think I can handle it." I watched while he unlatched then unscrewed the two front panels. "Next time, I'll remove the entire hard top so you can get the full experience. But only if you promise not to call my Jeep a convertible."

Grinning, I agreed. "Cross my heart."

Once we were on the road, Jackson looked over at me, his aviator sunglasses perfectly framing his sun-kissed face. "I need to make a stop before I take you back to the loft. Do you mind?"

"Nope." I figured he was picking up his dry cleaning or something, and I was perfectly content to ride along. The sun was radiant, warming my skin while the fresh air whipped through my hair. I felt a sense of freedom and abandon as strands blew around my face and shoulders. All the while, I was still trying to get used to the idea of him driving such a rugged and adventurous vehicle. I guess what Jackson told me at the party was true; I had a lot to learn about him.

We soon pulled into a large circular driveway where uniformed attendants opened each of our doors before handing Jackson a ticket and driving off. Too distracted by the building's appearance, I didn't have much time to dwell on how odd it seemed to trust a complete stranger with your car. Taken aback at our unexpected location, I wondered what exactly we were doing at "The Corinthian."

We scaled the wide steps that led up to the front of a stately stone building with large ionic columns and flags waving in the breeze. The historic exterior stretched several stories high, and on top rested a more modern building that somehow managed to complement the original facade. Between the valet service and the bellhops buzzing around with luggage, it was clearly a swanky hotel. I quickly tried to smooth my unruly hair. *That's what I get for not asking where we were going.*

Jackson held the door open for me and we entered the grand foyer, complete with an enormous crystal chandelier. I admired the patterned rugs, dark wood floors, and antique furniture of the ground floor. We passed the reception desk and an elevator bank before exiting through doors to a courtyard.

When Jackson slowed his pace, I circled the quatrefoil fountain, surrounded by lush, green plants and delicate orchids. It was peaceful and cool in the outdoor space, the sound of the water pleasantly dripping into the basin. Unable to quell my curiosity any longer, I said, "So what exactly are we doing here?"

"I believe Liam invited you to the fundraising gala at the end of the month?" I nodded, and Jackson continued. "Well, this is the event venue, and I wanted to get a feel for it so we can start preparing."

"He mentioned it was a work function."

"More of an assignment, actually. Our whole team and several members of Team Falcon will be there."

Well, that certainly cleared up the question of Liam's intentions. What appeared to be a romantic date at a glamorous ball was actually just another assignment. I was genuinely relieved that Liam didn't expect me to be a proper date *until* the real reason for his invitation dawned on me: all of the guys would be working that evening. And Liam was stuck babysitting me; he must have drawn the short straw.

When the frustration and uncertainty I'd felt at Theo's party tried to resurface, I immediately smothered my negative emotions, consoling myself with happy thoughts of the gala. At least I would finally have an excuse to wear a Halloween costume. And knowing my fairy godmother (a.k.a. Theo), I would probably be wearing something extravagant with the hairstyle and accessories to match.

I thought back to what Jackson just told me and was surprised at his mention of another team being present at the gala. I'd always gotten the impression that the teams worked independent of each other.

"I didn't realize teams worked together."

"Occasionally—when we have a large or complex assignment."

Knowing this was as good a time as any to find out more about Zenith, I decided to ask Jackson a few more questions. "Do you like those assignments or do you prefer the smaller ones?"

"That's a tough choice since I like variety and crave a good challenge. But, if I had to pick one or the other, I'd choose the ones that utilize part or all of our team. We work best together without interference from outsiders." Perhaps I was being paranoid, but I really hoped that wasn't a dig at me.

"That makes sense. I've seen you all in action, and it's obvious how in sync you are."

"Yeah, that comes from years of training and then working together. Uncle really knew what he was doing when he encouraged us to bond first as friends and then later as teammates."

"Really? I didn't realize that your uncle was so involved in the process."

Jackson laughed a little, scratching his chin. "He isn't normally, but once I convinced him that I was determined to follow in his footsteps, he couldn't help himself."

"He needed convincing?" I was surprised by the thought; Jackson seemed like a natural extension of Zenith.

"Mostly he just encouraged me to pursue a different path, but in the end, I couldn't resist the allure of Zenith."

I grinned. "I'm confident he got over any reservations." I wanted to ask more, but figured I was already pressing my luck.

We wandered around the rest of the ground floor and mezzanine. Oversized flower arrangements, large mercury glass mirrors, and worn works of art enhanced the historic feel of the original structure. Jackson glanced at his watch as we neared the entrance to the hotel restaurant. "I thought we could grab dinner before I take you back to the loft."

Not giving me a chance to respond, Jackson requested a table and we passed the host stand. Enormous lanterns of wrought iron and glass cast a warm and almost romantic glow about the majestic space. The incredibly tall ceilings stretched above us, the massive wood beams inset with alternating panes of blue glass and intricately detailed panels of gold like stars in the night sky. The rest of the hotel was beautiful, but the ballroom turned restaurant was magnificent.

We were seated in one of the banquettes along the side of the room, and I felt Jackson's eyes watching me. "Stunning, isn't it?"

"Yes, that's an excellent word to describe it." When I turned toward him, I was slightly unnerved by the look in his eyes. *He's referring to the venue, right?*

Perusing the menu, I racked my brain for something to discuss over dinner while trying to summon the courage to strike up a conversation. Fortunately, I remembered that Ethan had mentioned Jackson's bookworm tendencies. "Rumor has it we have something in common."

He cocked an eyebrow. "Is that so . . ." He paused, his expression almost playful. "You're obsessed with manga, too?"

I tilted my head. "Manga? What's that?"

"Apparently not the answer you had in mind. Manga are Japanese comics." *Is he teasing me or is that truly an obsession of his?*

"Um, I was actually referring to reading; Ethan mentioned you're a bibliophile."

"Ahh." He tilted his head back, and the way the

dimmed light bounced off the angles of his face was breathtaking. "How many books have you read?"

I laughed. "Are you serious? I could probably give you a rough estimate, but I don't know the exact number. Do you?"

"Of course; I keep a list." *He would, wouldn't he?*

"Well . . ." Jackson stared back at me, unanswering, before I finally said, "What's your number?"

"That's quite a personal question, Miss Jones. Maybe I'll tell you once I get to know you better." He smirked, and I rolled my eyes at his response. After all, he asked first.

We quickly dove into the topic of books, exchanging opinions and debating which reads were best. Although our tastes were mostly different, we had a few overlapping favorites. And Ethan was right; Jackson was definitely a voracious reader. He conversed easily about many of the books I had read and seemingly endless ones I hadn't.

When dinner arrived there was a momentary lull in the conversation while the waiter inquired if we needed anything else. Once the waiter left, Jackson resumed the conversation. "Considering your love of reading, I think you'll thoroughly enjoy the gala. Guests will be dressed as their favorite literary characters since the gala raises funds for children's literacy."

I smiled. "What a perfect idea. And who will you be dressed as?" I tried not to laugh as I imagined Jackson dressed as Frankenstein, before the image of him dressed as Mr. Darcy almost made me blush.

"No costume for me; I'll be working more behind-the-scenes this time."

"That's too bad, especially considering your love of literature." I thought about his admitted appreciation for the classics. "Let me guess, you'd be Odysseus?"

Jackson smiled a rare smile, "Maybe. You would make a fitting Penelope."

Trying not to read too much into his comment about Odysseus's virtuous wife, I looked away, feeling somehow comfortable and awkward all at the same time. Despite our surprisingly easy conversation, Jackson always managed to make me nervous.

"Haley, I hate to bring this up, but unfortunately it's necessary before the gala." He paused, waiting for me to face him. "Did you ever see the men that were chasing your dad on the day of the fire? Perhaps more importantly, did they see you?" My breath hitched at the unexpected question.

"No, although I can't be completely sure. What does this have to do with the gala?"

"As you know, we've been keeping an eye on the client that hired us to find your dad." I nodded, divided between fear and the desire to know something, anything, about my dad.

"That same client hired Zenith as private security for the fundraising gala Liam invited you to."

I twirled my hair. "Ohhh . . ." I said, my voice lifting slightly at the end.

"Both of those men will likely be at the gala, and I need to know we can protect you if you attend. Also, I want to be certain you can keep a level head under the circumstances." His indigo blue eyes assessed me, awaiting a response.

"Of course." I picked at the food on my plate. "Actually, I'm kind of surprised Liam invited me as his guest considering what you're telling me."

Jackson sighed, and I sensed a note of displeasure. "If it was up to me, you would be staying home or keeping a low profile at the gala, at the very least. But Liam invited you before we could even discuss the situation as a team." I bit back a smile; Liam was definitely earning brownie points with me at the moment.

"Is this the typical kind of thing you discuss as a team—the social calendar of the girl you're babysitting?" My tone was playful, but I was truly curious. How much did they discuss me?

He chuckled lightly as he leaned back in his chair. "No, fortunately most assignments don't come home with us." His tone was so serious, it wasn't until I saw the corner of his lip curling into a grin that I realized he was joking.

With Jackson more relaxed, I finally worked up the nerve to ask him what I really wanted to know. "So . . . considering I'm included in the assignment, will you tell me more about the client?"

"I thought you might ask that." He paused to take another bite of his meal. "Did your dad ever mention the name Gerald Douglas to you?"

"Doesn't ring a bell. But obviously there's a lot he failed to mention to me."

"Gerald Douglas is a California politician; the gala is his largest philanthropic event of the year. Years ago, he was a District Attorney in Los Angeles. Based on the dates of his employment, we believe this is the connection to your dad. We don't know whose side he was on then or now, and unfortunately, it's not the kind of question we can just ask him directly."

"Wouldn't that be nice." I tried to limit the sarcasm in my tone. "My dad did suspect corruption within his own department, so I wouldn't be surprised if he thought there was corruption at the DA's office as well."

"Look Haley, you don't have to go to the gala if you

don't want to. One of us can stay with you and get another team to sub in one of their members."

"I'll be fine. And I don't want to be responsible for disrupting the team more than I already have." As if I could pass up a chance like this to get closer to finding out where my dad was.

He leaned forward, his eyes piercing through me. "I appreciate that, but think on it. If you change your mind, just let me know." I nodded.

"Also, whether you're attending the gala or not, you need to be prepared to defend yourself." My stomach churned, anticipating what was coming next. "Ethan and I discussed it; I've scheduled time on your calendar beginning tomorrow for him to work with you on self-defense."

The best I could manage was "Okay." I doubted I could get out of it, and I knew it was something I needed to work on. Even so, I could feel my anxiety rising at the thought of spending time alone with Ethan. After seeing him with that other girl at Theo's party, I didn't know how to act around him. But like it or not, I may as well get it over with. If I could survive hours alone with Jackson, I could handle a few of Ethan's defense lessons.

Jackson moved in close, his demeanor playful. "Can you keep a secret?"

A secret from Jackson? I'm intrigued...

"Of course."

He whispered unnecessarily in my ear and my answering smile was wicked. Ethan wouldn't know what hit him.

12

TOUCHY

I sighed, opening my eyes and glancing at the clock on my phone even though I knew I'd regret it. Tonight even the playlist of relaxing music I'd been listening to at bedtime wasn't doing any good. As the notes of the last song on the list faded, I rolled onto my back and stared at the ceiling, the shadows mocking me in my frustrated state.

For the first time since the night Ethan stayed with me at the cabin, I was overcome with the desire to escape outdoors and seek comfort in the night sky. Surprisingly, I'd been falling asleep easily over the last month, and that knowledge alone was enough to keep me awake tonight. What kind of daughter was I that I could push my missing, endangered father out of my thoughts with so little effort?

It was like I'd been living in a blissful Santa Cruz coma, and Jackson's discussion of Gerald Douglas today shocked me awake. Now it was all I could think about. What *were* Douglas's intentions? Was he involved with the criminals my dad had so carefully kept us hidden from? And, if not, what did he want with Dad?

I felt like I should be doing something about the situation rather than stewing over it in bed. But what could I do, really? If the guys, with all their resources, had yet to put all the pieces together, what chance did I have to figure it out on my own?

At least I could take comfort in the fact that they were actually taking me with them to the gala. I didn't know how, but I was determined to discover Douglas's role in all of this and hoped the gala would finally provide some answers. If not, I wondered how I would go around the guys or even get another chance like this to access Douglas.

My phone vibrated once, indicating an incoming text message. I ignored it, debating whether to bother checking the screen. A text at this time of night was likely unimportant, and I wasn't really in the mood to banter with any of the guys.

But, my curiosity got the best of me, and I found myself opening my messaging app.

Ethan: There's a supermoon tomorrow night.

I smiled but closed the app without responding. Instead, I switched to e-mail and re-read Jessica's latest message. Ever since our first exchange, we had been e-mailing back and forth every few days, slowly adding in details about our lives. Probably overly paranoid that the "bad guys" could hack into Jessica's e-mail, I had been reluctant to give her many details. But, I did finally give in and subtly ask her if she'd heard anything about what happened to my dad.

Her response hadn't told me much. Apparently the assumption around Coleville was that he'd died tragically in the house fire and that someone had stolen his truck, later dumping it a few towns away. Jessica relayed that when her mother was questioned about Dad by two men, she said she didn't know anything. And, she didn't mention me. At least that was one less thing to worry about.

I knew I should share the information with the guys, especially since it meant they might lighten up on their babysitting duties. But, I doubted that they would approve of me contacting Jessica at this point, and I didn't really want to drag her into the middle of it anyway. And, knowing they were constantly keeping secrets from me, I felt no guilt about keeping a few from them...including my plans to escape to San Francisco.

After researching online, I had a tentative plan in place. Since the bus fare to San Francisco only cost around twenty dollars, that part wasn't a problem. I had saved a decent amount of money in the short time I'd been working at Zenith. The bigger problem was what to do after I got to San Francisco and accessed the safe deposit box. It was too expensive to stay in San Francisco, so I was planning on taking another bus to a town outside of Sacramento. I'd stay in a motel there for a few days while I figured out my next steps depending on what I found in the safe deposit box.

I just had to decide when to leave. Part of me wished that I could disappear tonight, to move on and attempt to forget the guys before they became even more entrenched in my life. After Theo's party, I was finding myself more and more torn about them. I tried not to overanalyze the jealousy I felt after seeing Knox with the bombshell, Ethan with the girl on his lap, even Theo with Kenzi hanging all over him. But, deep down, I knew that my feelings were growing for each of them. And they shouldn't, couldn't; it was too complicated, too impossible.

For now, I would just have to deal with the awkwardness I felt around them, constantly wondering if any of them saw me as more than a friend or if it was all in my head. Finding out that at least one of the men who chased my dad would be at the gala was enough to force me to stay. Halloween was less than two weeks away; I could hold out until then.

Finally deciding that sleep was unattainable, I climbed out of bed to hunt for a snack, a book, or just something to occupy me. Maybe a distraction would help quiet my thoughts. If nothing else, at least I wouldn't waste any more time agonizing over things I was currently powerless to change.

My bare feet padded against the cool floor as I headed down the hall toward the living room. Folding my arms across my chest for warmth, I tried to ignore how chilly it was after the coziness of my down comforter. I didn't often wander around the loft in my pajamas even though it felt more like my home every day.

One of the floor lamps in the living room was on as usual, and I walked to the kitchen feeling restless. I stuck my head in the fridge, the fluorescent light flooding the dimly lit kitchen.

"Can't sleep either?"

I practically jumped out of my skin and quickly closed the fridge. Scanning the room, I didn't see anyone. "Theo? I didn't notice anyone down here? Where are you?"

He waved his hand from one of the large leather couches, and I walked into the living room to stand at the back of the couch, looking down at him. Lying on his back, Theo had his knees propped up, holding a book. He looked different, but I thought perhaps he was just tired.

I couldn't blame him. Last week Knox and Theo had been away more often and for longer stretches of time. I was dying to know what they were doing, but I knew better than to ask.

So used to seeing Theo perfectly dressed and coiffed at all times, this was the first time I had caught him without his distinctive swooped hairstyle. Resting on the back of the couch, I leaned over and ran my fingers through his russet hair before mussing it.

"Nice hair!" I grinned playfully.

He glared at me, his hazel-green eyes blazing and his jaw set. Accustomed to Theo's upbeat nature, his sullen attitude took me by surprise. "Nice pjs," he snapped.

I looked down at my favorite sleepwear—a set of satin pajamas in sapphire blue covered with white stars in several sizes. The silky, button-down top had the tailored feel of men's pajamas from the 1950s and looked cute with the matching drawstring shorts.

"Is everything okay?" I asked somewhat hesitantly.

"Fine and dandy." He responded, but the tone of his voice indicated it was anything but.

Did I do something? I wondered. Having barely seen him since the party, I wasn't sure what, if anything, I could have done to upset Theo.

"I have something that might cheer you up."

"I doubt that." He flipped the page on the book, seeming disinterested.

"Don't go anywhere; I'll be right back." I heard a puff of air come from the direction of the couch in response.

I returned with a small box wrapped by the local gift store in vintage map paper with a red satin bow. Theo was in exactly the same position as when I had left him minutes before. I leaned over the back of the couch again, extending the gift to him. "It's not much, but I really wanted to give you something for your birthday."

His eyebrow raised as he reached out to take it from me before carefully unwrapping it. I sat perched on the couch, barely concealing my excitement and nervousness while I anticipated his reaction.

His somber expression finally gave way to a grin. "Awesome! Thank you, Haley." He held up the stainless steel bicycle keychain that doubled as a carabiner and built-in bottle opener.

I relaxed, relieved that he seemed to love the gift and that his mood had lightened, even if momentarily. A surly Knox was to be expected, but a grumpy Theo threw me for a loop.

He closed his book and sat up, wincing as he did so.

"Are you okay?"

He swung his legs to the floor and patted the couch next to him. "I will be."

"What happened?" I asked, genuinely concerned as I sat next to him and grabbed one of the faux fur throws.

Theo sucked in a breath. "Not much, just some stitches and bruises."

"Not much?" I exclaimed. "Um, yeah, I totally disagree. Did you have a bike accident?"

He looked away and spoke softly. "No; I can't really talk about it."

I furrowed my brow, trying to read between the lines. "Oh . . ." I said, realization dawning on me. "Was it a work thing?"

He nodded, biting the corner of his lip. *Stupid confidentiality agreements,* I thought, wondering what he had been doing for work that resulted in stitches. Would I ever really know what the guys did in their work for Zenith?

He sighed. "I'm sorry I was short with you. It's just training for El Gigante was going so well, and now . . ." He threaded his fingers through his hair much like Knox did when he was agitated. "Now I'm going to be set back for at least a week, if not more."

"At least you still have two months or so to heal and train." I said encouragingly.

"Yeah," he sighed. "I guess you're right."

I sensed that talking about it wasn't going to make him feel any better; we sat in silence for a moment before Theo spoke again.

"Enough about me. What's bothering you, Haley?"

I ran my hand along the blanket, comforted by its warmth and softness. "I was just worrying about my dad."

"You want to talk about it?"

"Not really. I think I'd prefer a distraction, honestly."

He grinned mischievously. "That's the best idea I've heard all day. Let's go upstairs; I'll show you embarrassing photos of Knox as a kid."

I laughed. "Really? Will you show me some of you too? I want to see a five-year-old Theo in bowties and retro hair."

He shook his head and laughed noiselessly. "We'll see."

Theo rose cautiously from the couch, grimacing as he did so, and I wondered if he would be able to make it upstairs. I immediately took his arm and wrapped it around my shoulder so he could lean on me for support.

Hoping to distract him from his pain, I asked a question that had been in the back of my mind since my first days at the loft. "Speaking of photos . . . I've been meaning to ask. Did you take all the photos displayed on the wall above my bed?"

Through clenched teeth, Theo answered. "Yep, as well as pretty much every other photo in the loft."

After we slowly climbed the stairs and finally made it to his room, Theo was practically panting and perspiration beaded along his forehead.

"Theo?"

He nodded and said, "I'm fine, make yourself comfortable," before disappearing into the closet.

I perched on the foot of the bed and leaned back on my forearms, my feet dangling over the edge. I hadn't been in Theo's room since my snooping expedition, so I scanned the room to re-acclimate myself. When my eyes fell on Theo's previously full cork board, I sat up in surprise.

Where there used to be a collection of magazine clippings, there was now an eight by ten photo of me and a few remaining quotes. The photo was zoomed in, featuring an up and personal view from my forehead to shoulders. My body was angled away from the camera, but I was looking over my shoulder with a close-mouthed grin and pink in my cheeks. The background was blurred, and the sun provided the perfect light to showcase the red strands in my dark hair.

Overall, the effect was stunning. Somehow the photo made my natural look—disheveled braid, no makeup—appear almost glamorous. I thought back and remembered Theo taking seemingly careless close-ups of me while we were walking along the boardwalk. How was it possible that he could capture such an amazing photo without even trying? And why was mine the only portrait on display? Maybe he just really loved the composition?

When I heard the closet doorknob turn, I snapped back around, feigning boredom. Theo returned with a black box and a serious look.

"Haley, you have to promise you won't tell Knox I showed you these. He would kill me."

"Okay, I pinky swear."

I moved up the bed until my back was against the headboard, and Theo sat next to me, opening the lid to reveal a disorganized stack of photos. When he held up the first photo, I let out an involuntary, "Awwww." Knox looked to be about eight, his blond hair lighter and his cheeks much chubbier. He was wearing an oversized backpack and frowning like he couldn't believe he was being forced to pose for a picture. Some things didn't change.

As Theo and I pored over the rest of the photos, I found myself giggling at young Knox and Theo—their bad haircuts, missing teeth, silly expressions. I couldn't believe the number of freckles Theo had as a kid; pale-skinned and shirtless, his face and body were covered in them. I glanced over at him; he still had a dusting across his nose and cheeks, but they were minimal in comparison.

Whenever a photo included a woman I assumed was their mother, he would silently place it face down in the box and move on. I wanted to ask him about his parents, but after his surly mood earlier, I didn't dare bring up the obviously touchy subject tonight.

Once we finished with the stack, Theo returned the box to his closet before turning off the overhead light and sprawling on the bed, releasing a pained moan as he did so. His left arm rested palm-up on my knee, and from the dim light shining from his desk lamp, I could just barely make out the array of shapes on his forearm tattoo.

I lightly ran my fingers down his arm, following the lines of a geometric design that weaved through his other tattoos. His eyes shot to mine before adjusting them to follow my fingers moving over his warm skin. I ignored his look of curious surprise and asked, "Will you tell me about one of them?"

"Of course." He patted the pillow on my side of the bed. "You might as well get comfortable. It's practically the middle of the night, you know."

I shifted down so that my head could rest against the

pillow and turned on my side to face Theo. He held his forearm close to my face and pointed to a tattoo right in the middle. Finally seeing the shape up close, it was obviously a jaguar. Team Jaguar . . . of course.

Studying the tattoo, I was impressed by the simple yet artistic design. The outline was drawn in thick, black strokes with an intricate tribal design filling the body of the cat. The tattoo was positioned so that it appeared like the jaguar was climbing up Theo's arm.

"It's beautiful," I whispered.

"Thank you. I got it when I became an official member of Team Jaguar. It was one of the best days of my life."

"Really? Why is that, exactly? I mean, I get that you guys are close. But, is your job really so important to you to justify inking a permanent symbol of it on your body?"

Theo lowered his arm and angled toward me. "It's more than a job, Haley. Zenith basically saved my life. Knox did his best to keep me straight, but the truth is, I was headed down a pretty dark path."

"You? But, you're so happy and so . . . not dark."

Theo's smile was amused but grim. "Clearly, I still have my moments—I really do like those pjs, by the way—but I was a different person back then. I hung out with the wrong crowd and constantly got into trouble. You would not have liked the pre-Zenith trained and educated Theo."

"Are you referring to the youth outreach program?"

He tilted his head. "Yeah, you've heard about it?"

"Not really; Melissa just mentioned it in passing."

"It's an amazing program. The founders of Zenith started it about ten years ago as a way to encourage teenagers to learn life skills they wouldn't have otherwise. It's sort of a training ground for future security personnel, but you don't have to commit to working for Zenith. And just because you go through the program doesn't mean you'll automatically be hired. It just turns out that most people who complete the program want to come work for Zenith anyway."

"Wow, I've never heard of anything like it. So, is that how you met the rest of the guys on the team? You were all in the program together?"

"Yeah. The training is pretty intense, so you get to know all of the other trainees pretty well. But, the group of us that eventually became Team Jaguar were unusually close. It's like it was meant to be."

I remembered what Jackson said about his uncle, Patrick, encouraging the guys to be friends then teammates. Even if destiny wasn't involved, clearly the guys were shoved in the right direction.

Quoting Theo from weeks ago, I said, "Your own little island of misfit orphans."

He smiled then, the first genuine smile I'd seen from him all night. "Indeed."

Thinking about my own situation, I asked, "The misfit thing . . . does it bother you?"

"Who, me?" He laughed. "Haley, have you seen me? My tattoos, hair, clothes, freckles, bikes, hobbies, friends. Does it seem like I'm trying to fit in?"

I giggled, "No, I guess not."

"Why bother? I'd much rather be myself even if it means attracting attention or standing out."

He had a point. All of Theo's quirky traits came together to create his unconventional personality, and they were all things I adored about him. If Theo could be so secure in his uniqueness, why couldn't I?

"You know, if you're worried about being too normal to

fit in with us misfits, we could always shave one side of your head. You'd look badass like that."

I scrunched my nose and pulled on a piece of Theo's hair that was now hanging in his face. "Um, are you sure you didn't hit your head?"

He tickled my side in response and I writhed and giggled, reaching out automatically to retaliate. When I gripped his side, he started to laugh, but it quickly faded to a groan. I bit my lip, feeling guilty that I may have caused him pain.

He sighed, "Fine, have it your way. You'll just have to go on being beautiful and boring. It's such a curse."

Then he had the nerve to resume tickling me, and I was helpless to do anything but laugh while he grinned mischievously, clearly milking his injury. I probably would have been annoyed if he wasn't so cute.

13

DOWNTIME

Half-asleep, I turned onto my left side and nuzzled into the pillow, inhaling traces of citrus and lavender. The room was quiet, and I sensed that something was different without realizing what it could be. When I opened my eyes, Theo was sitting across the room at his desk, the lamp on and the blinds drawn, focused on what I assumed was homework.

It took me a second to remember that I had fallen asleep in his room last night. Theo must have heard me stir because he rotated in his chair and smiled.

"Good morning, pretty bird," he said in a cute, sing-songy voice.

In spite of feeling slightly awkward, I smiled. I was glad that he seemed back to his normal self again. He was already dressed and his hair was styled; I wondered how long he had been up and why he hadn't kicked me out of his room sooner.

I sat up in bed, rubbing the sleep from my eyes. "Have you been up long?"

He shook his head and I stood, smoothing the hem of

my shirt before running a hand through my hair. I felt his eyes graze the length of my body, and I wondered how disheveled I looked. It couldn't possibly be worse than the first time he met me—when I was wearing borrowed clothes and in desperate need of a shower.

He seemed abnormally quiet, but maybe he was being considerate and letting me wake up at my own pace.

"I'm going to make breakfast. Want some?"

"I already ate, but thanks. I have a test so I'll be up here studying most of the day." He stuck out his bottom lip, and I pouted playfully in return.

As I walked downstairs, I fervently hoped I wouldn't run into Knox. He didn't need to find out I spent the night in Theo's room. It was already bad enough that he knew Chase had stayed with me only a few nights before.

I massaged my temples. *Haley, Haley.* First I shared a bed with Ethan, then Chase, now Theo. *Who next? Jackson?* I laughed at the thought; I was almost certain that would never happen.

I grabbed clothes out of my closet and headed to the bathroom. The tile was cool beneath my bare feet, and sunlight poured through the frosted window. Off-white subway tiles lined the shower, contrasting with the slate gray floor and the almost-black metal accents framing the shower, sink, and mirror. Standing under the large, antique brass shower head, warm water gently fell on me. With no plans for the day, I leisurely closed my eyes and cleared my mind; it felt like I was standing outside in a peaceful rainstorm.

I looked forward to the rare days when I was mostly on my own; as much as I liked the guys and working at Zenith, I craved time alone to recharge. And considering how many new things I had experienced lately, downtime at the loft was exactly what I needed.

I shut off the faucet and toweled off as a few remaining drops of water dripped slowly out of the the shower head. I smiled at the cheerful yellow orchid adorning the white marble countertop; it was in bloom, thriving on the diffused sunlight and high humidity. After pulling on my clothes and hanging my towel over the bar to dry, I combed my fingers through my wavy hair. I was more than overdue for a trim.

Standing at the stove, I whipped up an omelet and consulted the calendar on my phone. *Great,* I thought. Self-defense lessons with Ethan were scheduled for this afternoon. I hadn't seen him since Theo's birthday party and wasn't really sure how to act around him. When we were alone, he always seemed interested in me. But after seeing him with another girl at the party, I realized maybe he was like that with everyone.

After breakfast, I grabbed Theo's spare laptop and sat on the couch facing the stairs. Since Jackson had finally told me the name of their client, I couldn't wait to find out as much as I could. I didn't want anyone to come up behind me while I was cyber-stalking Gerald Douglas, although I preferred to call it investigative research.

Skimming his campaign site, I tried to see past the political propaganda; currently a legislator in the California State Senate, he had aspirations of becoming a U.S. Senator. Gerald Douglas was handsome in that suave politician sort of way. He had the kind of picture one would expect— posed in front of an American flag, he smiled at the camera and looked polished in his navy blue suit, white shirt, and red tie. His full, dark brown hair was parted to one side and smoothed into place. He looked older than my dad, closer to fifty. His brown eyes sparkled behind rimless glasses, his smile reminiscent of the Cheshire Cat.

I stared at his face and felt like I was struggling to work out the solution to a complicated math problem. I didn't recognize him, but it was unlikely I would have met him when my dad was a detective. Even if I had, I was probably too young to remember.

Scrolling through the site, I read the rags to riches story of his parents, the fairy tale story of his marriage, and the ideals and optimism he wanted to impart to the nation. There was a brief mention of his time as a district attorney in Los Angeles but not much else; while interesting, it really wasn't helping me figure out his agenda. Was he trying to hurt or help my dad? Or did he even care?

I returned to the search results to see what other items showed up. Unfortunately, apart from his political history and some news articles, there wasn't anything of substance to be found. After a while it was clear I was spinning my wheels, so I checked my inbox for any messages from Jessica before clearing the browser history, something my dad always insisted on.

When my phone buzzed, I tapped in the passcode and saw a new alert from my *Words With Friends* app. Chase had introduced me to the game a week or so ago, and I was addicted.

I grinned and tucked my feet under me; he must be in philosophy class.

We played a few quick rounds before I stood and slid the phone in my back pocket.

Chase may have been bored in class, but he still had to pretend to participate every so often. Knowing it would likely be a few minutes before he played his next turn, I perused the bookshelves seeking a new subject to study.

Running my eyes along the book titles, I debated between the endless options—home design, art history, criminal justice, biographies. I finally settled on a book titled, "The Field Guide to American Houses." I had studied a few architecture books in the past, but this looked different with its focus on domestic architecture. I guessed this was a Theo book, but considering their mutual interest in renovation, restoration, and design, I wouldn't be surprised if Knox had read it as well. I wanted to know more about all of the guys' interests, and this seemed as good a place as any to start.

Around noon, I peeked my head around the door to Theo's room. "Hey, Theo, want some lunch?" I held up a plate with a sandwich and a sliced apple.

He looked up and shut his laptop quickly. "Awesome, thanks!"

"How's the studying going?"

"Pretty good. I can't wait to be done. I have more important things to focus on." He paused for a bite of the sandwich and grinned. "Like taking you shopping for a costume."

"Any ideas?" I leaned on the door frame.

"A few," he answered before taking a big bite.

"Would you care to share them with me?" I crossed my arms.

He shot me one of his mischievous grins. "Nope."

I rolled my eyes and smiled before walking off to leave him to his studies and his secrets.

* * *

WHILE I WAITED for the oven to finish preheating, I gathered the ingredients for a batch of chocolate chip cookies.

Grabbing the flour and sugar, I felt my back pocket vibrate and figured it was Chase's latest *Words With Friends* turn. I set the canisters on the counter and pulled out my phone, surprised to see an incoming text message instead.

Liam: What are you up to today? Wish I could play hooky with you.

Me: The usual - baking cookies and kickin' butt.

I grabbed the rest of the ingredients and waited for the butter to melt in the microwave.

Liam: Seriously, cookies? What kind?

Me: Chocolate chip

Liam: My favorite! Save me some? You can give the butt kicking to someone else.

Me: Ethan's on deck for today, but don't get too comfortable. You could be next.

Liam: Bugger. He better not eat all the cookies.

Me: Don't worry; I'll hide a few for you.

Liam: Thanks, gorgeous!

Although Liam had taken to calling me "gorgeous" lately, I didn't take it too seriously. I figured it was another one of his pet names for girls, like "kitten" or "love."

When the butter was sufficiently melted, I measured the dry ingredients before switching on the mixer and beating the butter and sugar together. With the mixer on medium-high speed, it was hard to hear much else as the beaters clanged against the bowl. But the noise was meditative somehow, soothing and reminiscent of baking cookies in Coleville.

I knew the recipe by heart and my body functioned on autopilot, freeing my mind to wander. What would Jessica think of the guys? Would she have a favorite? I added the vanilla extract, egg, and baking soda. Switching the mixer to low speed, I slowly poured in the flour mixture, incorporating it a little bit at a time. Knowing Jessica's penchant for tall blonds, she'd likely start flirting with Chase or Knox—or both—within minutes. I laughed at the thought; I doubted either guy would be particularly receptive to Jessica's exuberant personality.

After the ingredients were fully incorporated, I shut the mixer off and measured the chocolate chips. I couldn't help but snitch a few as I stirred them into the thick batter with a large spatula. The oven beeped, alerting me that it was ready for baking. I grabbed the cookie sheets and a metal spoon and began scooping the dough into balls before placing them on the baking sheet.

Once the cookies were in the oven, I grabbed my phone and opened a group text message before hovering over the keys. I hesitated between my desire to invite the guys to dinner and my discomfort at initiating text messages absent an emergency. But, I'd been wanting to cook dinner for all of them; it was something small I could do since they still refused to let me pay for anything. So, I typed the message and quickly hit send before I could over-think it any more than I already had.

Me: Dinner tonight at the loft at 7:00pm. Hope you can make it!

A few minutes later, my phone chimed several times, signaling incoming messages.

Knox: Count me in.

Theo: I'm stuck on campus. Save me some leftovers. :(

Chase: Can't wait! Thanks, Haley.

When the kitchen timer beeped, I pulled the last sheet of cookies out of the oven. They smelled like sugary-choco-latey deliciousness, and I resisted the urge to eat one while I shifted them to the cooling rack.

Ethan walked in and set his satchel and gym bag on the

floor near the couch. "Awww, cookies—for me? You're too sweet."

I smirked in response but avoided eye contact. I spent most of the afternoon trying to block our upcoming alone time, and now that it had arrived, I felt unprepared.

"Unless you're planning to weaken all your would-be assailants with freshly-baked cookies, you don't look very ready for self-defense training."

I took a second glance at Ethan, and it was clear he had just come from work in his slacks, subtly patterned button-down shirt, and trademark glasses. "I could say the same about you."

Feeling awkward, I almost preferred the thought of hand-to-hand combat over conversation. I wiped my hands on the kitchen towel. "I just need to change; be right back."

When I returned to the living room in running shorts, a sports bra, and tank top, Ethan was scrolling through his phone. He had removed his glasses, and I almost halted at the sight of him in gym shorts and a fitted T-shirt that clung to his every muscle. *Whoa.*

He looked up from his phone, and his rich brown eyes scanned the contours of my body and lingered on my legs. "You certainly make an attractive target."

I tried to hide the color rapidly flooding my neck and cheeks by quickly turning toward the stairs to the basement. Hand on the rail, I focused on the steps as I led the way, feeling my loose braid bounce gently on my shoulder.

After Knox had first shown me the basement, I started visiting it several times a week to work out. Despite being mostly below ground level, natural light streamed in from the rectangular windows located near the surprisingly tall ceilings. Part of the basement served as a gym, complete with workout machines, free weights, a punching bag, and a padded area for combat practice. The other section housed a pool table, air-hockey table, leather sectional, television, and bar area with a sink and mini fridge. Stained concrete floors kept the area a nice, cool temperature despite the openness.

While Ethan hooked his phone up to the speaker system, I walked to the padded flooring and stood silently, awaiting his instructions and fiddling with my braid. A song started playing over the speakers—a fast-paced tempo with an edge—the perfect workout music.

Ethan adjusted the volume and then crossed the room to stand facing me. "Let's start with some basic moves? I'll try to attack; you defend. It will help me assess your strengths and weaknesses."

My dad taught me a number of basic self-defense moves, and we practiced occasionally, but I was pretty sure I was out of my league with my new mixed martial arts master. I nodded and could feel the butterflies flitting around my stomach as I waited for his first move.

When Ethan's hand sprung in my direction, I successfully darted out of the way to avoid it.

"Good. Quick reflexes." he said.

He reached toward me again, much faster, attempting to grab my throat. Immediately, I shoved my right wrist toward his nose, and he backed away before I could actually strike.

When Ethan tried to put his hands on my waist, my knee jerked towards his groin. "Alright, point taken; no need to demonstrate." He smirked.

All the while, I remained quiet, focused. It was clear that he was holding back, and I was waiting for him to launch his attack. He stepped back a few feet, giving me space, but I could feel an undercurrent of energy, tension, surging between us.

"Unlike most of my first-time students, you don't shy away from hitting me."

I took that as a compliment and smiled, my muscles warmer and my pace faster. "Well, I'm not completely inexperienced," I said. "And it's a lot easier to practice hitting you than my dad, although I eventually got over that too." I flipped my braid behind my shoulder.

He pulled his shoulders back, stretching. "Actually, if I didn't know better, I'd say you *want* to hit me." He cocked his head, leaving the unspoken question hanging in the air. I shrugged my shoulders; he was more on point than he realized. I couldn't decide if he was the source of my pent up frustration or just an outlet.

"You clearly understand the basics. Now that we're more warmed up, let's work on more advanced maneuvers."

I grinned. "Bring it on."

We executed a series of maneuvers that were increasingly complicated; it was almost like a dance. Ethan would occasionally stop me mid-attack and give pointers—how to strengthen my stance, weaknesses to focus on, alternative counter-measures.

"Don't forget, Haley, your first goal is always to evade and run away. Don't engage if you don't have to." I nodded.

I felt hot, sweat prickling my skin; I inhaled deeply to catch my breath. Competitive by nature, my anxiety over being with Ethan faded as I focused on how to take him down. He was a good teacher, patient and very knowledgeable; he was also very strong and very quick. Now that we had moved past the warm up, it was getting increasingly difficult to combat him.

Ethan came up beside me and attacked so suddenly that

I was caught off guard. Left with limited options, I flung my elbow at him but to no avail. Before I knew it, Ethan stood behind me, one of my arms locked behind my head and around his neck, the other pinned to my side beneath his forearm.

Trapped against Ethan, I could feel his muscles pushing against my back as we breathed heavily, our chests rising and falling almost in unison. His nose grazed my temple and cheek before his mouth hovered next to my ear, his baritone voice low. "I like this feisty side of you."

My heart clenched and then started beating even faster. *Can he hear it racing?*

His arm wrapped around my waist held firm, keeping me close to him as his other hand trailed gently down the inside of my arm that was around his neck. My body shivered, unable to hide my obvious pleasure at his touch.

"But our time is up. So . . . better luck next time, Buffy."

Poof! In an instant my thoughts completely changed, and I felt like a bull facing down the red cape of a toreador. I couldn't let Ethan have the satisfaction of winning. Ethan's grip loosened, but his hand remained on my side.

Jackson's wicked suggestion popped into my head, but I knew I only had a moment to act before the opportunity vanished. Ever so slowly, I shifted my right side down, running the palm of my hand on the outside of his thigh. His breathing got heavier, and he dipped slightly to accommodate my movement.

I struggled to stay focused as his face brushed against my neck, tickling me. I reached behind his knee, running my fingers along the sensitive skin. He laughed and squirmed, loosening his grip on me even more. I used the opportunity to crouch down and jab him in the solar plexus, perhaps a little harder than necessary, before stomping on the instep of his right foot.

Ethan grunted and stepped back, releasing me from his grasp. "Whoever told you about that is going down." He sucked in a deep breath.

I grinned, feeling empowered by the self-defense lesson and perhaps braver than was wise. "No, you are," I said as I kicked his legs out from under him.

Looking down at his sprawled figure on the mat, I stretched my hand out to help him up.

He grasped it, his large, strong hand closing over mine. "You're ruthless, Haley." Ethan gave me a devilish side-eye, but I could see the edge of his lips curling up

"Don't even think about trying that again in the future." He yanked my arm. Unprepared and powerless against his strength, I landed on his chest, our faces inches apart. In real time, the moment probably lasted fifteen seconds, but it felt like a solid minute.

When I heard a door close upstairs, I jumped to my feet. I smiled sweetly and said, "No guarantees," as I sauntered off toward the stairs.

PARTY OF FIVE

I PRACTICALLY LEAPT up the stairs two at a time, grinning at the success of my suprise attack on Ethan. When I reached the first floor, I swiped my phone off the kitchen counter, hoping to get a final headcount for dinner. Sure enough, there were several new text messages.

Jackson: See you at 7pm. Let me know if I can bring anything.

I smiled, glad to see Jackson had accepted my invitation. I couldn't believe I was actually kind of nervous-excited about seeing him, instead of just plain nervous.

Liam: Can't tonight. Raincheck?

Liam: Preferably for dinner for two.

I huffed out a laugh. *Typical Liam.*

Ethan appeared in the kitchen. "What's for dinner, and what can I do?"

I glanced at the clock and realized we had an hour, hour-and-a-half tops, before the rest of the guys would arrive. "That's a very good question," I said, tapping my fingers on the counter.

I quickly inventoried the fridge and pantry, hoping we

had the ingredients for tacos. *Jackson, Ethan, Knox, Chase, and me—five*; we would need a few more items from the store. I looked over at Ethan and he was standing patiently at the counter, checking his phone. A flash of concern crossed his face before he looked up at me, his face composed once more.

"Everything okay?"

He ruffled his hair with his fingers. "Yeah, nothing to worry about."

Did his hair just look like that when he rolled out of bed, or did it require effort? Even after the self-defense lesson, it looked perfectly styled yet messy. My hair, on the other hand, felt beyond messy with my braid in drastic need of repair.

"So . . . dinner?" He asked.

Crap! How long had I been standing there staring at Ethan? I shook my head to clear the image of Ethan's fresh-out-of-bed hair, and I saw the corner of his lips lift into the beginning of that irresistible smirk of his.

"Oh, um, yeah. I think we need to make a quick run to the store," I responded.

When Ethan started the car, the radio was blaring. He hurriedly reached for the controller and turned it down. Was that Katy Perry? The radio station switched to another song, just as catchy, but not quite so loud. About three songs later, we pulled into the parking lot of the grocery store.

Ethan stopped at the sliding doors. "Cart or basket?"

"Basket should be fine," I said and walked toward them. But Ethan's long stride beat mine and he picked up a basket before I had a chance. "Lead the way, Supergirl."

I laughed, surprised that Ethan had called me by a nick-name. "Actually, that's what Theo calls me. Well, that and other nicknames." I bit my lip, not realizing what I was saying until it was too late.

"Oh really?" He said as his eyebrow lifted. "Such as?"

Pausing in front of the tortilla chips, I racked my brain for a suitable answer. The longer I delayed, the worse it seemed. "Oh, you know Theo; he likes to change it up." I hoped that he wouldn't push the issue further; admitting some of Theo's pet names such as "pretty bird" and "cutie pie" to Ethan was out of the question.

"Theo can't possibly have a monopoly on all nicknames," he said, maintaining a firm grip on the basket handle.

Ethan threw out a few names like he was trying them on for size. But each time, he shook his head and pursed his lips, dissatisfied with the option. I even scrunched my nose at a few of them.

When we passed the candy aisle, I laughed as Ethan wandered off without me. "Hey! Where do you think you're going? We have dinner to make."

Ethan stood mesmerized by the endless choices in front of him. After a minute or two, I tugged on his arm, feeling his large bicep flex beneath my hand. He quickly grabbed a few packages of Peanut Butter M&M's before letting me playfully drag him along.

"Ready to check out, Starburst?" He grinned, clearly pleased with his latest suggestion and awaiting my reaction.

"Absolutely, Milky Way."

Ethan laughed, the rich timbre of his voice warming me. "Um, yeah. I don't think so." He placed a few items on the conveyer belt as the cashier started ringing them up. "But actually, I like Starburst."

None of the other guys had arrived at the loft by the time we returned. Ethan switched on some music and then started mashing avocados for guacamole. I stood at the stove cooking peppers and chicken; my stomach rumbled in response to the sizzle and hiss of the food in the pan. Working together to make dinner, it didn't take long before most of the food was ready to go.

"Looks delicious." Ethan practically purred in my ear.

I jumped and almost lost hold of the tongs. *How did he sneak up on me like that?*

He placed his hand on my waist, and I felt a jolt of electricity as he stood behind me, my heart kickstarting into high gear. His lips felt like they were touching my ear when he spoke. "Nice work today. I was impressed, despite your unsportsmanlike conduct near the end. Tsk-tsk." The wisps of hair that had fallen out of my braid tickled my face, compounding the effect.

Hoping my voice at least sounded steady, I responded in a sweet and coy voice. "Unsportsmanlike? I thought you would want me to use an adversary's weakness to my advantage."

I could hear the smile in his voice. "That's true, but . . ." He placed his other hand on my hip and spun me around to face him. I blinked rapidly, surprised by the shift in my position. "That doesn't mean I want anyone else to know about it." His hands remained on my hips as I leaned slightly backward to avoid touching either of us with the tongs still in my hand.

I tilted my head and raised an eyebrow. "So, I'm just supposed to keep quiet about the fact that I took you down?"

"That would be great." He said it in such a matter-of-fact tone, I couldn't help but laugh.

"Seriously?" I wasn't going to gloat about it, but I felt entitled to a little bragging at the very least.

"Yes," he squeezed my hips gently, "It will be our little secret." He held eye contact, pulling me in like a magnet.

Out of the corner of my eye I noticed Jackson walking in the door and cringed. *This is so not what it looks like*, I thought, for once wishing Jackson could hear my thoughts. Ethan must have sensed the change in the atmosphere, or perhaps saw my deer-in-the-headlights look because he turned around, shielding me behind his back.

"Hey, Jackson." Ethan said easily, before shifting out from his attack-dog stance. Ethan looked back at me and raised his eyebrow, silently asking me if I would keep his secret. Flustered, I turned around and quickly busied myself with cooking without giving him the confirmation he sought.

"Let me guess . . . Taco Tuesday?" Jackson said.

I looked over my shoulder, hoping my face had returned to its normal color. "You got it!" I smiled and turned back to the chicken that was almost finished before turning off the stove.

Jackson and Ethan were pulling everything out of the fridge for dinner when Knox and Chase walked in.

"Smells fantastic." Knox's voice practically growled, betraying his hunger.

Chase looked stressed, tired maybe. But when he noticed me looking his direction, his face lit up into a smile, and he moved closer to say hello. Before I could wonder if he would give me his usual one-armed hug, Chase scooped me up in his arms, wrapping them around me and squeezing tight. He gave me another quick squeeze before releasing me, and I wobbled, struggling to remain upright after such an intense hug. *What was that about?* I scanned each of the guys' faces, trying to figure out what they were thinking, but they carried on as if nothing out of the ordinary had happened.

With dinner ready, I placed the final dish on the counter. "Dig in," I said, before the guys swarmed the food. Jackson went last, facing me across the kitchen island while Chase, Ethan, and Knox took seats around the large wooden dining table.

"I brought you that Napoleon book I mentioned at dinner," Jackson said as he spooned salsa onto his tacos. "Thanks for dinner; this looks delicious."

Jackson and I joined the others at the table where they were discussing college football and fantasy teams. It all sounded like gibberish to me so I was thankful when Ethan changed topics to campus Halloween pranks. I couldn't believe some of the outrageous stunts students pulled. And while I laughed at many of the hijinks, some made me almost thankful not to be a college student.

Throughout dinner I noticed Chase laughing, but he seemed distracted. He kept crossing his arms, rubbing his thumb over his bicep, lost in his thoughts.

We were all laughing over Knox's latest tale when he turned to me. "So Haley, pulled any good pranks, Halloween or otherwise?"

I shook my head. "Unless you count putting plastic spiders on my dad's pillow, not really."

Knox threaded his fingers through his hair, laughing. "Not exactly what I had in mind," he said before Chase and Ethan drew him into their sports conversation that had resumed.

I pulled my braid over my shoulder and started playing with the ends of it, thinking about the Halloweens of years past. Since trick-or-treating was out of the question, my dad made going to the pumpkin patch a special event.

Jackson interrupted my thoughts. "What are you thinking, Haley?"

I pushed some wisps of hair out of my face and smiled wistfully. "Oh, nothing."

"I doubt that." He pressed, his indigo-blue eyes searching my own.

Sighing, I said, "I was just thinking about all of the great Halloween traditions my dad and I have . . . had."

He was silent, listening, inviting me to continue talking. "It's my favorite time of the year. I'm sure that sounds silly; most people love Christmas or Thanksgiving, some family holiday with great food. But for us, Halloween was the one holiday we made a big deal of—decorating the house, watching scary movies, eating candy. And most importantly, visiting this amazing pumpkin patch—outside of our town, of course."

"Did you carve jack-o'-lanterns?"

"Yuck. Are you kidding? I hate getting my hands covered in pumpkin guts."

Jackson laughed almost noiselessly before I continued. "No, we decorated them with paint or hot glue and things like googly eyes a few days before Halloween."

"Googly eyes?" He asked, looking puzzled.

I giggled. "Yeah, you know. The little plastic eyes that move when you shake them." I shook my head and rolled my eyes around to demonstrate."

Jackson smiled, his features transforming into something softer. *Great, now he thinks I'm a complete goofball.*

* * *

ETHAN PULLED two pool cues off the rack. "Who's up first?"

Chase headed straight for the couch and turned on the TV. "You guys go ahead. The Angels are playing tonight." He stared straight ahead as he switched the channel to the baseball game and turned the volume on low.

Although I knew Chase was a baseball fan, I was surprised that he was being so anti-social. Whatever was bothering him must have been pretty serious. I wanted to ask him about it but decided to give him time to snap out of his funk.

Jackson took the other pool cue. "I'll take you on, Ethan. I need to redeem my standing after you beat me last time."

Ethan snorted. "Don't count on it."

"Be careful," Jackson responded. "Your overconfidence has been known to bite you in the ass now and then."

Knox chimed in, his smug grin evidence that Ethan wasn't the only overconfident player. "I don't know why you two even bother. Neither of you has a chance against me."

Ethan glared playfully. "Says the man who has a pool table in his basement. It's not exactly a fair competition, now is it?"

I rolled my eyes at their banter. Were all guys so competitive?

Knox turned to me. "Up for a game of air hockey? Theo told me you're not bad."

I wasn't particularly familiar with proper air hockey trash-talk, but I decided I might as well fake a little confidence of my own. "Not bad? That sounds like the kind of challenge I couldn't possibly turn down."

Ethan snickered and said, "Five dollars on Haley." He gazed at me knowingly, "She's tougher than she looks."

I smiled at his comment. Despite basically begging me to keep "our little secret" from the self-defense lesson,

Ethan was acknowledging my abilities. Obviously I wasn't anywhere near Ethan's level, but I could hold my own.

Air hockey, on the other hand, was a different story. Even though I'd won several games against Theo, I suspected that he was taking it easy on me, and I had no doubt that Knox would trounce me. *Oh well; hopefully Ethan isn't too attached to that five dollars.*

Knox hit the button to turn the table on and handed me a mallet as the cool air rushed through the vents. "First player to seven wins." He slid the puck toward me. "I'll even be nice and let you take possession first."

"Wow, so generous."

Remembering one of the tips Theo had given me, I slid my hand behind the knob instead of holding the top of it. Knowing that it was more important to make my shot accurate than incredibly fast, I aimed the puck for the left corner of Knox's goal. Surprisingly, it slid right in and I scored my first point.

Jackson and Ethan—apparently more interested in the showdown between me and Knox than their game of pool—both cheered loudly. I smiled but didn't let them distract me. I positioned my mallet about a foot away from my goal like Theo had instructed and waited for the shot. When Knox aimed the puck for just off of the table's center, I was able to slightly move my wrist to knock it away. I quickly gained control of the puck and aimed for the opposite corner as last time, but Knox blocked it easily. In a blink, the puck was soaring back toward me and slid right into my goal.

As the game continued, it was obvious that Knox was the more experienced player. By the end of the first game, I had only scored three goals to his seven. During our second game, Knox gave me a few more tips that proved helpful, and I only lost by two points.

Ethan groaned and pulled a ten dollar bill out of his wallet before slapping it down on the table. "Clearly I shouldn't have agreed to double or nothing on the second game." Turning away from Knox, he winked at me, letting me know he didn't actually care about the money.

I watched as Jackson and Ethan played pool. Jackson was relaxed and carefree, playing and chatting all the while. With Ethan, however, I detected an undercurrent of intense competitiveness. Unlike the poker game at the cabin, Ethan seemed invested in winning, especially as Jackson sunk consecutive balls in the pockets of the table. *What is Ethan trying to prove?*

Knox gave Jackson an amused look. "So, Jax, are you still having dinner with Uncle and Kenneth tomorrow night?"

Jax leaned over the table and shot a red solid ball into a side pocket. "Yes, I can't wait." His dry tone gave away his sarcasm. "Thankfully, Liam will be there as well. He's always useful for dinner meetings; I swear he could charm the stripes off a zebra."

Knox chuckled, "True. Where is Liam tonight, anyway?"

Ethan smirked, "He has a hot date, of course. Apparently her trust fund is as big as . . ." he glanced at me and cleared his throat, ". . . her hair."

My stomach dropped. Liam was on a date? I'd always known about his playboy reputation, but it was still strange listening to the guys discuss his exploits. Deep down, I knew that some—if not all—of the guys were dating. But, I wasn't used to hearing about it. *I guess the gala really isn't a date.*

Knox, Ethan, and Jackson changed the subject to sports and I zoned out. I couldn't help but notice Chase hadn't spoken a word during the entire exchange. I grabbed a couple bottles of water from the mini fridge and sat down in the corner of the sectional, facing him.

"What's the score?" I asked, handing him one of the bottles.

Chase took the water and looked up at me, but his eyes were glazed over. "What? Oh, um . . ." He glanced at the TV before responding. "The Angels are down by one."

I lowered my voice so the other guys wouldn't hear. "I can tell something is wrong. Do you want to talk about it?"

Chase grimaced, and I immediately knew what he was going to say. "Right. You *can't* talk about it."

He shook his head. "Sorry."

I forced down my frustration at once more being kept in the dark and tried to cheer him up instead. "Do you want to play pool? I've never played, so you're guaranteed to win."

Chase stared down at his phone. "I'm not really in the mood tonight."

"You sure?"

He finally returned my gaze. "Yeah."

Searching his crystal blue eyes, it was clear that he would sincerely rather be alone. I rose from the couch and had just barely turned away when Chase caught my wrist in his hand. He gave me a forced smile and quietly said, "Thank you for caring, Haley. Really."

Knowing nothing else needed to be said, I nodded and headed back to watch the guys play pool. It was Knox's turn against Jackson, and he was sinking ball after ball with what appeared to be very little effort. In this case, it seemed that his confidence was absolutely deserved.

When Jackson finally had a turn, he stretched over the

table right in front of me, and I couldn't help but stare . . . his polo drifted up and I could see the dips and curves of his muscular lower back. The exposed skin was as tan as his arms, suggesting that he spent plenty of time outside with his shirt off.

"Want me to teach you?" Ethan's deep voice snapped my attention away from Jackson. *Oh god, did he notice my wanton staring?*

"I don't know . . ." I tried to stall as images of Ethan "teaching" me to play pool flooded my head. Somehow I didn't think he would be able to resist getting physical with his lessons, and I really didn't want to act out that particular scene from pretty much every cheesy romantic comedy.

Chase's phone rang, providing a reprieve from Ethan's question. His voice sounded concerned when he spoke, "What's going on?" After a short pause his voice rose, his tone transforming to panicked. "WHAT?"

Chase ran from the room with the phone to his ear. Jackson, Knox, and Ethan shared looks of silent communication that I couldn't decipher before getting back to the game. *Seriously, what is going on?*

After a few minutes, Chase reentered the room, agitatedly rubbing the back of his neck. "Jackson, I need to speak with you."

Jackson handed his pool cue to Ethan, "I'm going to call it a night. Haley, thanks again for dinner."

After Chase and Jackson left, my mind churned with the possibilities. Did the apparent crisis have something to do with Theo? His text said that he was stuck on campus, but who knew if that was the truth. *Of course, if Theo was in trouble, Knox would be involved, so that can't be it.*

Knox's voice jolted me out of my ponderings. "So,

Haley, I'm going running in the morning around seven-thirty. Do you want to join me?"

I didn't even take a moment to think about it before exclaiming, "Yes!"

Ethan's lips tipped into his trademark half-smile. "You may need to repeat that. I'm not sure the next town over heard you."

I scowled and punched him lightly in the arm. He slowly backed away with his hands up, "No need to be violent."

Knox shook his head before saying to me, "Oh yeah, how did the self-defense training go?"

This time I stole Ethan's smirk while he just watched me with a pleading look on his face. "I don't know . . . you'll have to ask Ethan how I did."

Ethan responded, all signs of amusement gone. "She was great. A regular pro."

Knox looked back and forth between us. "Nope. I'm not buying it. Something happened."

I crossed my arms and glared at Ethan, patiently waiting for him to explain. He copied my stance and crossed his arms over his chest, his biceps straining against the fabric of his T-shirt. When it was clear that Knox wasn't going to let the issue go, Ethan finally relented.

"Fine. Haley may have distracted me and taken me down." He spoke the last few words quickly, as if to disguise their meaning, before looking at the floor.

Knox stared at him in shock before exploding in laughter. Between guffaws, he said, "Haley, you are . . . without a doubt . . . my favorite girl. Ever."

15

HOLDING ON

I IGNORED the chilly air stinging my cheeks and relished in the crispness of early morning instead. Even though it had only been a little over a month since my last run outdoors, it felt like a lifetime ago. Thankfully, I'd been able to use the treadmill in the loft for the last few weeks to build my endurance back up, but it wasn't the same.

Heading away from the loft, I took in the unfamiliar landscape. We'd passed mostly industrial buildings for a couple of blocks before following a windy road through Natural Bridges State Park. The trees obscured the view of the ocean, but I knew we were closing in on it; the smell of the salty sea air was getting stronger, and I could hear the distant squall of seagulls.

I stole a look at Knox, trying not to stare at the way his snug navy T-shirt molded over his broad shoulders and sculpted chest. At first glance—especially in his usual jeans, boots, and leather jacket—I wouldn't expect him to be a runner. A weightlifter or a boxer, sure. But after watching his powerful stride eat up the first mile without so much as a heavy breath, my opinion had definitely changed.

Bursting through the trees, we caught our first sight of the ocean and I gasped in wonder. Just a few minutes past sunrise, the sky was a symphony of muted colors; soft shades of orange, pink, and blue reflected in the mostly calm water. It was stunning in a completely different way than the magnificent sunsets California was known for. There was a peacefulness to it that made me feel both relaxed and happy.

Knox paused at the edge of the sidewalk. Pointing to the right, he said, "Sometimes I run on the beach but only during park hours. We can go another time if you'd like. It's actually a great place to look for whales."

"Really? I've never been whale watching, obviously, but it's something I've always wanted to do."

He turned the opposite direction and started jogging along a designated pedestrian path. "Fortunately, there's whale watching practically year-round in Santa Cruz, so that shouldn't be too difficult."

I soaked up the view of the rocky cliffs along the shore while we ran. Knox set the pace, and I could sense his surprise that I was so easily keeping up with him. Inwardly, I was gleeful. It was gratifying to be equal to Knox at something like running, especially considering his undeniable athleticism.

Noticing a few surfers wading in the distance, I asked, "Isn't it too cold for surfing?"

"Nah, it's really not that bad with a wetsuit on."

"Do you surf?"

"Sometimes I go surfing with Jax, but mostly I go kite-boarding."

"Oh yeah, I've been wondering about that ever since Theo mentioned it. What exactly is kiteboarding?"

"It's kind of a combination of wakeboarding and surfing with a really powerful kite attached."

"That sounds dangerous."

"It is considered an extreme sport, but it's not horribly dangerous as long as you're properly trained. Not that I'd recommend it for *you*, of course." He gave me a stern look, almost daring me to disagree.

I smiled at his protective response. "No worries. I'd be happy just to swim in the ocean at this point. But, I would like to watch sometime."

We passed a few runners and people walking their dogs, but we mostly had the trail to ourselves. I thought more about kiteboarding, and while it sounded exciting, I had a feeling it would be nerve-racking to watch.

"What is it with you guys and extreme sports, anyway? Kiteboarding, surfing, rock climbing, martial arts? Anything else I don't know about?"

"Hmmm...not unless you count sailing, and I don't."

"Ooh, let me guess. Sir Liam is the sailor?"

Knox chuckled. "Liam and Jax are both pretty into it. They've gone sailing with Uncle for years, but now they usually just borrow his boat."

Would Liam offer to take me sailing? The idea was appealing, but I knew I shouldn't get ahead of myself. Liam had yet to give me the tennis lesson he promised and I was already imagining him teaching me to sail as well.

"Speaking of Liam, he wants to teach me how to play tennis. I'd like to learn, but I'm assuming he's good, and I could be embarrassingly awful."

"I doubt that. Running is a big part of tennis, and clearly you have that skill down. As long as you have decent hand-eye coordination, you should pick it up fairly easily." He paused, "You know, I could give you a few pointers beforehand. That way you'll feel more comfortable for the lesson, and Liam will be surprised by your 'natural' talent."

I smiled at the slightly devious suggestion. "That would be great."

"No problem." Knox grinned, "We can't let Liam's ego get any bigger than it already is; any chance to knock it down a peg is a win in my book."

Choosing to stay near the water, we turned around and ran back the way we came. The sun was higher above the horizon, and while the sky was still beautiful, it was nothing like the initial sunrise. My heart was pumping and I felt energized, my mind clear. Returning to the industrial area and streets near the loft, our paced slowed until we were walking up the sidewalk to the loft.

Knox stopped at the front door of the loft and gently nudged my shoulder with his. "I'm impressed. I wouldn't be surprised if you could outrun me given the chance."

I bit my lip, holding back a huge grin that was begging for escape. "Thanks; I had fun."

"I usually run four or five days a week. You're welcome to join me if you want."

"Really?" This time I didn't even try to contain my smile. "I'd love to; I really miss running outside."

Knox turned to unlock the door and held it open for me. "As long as you're okay with early mornings. On days I go in to Zenith, I usually head out around six-fifteen."

I groaned inwardly. I would definitely have to start going to bed earlier. "I'm not that much of a morning person, but I'm sure I can handle it."

"Good. I need to take a shower and get a little work done. But after that, I thought we could go for a ride on the black beast. What do you think?" Knox's expression was a tad mischievous, hinting that he thought I might chicken out.

My heart leapt and my stomach dropped simultaneously. I'd wanted to ride on Knox's motorcycle ever since I found out about it, but the thought of actually making myself so vulnerable to the open road was intimidating. Not to mention holding on to Knox for an unknown length of time.

I attempted a steady voice. "Sounds great."

"Okay, meet you back here in an hour and a half. Make sure to wear jeans, boots, and a jacket."

After washing and drying my long hair, I braided it tighter than usual to make sure it would stay out of my face. I slipped on a hunter green fitted tee and skinny jeans before pulling a pair of camel-colored riding boots on over my jeans. I checked out my outfit in the full-length mirror and decided Theo would approve. It didn't exactly scream "biker chick" but it would do. I grabbed my only jacket—a thin rain jacket—and hoped it would be warm enough.

With about thirty minutes to kill, I got comfortable in my favorite chair in the living room and opened a book. After reading the same paragraph at least three times, I closed the book and grabbed the remote. I tended to only watch TV when one of the guys turned it on, but I was too anxious about the black beast to focus on anything else.

After watching an episode of *Family Feud*, I flipped through the channels until I landed on local news. On the screen was a photo of a smiling, pretty, blonde girl about my age and the headline, "Tragedy on UCSC Campus." The news anchor explained that the nineteen-year-old student was reported missing on Friday night, and her body was discovered in the woods just off campus yesterday evening. Her cause of death was suspected to be blunt trauma to the head; the police were urging anyone with information about the incident to contact them immediately.

As more details of the incident were shared, I shuddered. Even though I'd seen heart-breaking news reports before, this one felt so close. I was used to my quiet little valley where violence was a rarity.

Knox came up behind me and took the remote from my hand before powering off the TV. I twisted my head around and looked up at him. "Did you hear about that girl on the UCSC campus? It's horrible."

His face was as stoic as I'd ever seen it. "Yes. And it's a perfect example of why you shouldn't go out alone, especially at night." He tugged on my hand, "Come on, let's go."

I forced the girl's photo out of my mind and followed Knox to the garage. When we stopped in front of the huge black and chrome bike, I groaned. How did I get myself into this?

Knox must have read my worried expression because he moved in close and held my shoulders. "Haley, look at me." I peered up into his startlingly green eyes. "I promise that you'll be perfectly safe. But I know it's not for everyone, so I'll understand if you'd rather go for a drive in the Mustang."

For a moment, I considered agreeing to his alternative. But then I remembered my birthday wish; undoubtedly that past Haley would be disappointed in me for giving up a chance like this for an adventure. I couldn't let her down.

I pasted on a smile. "Are you kidding me? You're not getting out of this now."

I'm sure he saw right through my false bravado, but he just held out a helmet and said, "Okay, let's do this."

After helping me properly adjust the helmet, Knox climbed on the bike and waved for me to get on. I gingerly lifted one leg over the side and settled in behind him. I knew we'd be close, but I still wasn't prepared for the feeling of being pressed up against his back. I instinctively stiffened and attempted to hold my body away from his.

Knox took hold of my arms and wrapped them tightly around his stomach. Over his shoulder, he said, "You're going to have to hold on."

The bike rumbled to life beneath us, and my heart started racing faster than when I'd reached the top of the Boardwalk roller coaster. Knox drove out of the garage and onto the street before slowly increasing his speed. I could tell he was holding back on my account, and I silently thanked him for being so considerate.

As we made our way through city streets, I started to relax. Unclenching my hands, I spread my palms flat against Knox's stomach. Instantly feeling the hard ridges of his abs, I realized my mistake too late. *Great, now his ridiculous body is all I'm going to be able to think about.*

But, when he turned onto a two-lane highway and began to deftly take the curves of the very windy road, I was sufficiently distracted. I tightened my hold on him, closed my eyes, and squealed. Even though our speed had barely increased, it felt like we were moving exponentially faster.

When I forced my eyes open, my fleeting moment of panic transformed into one of thrilling danger. I relaxed my body and attempted to lean into the curves of the road, following Knox's movements. Finally calm enough to actually observe my surroundings, I realized that the road was enveloped by redwoods.

Entranced by the scenery, I began to truly enjoy the ride and the feeling of the air rushing by as we cruised along. I could understand why Knox loved it so much; it was like we were one with the road. Sure, there was risk involved, but there was also something so sensory, so tangible, that was unlike anything else I had ever done. The whole experience was exhilarating.

After about thirty minutes on the road, Knox pulled up to a ranger's station for the Henry Cowell Redwoods State Park. He paid the day use fee before parking and turning off the bike. He motioned for me to climb off first and held out his hand to steady me. When I stood up, my legs were shaky; from nerves or excitement, I wasn't sure.

I took off my helmet and pushed back the stray hairs that had fallen from my braid. Knox removed his helmet and ran his fingers through his hair once to smooth it away from his face. *How does his hair always look perfect? So not fair.*

"What'd you think? Ready to go out and buy a leather jacket and real boots?" He said, glancing down at my riding boots.

Ignoring his jab at my unquestionably stylish boots, I said, "What a rush," before exhaling loudly and then grinning. I could feel the warmth flooding back into my body, replacing the shaky feeling that had been there only moments earlier.

"Yeah, I could tell when you finally loosened up. Hopefully now that you've gotten past your initial fear, you'll be able to relax easier."

"Let's hope so."

Knox pointed toward a map marking the beginning of a trail. "There's an easy hike through old-growth redwoods. You interested?"

"Absolutely! I loved seeing all the redwoods at UCSC, so I can only imagine how stunning the old-growth must be."

"It is pretty spectacular. That was one of my favorite things about UCSC, actually."

"Really? I didn't realize you went there as well. What did you study?"

"Electrical engineering."

I stopped in my tracks. "Wow, I had no idea. Isn't that a pretty challenging program?"

Knox chuckled. "Why? Don't you think I'm smart enough?"

My cheeks flushed as I tried to put my meaning into words. "I didn't mean it like that. I just never imagined you spending that much time studying."

He started walking again. "I admit that I didn't love the studying part, but I liked the subject. I've always been interested in how things work."

"That makes sense considering your interest in cars. Have you thought about finding a job in engineering?" I was starting to sound like a broken record. First Ethan, then Tyler, and now Knox.

"No, I always planned on working full-time at Zenith after graduation. But, I felt like I should earn a degree while I had the chance."

"Back-up plan?"

"Not really. More like a 'to better myself' plan. Zenith actually encourages their recruits to study whatever subject they're interested in, even if it's not directly related to private security."

"I guess that explains Theo majoring in the history of art and visual culture."

Knox groaned. "Don't even get me started. Sometimes I want to smack some sense into my brother. I doubt he could have picked a more ridiculous degree even if he tried."

Noticing the pained look on Knox's face, I laughed.

"Well, at least he seems to enjoy it, and it's not like he'll have to search for a job after college anyway."

"Thank god."

"So did you, Liam, and Jackson all go to college together and party all the time?"

Knox halted. "Please don't tell me you just accused me of partying. I despise parties. I always end up cleaning up messes and taking care of annoying drunk girls."

"Now that you mention it, you did seem pretty stressed at Theo's party."

He shook his head. "It was awful. Be glad you left when you did. I found a wasted girl wandering around upstairs, and I'm pretty sure she would have tumbled down the stairs if I hadn't caught her just in time. Stupid high heels."

Wasted girl? Upstairs? The pieces clicked into space and I bit back a smile. Knox wasn't getting intimate with the blonde bombshell at the party; he was just being a good guy. I felt like a weight was lifted off my shoulders and tried not to analyze why I cared so much.

"And, we probably wouldn't have partied together anyway. Liam and Jax both got degrees in business from Stanford."

My head snapped back in shock. "Stanford? I can't believe I didn't know that."

"Well, Jax doesn't exactly go around bragging about his alma mater." Knox grinned, "Liam, however, is a different story. I'm surprised you haven't yet heard all about his Stanford glory days."

We wandered along the path sprinkled with fallen leaves, and I found myself enchanted by the massive redwoods. There was something about standing amidst trees that had lived for a thousand years that made me feel all at once insignificant and honored. With bursts of sunlight filtering through the canopy, the effect was nothing less than ethereal.

When we stopped by a stream, I wished Theo was there to capture the picturesque scene. Knowing I wouldn't do it justice, I pulled my phone from the inside pocket of my jacket and snapped a few photos.

"Do you want me to take a picture of you?" Knox offered.

"No, but we could take one together?" My voice squeaked a little on the last few words. I seriously doubted Knox would agree.

"Okay, just don't use the 's' word. I really hate that word."

I laughed at his reference to "selfie." "I promise."

Knox wrapped his arm around my shoulder and pulled me in close for the photo. Beneath the redwoods, it was cool and his body was warm against mine. The closeness felt intimate yet comforting. Perfectly positioned in the crook of his arm, I could have stayed there all day.

We settled on a patch of soft grass near the stream and relaxed in silence. I was startled when Knox spoke, his deep voice louder than usual in the quiet forest. "So, Haley, how are you adjusting to Santa Cruz?"

I shifted so that I could look him in the eye while attempting to form a response. If anyone other than Knox had asked, I likely would have provided a surface "everything's great" reply. But, I could tell that he sincerely wanted to know, and I couldn't give him less than the truth.

"Some days I really love it. There are so many interesting new things to do and see. That part of it is practically a dream come true for me."

"But?"

I blew out a loud breath before finally responding. "But,

I feel guilty anytime I'm truly enjoying myself. I'm not even supposed to be here in the first place; I didn't choose this. And, I don't know that I should have given in so easily. I should be out there actively searching for my dad instead of having adventures and making cookies."

"Don't be so hard on yourself. I haven't met your dad, but from the way you speak about him, I can tell that he's a good man. He would want you to be protected and happy. And, honestly, he's probably safer if you don't know where he is."

I sighed. I knew he was right, but it was still hard to hear. "I just worry that I'll never see him again." *Did I really just admit that out loud?* I had barely admitted that fear to myself.

I felt a lone tear roll down my cheek. Knox gently caught it with his thumb before pulling me into another one of his bear hugs. Held tight against his chest, Knox spoke in my ear, his voice heavy with promise. "Haley, we will find him. And I'm here for you—anytime you want to talk about it. You can come to me about anything."

16

A PERFECT FIT

SITTING in the leather salon chair facing the large mirror, I wondered at my surroundings. I had barely mentioned the need for a haircut to Theo and now we were at a salon, awaiting the arrival of my new stylist. "*Stylist*," I thought, *it sounds so fancy*. Used to a no-frills walk-in shop in Minden, the price of the entire haircut there would maybe cover the tip at this salon. *Maybe*.

Theo stood behind the chair chatting with another employee while I sat quietly. I had seen too many episodes of *America's Next Top Model* with Jessica to stay calm; I knew what often happened to the girls with long hair —*whack*. They often got the shortest and most severe haircuts.

When Theo finished his conversation, he turned to me and placed his hand on my shoulder. "Everything okay? You look like you're getting ready to jump out of a plane."

I bit my lip. "Just a little nervous about having a new person cut my hair."

Theo smiled, gripping both my shoulders while he stood behind the chair and met my eyes in the mirror.

"Don't worry, Haley. Max is the best, and you'll look great." Under his breath, I thought I heard him say, "Not that you could ever *not* look great."

A stunning girl with olive skin and a long raven ponytail walked up to Theo. He immediately smiled and turned to hug her. "Max!" *Max is a girl?* If I hadn't been so apprehensive about the whole thing, I probably would have felt more jealous at their interaction.

Max turned toward me. "You must be Haley." She smiled warmly, relaxing me almost instantly.

Her high cheekbones and long black eyelashes were stunning, exotic even. It took me a minute to realize that the sides of her hair were shaved, giving her otherwise girly look a serious edge. And while her black clothes conformed to the uniform of other salon employees, in skinny black jeans with black leather ankle boots and a loose black top banded at her waist, her personal style made an impression. As she moved, her shirt slipped off the edge of her shoulder, revealing a bra strap and a tattoo.

"Theo, are you going to hang out here or let us have some girl time?" Max shot him a mischievous grin.

Theo pulled his phone out of his pocket and glanced at it. "Actually, if it's okay with you, Haley, I may run a quick errand." I nodded; if Theo trusted Max, I could too.

Theo squeezed my shoulder and then headed for the door before quickly turning back. "Don't let me forget to discuss those hairstyles for the gala when I get back." Max nodded, shooing him away.

Max gently ran her fingers through my hair. "Your hair is beautiful, Haley. I love the subtle complexity of the color, and it has the best texture. You have gorgeous waves; I bet you drive all the boys crazy."

"Thank you." I smiled. "I love your hair, although I'd

never be brave enough to do it myself. But you really pull it off."

"So what are you thinking you want to do today? Just a trim or something more . . . daring?" She raised an eyebrow.

"It's long overdue for a trim, but I don't want to do anything drastic."

"Okay," Max said. "So maybe keep the long layers, but shape it up and take off an inch or two. Sound good?" I nodded. "Great. Let's get you back to the shampoo area."

I followed Max to the back of the salon, the noise intensifying as we passed people chatting and blow dryers humming. A clean, calm scent perfumed the air and everything looked fresh and new. It was somewhat chaotic, but there was still a sense of relaxation and rejuvenation.

I leaned my head back and closed my eyes while Max shampooed my hair. The water was pleasantly hot and her hands were adept at massaging my scalp; I felt like I was melting into a pool of butter. It ended all too soon and we headed back to her chair where she draped a cape over me before combing out my hair.

She circled my head, combing and cutting my wet hair. "So, Haley. Theo tells me you're new to the area. How do you like Santa Cruz?"

"It's beautiful here, I love it."

"Have you been to the Boardwalk yet?"

I smiled, remembering the night Theo, Chase, Jackson and I spent there. "Yes, we had a blast."

"How about whale watching at Natural Bridges?"

"I just found out about that, actually. I'd love to go."

"I'm sure Theo would be happy to take you," she said, giving me a slightly inquisitive look before continuing. "He clearly adores you."

I squeezed my hands together under the cape, trying to

remain composed. *Does she mean he adores me as a friend-sister-type-thing or something more?*

"Have you known each other long?" I asked, hoping to deflect from me and Theo.

"We met through my boyfriend, Chad. Chad's a tattoo artist and when Theo found out I cut hair, he started coming to me. But he's never brought a girlfriend to see me."

"Oh . . . we're not dating." I quickly blurted out.

"Shame," she said, pulling two pieces of hair near my face down to make sure they were even, "You would be really cute together."

Fortunately, Max switched on the blow dryer, leaving me alone with my thoughts. If Max thought I was dating Theo, did that mean he was single? If so, what was up with the whole Kenzi situation? Despite all my questions, my mind kept coming back to one thing: *Max thinks we would be cute together?*

I felt lighter after the trim. As I admired my reflection I was reminded, yet again, at how good Theo was at making me look and feel better. He returned just as Max was putting the finishing touches on my hair.

"Lookin' good!" Theo said, his face lighting up into a grin. "Nice job, Max."

I blushed at Theo's compliment, wondering if Max was watching our interaction more closely now.

Theo pulled out his phone and showed something on the screen to Max. "Ooohhh, that's fantastic, Theo."

Assuming he had just shown her my costume for the gala, I glared playfully at Theo. Theo continued to focus on Max, but in the mirror I saw him grin, fully aware that I was watching him. Despite my persistent efforts, Theo continually refused to tell me anything about my costume for the gala; he said he wanted it to be a surprise. Since we were going to the costume shop this afternoon, I hoped I wouldn't have to wait much longer.

Max and Theo were lost in their own world, whispering behind their hands and pointing excitedly at the screen. They walked over to me and started talking in vague messages as they alternated pulling back sections of my hair. Finally, they looked at each other and nodded in unison, clearly pleased with whatever grand plans they had concocted.

Before we left, Max hugged both me and Theo and said she'd see us next week for the gala.

When Theo and I stepped outside, a gentle breeze blew through my hair, the clean scent swirling around me. I felt happy, content.

"How'd you like Max?"

"She's great! Very easy to talk to and I really love my new haircut. Thanks again, Theo." I smiled.

He tugged a piece of my hair. "See. I told you not to worry."

"I know," I said, lightly butting my shoulder into his. "You were right, *as always.*" He beamed, clearly pleased by the compliment.

"Did she tell you about Chad?"

"Yeah, she mentioned he's a tattoo artist. She also talked about you."

"Oh really?" He asked, his voice raising slightly at the end—sounding more lighthearted than surprised.

Theo opened the car door for me before walking around to the driver's side. After he was buckled in, I said, "Yeah. She thought I was your girlfriend." I hesitated for a moment before continuing, "Does she not know about Kenzi?"

Theo paused with the key in the ignition, then quickly turned the key to start the car. "What about Kenzi?"

"I just thought after your party that you and Kenzi were dating or something."

Theo laughed nervously. "She's part of my group of friends, that's all."

"So that's why she was practically co-hosting your birthday party?" I asked, teasing him although I really wanted to know.

When he responded, his tone was playful. "Why are you so interested in my love life?"

"I was just curious." I paused, wondering if I should even say the rest of what I was thinking.

"Haley?" He quickly glanced over.

"Other than Jessica, you're my best friend. And I'm not sure a girlfriend would like or understand how close we are; she might get jealous." *Kenzi definitely would,* I thought.

"Oh." *Was there a note of disappointment in his voice?*

Theo pulled into a parking spot between a Prius and a car with a "Santa Cruz" sticker on the rear window. "Now, you have a ball to attend a week from today, and Liam will not be pleased with me if I don't have you properly outfitted." He quickly launched into an overview of the history of masquerades and masks. It was quite fascinating, but I wondered why Theo was so desperately trying to change the topic from dating.

When we walked into the costume shop, I couldn't help but get excited. Having never really had the chance to dress up, I relished the thought of wearing a costume and attending a ball. Surrounded by racks and racks of costumes, they ranged from hideous and scary to fabulous and glamorous. I trusted Theo, but I was dying to know what my costume was.

"This place is awesome." I said, still gazing around in

wonder at all the costumes, accessories, hats, swords, you name it.

"I knew you would love it." Theo grabbed my hand, pulling me through the over-stuffed shop toward the back. "Now come on, we have a fitting."

"Hello, Theodore," said an older woman with a Polish accent. I smiled at her use of Theo's full name.

"Nice to see you, Madame Walska." Theo leaned forward and kissed her on the cheek before stepping back. "This is Haley; we are here for her costume fitting."

"Yes, yes, of course. Lovely to meet you, Haley. Follow me, please."

Theo and I followed Madame Walska behind a plum-colored velvet curtain to a large space filled with chairs, mirrors, and several smaller changing rooms.

"Would you like to sit, Theodore?" She gestured to one of the large antique upholstered couches where Theo promptly sat.

"Through here, my dear," she said as she held back another curtain that blocked off one of the fitting rooms. Stepping inside, I saw three costumes laid out with matching shoes and could barely contain my excitement. There was a large ball gown that looked like it belonged on the set of *Gone with the Wind*, an elegant velvet dress inspired by the Middle Ages, and a satin and glitter dropped-waist dress perfect for Daisy Buchanan. *Where do I even start?*

As if reading my mind, Theo called from outside the curtain, "Start with *Gatsby*." I grinned.

Madame Walska stepped outside and closed the curtain. "Let me know if you require assistance."

I slipped into the dress, the smooth silk fabric sliding deliciously over my skin and clinging to my curves. I felt comfortable and sexy. I looked at my reflection wondering what Liam and the others would think. I took a breath and opened the curtain.

Madame Walska led me to a raised platform in front of a trio of mirrors. "Yes," she paused, evaluating. "This is nice."

I could see Theo's face in the mirror, and he stretched his arm over the back of the couch, watching me thoughtfully. "Definitely an option. What do you think, Haley?"

I turned and admired the dress in the mirror. "It's beautiful."

"It is, but you still have two more dresses to try."

I selected the ball gown next. I stared at it, trying to decide where to begin when Madame Walska peeped her head in the curtain. "Would you like assistance?" I nodded, grateful for her perceptiveness.

After layering a corset with an under petticoat, hoop skirt, over petticoat, and finally the overlay, she put the finishing touches on the costume. How did women of the past wear all of this every day? How would I wear this slightly simplified costume version for even one day? Using the bathroom would be a major production.

As I walked out to the platform, the skirts swished around me, and I couldn't help but laugh when I looked in the mirror. I looked every inch the Southern belle, and it was hard to believe that the girl reflecting back was me. It was amazing how transformative clothes could be.

"My, my, Miss O'Hara, you sure look mighty pretty," Theo said with a fake Southern accent.

I laughed and spun around, feeling the skirts follow a second later. "This dress is definitely dramatic but perhaps a little much." He nodded.

Back in the dressing room, Madame Walska helped

remove layer after layer of the costume before leaving me alone again. I had saved the best for last—a beautiful sapphire gown with beading around the neckline and a metallic belt. I fingered the soft velvet fabric, trying not to let the color of the dress cloud my judgment.

Madame Walska came in and zipped up the back, appraising me in the mirror. "Yes, yes. This is very nice."

I had to agree with her. The fabric clung to my curves without feeling restrictive, and the neckline draped perfectly around my shoulders. The dress was sexy, dropping toward the center of my bust but holding me in tight. I smoothed my hands over my stomach, gingerly touching the delicate design of the embellished belt. And the beaded sleeves were magnificent; their bell shape fluttered like wings. The overall look was one of elegant simplicity, and I felt regal.

Madame Walska opened the curtain and I walked out toward Theo. He looked up from his phone and simply stared at me, his hazel-green eyes burning into mine. Silently, I walked to the platform and stood in front of the mirror. Just wearing the dress, I felt like I could rule the world.

"Well . . ." I finally asked, surprised Theo had stayed silent for so long. "Who's the winner—Daisy, Scarlett, or Lady Guinevere?" I held my breath, hoping he would agree to Guinevere.

"Without a doubt, Lady Guinevere; I knew the dress would be perfect. You look magnificent, Haley. And we haven't even done hair, makeup, and accessories." I was so excited, I barely heard what Theo said after he agreed to the Guinevere costume.

After I changed, I met Theo at the front of the store. He had already made the arrangements for the rest of the costumes and was ready to head home. As we walked down the sidewalk, I replayed Theo's words in my head.

"Wait. What did you show Max at the salon earlier?"

"The Guinevere costume and some hairstyles," he said casually.

"Theodore whatever-your-middle-name-is Bennett! You had already picked this costume before we walked in? Why even have me try the others?"

"I wanted to be sure. And, besides, I couldn't deny you the fun of playing dress up."

I laughed. "All right, it was fun. So is Liam going as King Arthur or Lancelot?"

"Are you kidding?" He inclined his head. "Do you really think Liam would give up the chance to dress as a knight who steals the queen's heart and rides off into the sunset with his forbidden love?"

Before I could respond, a male voice interrupted us. "Theo. Hey, Theo. Wait a sec."

Theo and I turned around as a tall, lanky guy crossed the street to meet us on the sidewalk. He wore black slacks, a white button down shirt and tie, and a badge with the name "Andrew" on it.

"Hey, Drew," Theo said, shaking hands with him. "Good to see you."

"Same here, man." Drew said before looking toward me.

"Drew, this is Haley."

Drew and I shook hands before he dug in his pocket for something. "I only have a minute, but I saw you through the bank window and wanted to give you this."

He handed Theo a flyer printed on white paper with black ink; the design was clean and advertised a concert at some jazz club. Theo glanced over the flyer. "Awesome. Is this your band?"

"Yeah. We're playing there next Tuesday. I really hope you can make it. Feel free to bring friends. You're welcome to come too, Haley."

Theo grinned. "I'll be there!"

He turned to me. "How do you feel about jazz?"

17

STRIKE A CHORD

THEO WAS TALKING about jazz music, but my mind was a million miles away as I followed him up the stairs to Chase's apartment. My apprehension mounted with each step. Chase had gone almost radio silent since the Taco Tuesday incident, and I wasn't quite sure what to expect for the evening. Was he still upset about whatever happened that made him flee the loft? And what exactly had happened?

When we reached the second floor landing, I started thinking less about Tuesday and more about today. Having never been to Chase's apartment, I knew that he lived with his older brother, but I had yet to meet Kyle. Would he be there tonight?

Despite all these questions, the one thought that kept tugging at the back of my mind was the sleeping situation. I had gotten so used to sleeping at the loft that spending the night at any of the other guys' houses hadn't really crossed my mind. Would Chase just assume we would share a bed since we did the night of Theo's party? My mind drifted back to that night and how cute Chase looked with his messy blond hair and sleepy blue eyes. I could already feel butterflies taking flight at the thought of lying next to him.

Theo stopped walking and looked at me like he was expecting an answer.

"What? Sorry." I said, shaking the image of Chase from my mind.

"Do you have everything you need?" I nodded, looking toward the overnight bag Theo carried for me.

Theo put his hand on my arm, his hazel-green eyes filled with concern. "You okay, Haley?"

I forced a smile. "Yeah. I'm good."

Theo dropped the matter and was pulling a set of keys out of his pocket when I heard feet moving quickly down the hallway behind us. I turned to see Chase approaching, his backpack swinging behind him.

Chase called out, "Hey, guys, sorry," before blowing out an exaggerated breath. "My professor kept us late going over exam materials," he said as he unlocked and opened the door. He caught me in a quick hug then ushered Theo and I into the apartment.

A small entryway led to a kitchen which opened into the living and dining space. The apartment complex seemed fairly new, and the design felt fresh thanks to light floors and countertops that contrasted with the dark cabinets. I was already feeling relaxed in his cozy apartment, the atmosphere calm and welcoming. Chase dropped his keys on the counter and set his backpack by one of the bedroom doors while Theo walked off with my bag and returned a moment later, empty-handed.

"All right, cupcake," Theo said, grinning. "It's been fun." He reached out and gave me quick squeeze before heading for the door.

"Thanks for a nice day." I smiled and gave a little wave as he closed the door leaving me and Chase alone.

Hoping to avoid the inevitable awkwardness, I looked around, familiarizing myself with his apartment. As Chase leaned against the kitchen counter with his arms crossed, I tried not to focus on his broad shoulders and lean waist that were accentuated by his raglan T-shirt and light-wash jeans.

"Are you hungry?"

I nodded, realizing just how hungry I was after the excitement of the day. We decided to order takeout and switched on the TV while waiting for it to arrive. I sunk into the navy canvas sectional. I liked the square shape of the cushions and the more modern feel mixed with such a traditional fabric; it felt like sitting on a giant plush pillow.

I snuck a glance at Chase and noticed dark circles under his eyes. He was never what I would call chatty, but tonight's lack of conversation was notable. Something was weighing on him, and my guess was it had something to do with whatever happened on Tuesday.

After the food arrived, we filled our plates and headed back to the couch. I finally worked up the courage to approach the elephant in the room. "So . . . you want to talk?" I stayed silent, waiting as the anticipation built within me.

"About what?"

"Whatever it is that's clearly bothering you?"

He shrugged his shoulders.

"You know, you're kind of stuck with me all night," I said playfully, hoping he'd lighten up. I was rewarded with a small smile that touched his lips, but he remained silent.

"Alright. We can do this the easy way or the hard way." He looked over at me, his eyes questioning what I was up to.

"We can study for your exam or you can tell me what is bothering you. Take your pick."

"Wow, you're tough." He paused, assessing me. "And what if I choose neither?"

"Not an option." I grinned but stood my ground.

"Fine," he said, picking up our plates and heading to the kitchen, "I really could use some help studying for my Spanish exam." He looked back over at me. "That is, if you don't mind."

"Are you kidding? Where are the flashcards?"

Chase laughed. "Whoa there, let's not get too excited. It's a Friday night and you're helping me study for an exam; I'm guessing that was not on your list of top things to do in Santa Cruz."

"Maybe not," I smiled, "But only because I didn't realize it was an option."

Chase grabbed his backpack before returning to the couch. He pulled out a stack of colored flashcards and handed them to me. "Are you sure, Haley? You really don't have to."

"Quit stalling . . . you know what, I'll make you a deal. For every answer you get wrong, you have to answer a question of mine before I leave tomorrow."

He rubbed the back of his neck, looking slightly nervous. "And what about the ones I get right?"

I shrugged my shoulders. "Gold star?"

He laughed. "I think it's only fair that you should have to do the same for me."

I rolled my eyes. "Fine, if that's how this is going to be. But I'm limiting you to two questions since I'm expecting you to give me all the right answers."

He started off well with a string of right answers and I could see him relax a little.

"What is the word for confidence?" I asked and flipped over the card after answering it correctly in my head. Sure I was helping Chase study, but I had been brushing up on my Spanish as well and it was good to put it to the test.

Chase sat quietly, thinking. When he finally answered, it was incorrect.

"Bzzzz." I grinned. "Looks like you owe me an answer!"

He laughed and I tucked my feet under my legs. I was startled when the door opened and a guy with light brown hair and pale blue eyes walked in. He stopped when he saw us sitting on the couch together.

Chase spoke while signing to the stranger. "Hey, Kyle. This is Haley."

I cocked my head, surprised by the sign language; not wanting to be rude, I waved. "Hi, Kyle. Nice to meet you." Chase translated my words into sign language.

Kyle spoke and signed simultaneously. "Sorry to interrupt. I'm just showering and then heading out. I won't be back until late." Chase nodded before Kyle walked off to his bedroom. Not long after, Kyle left again with fresh clothes and wet hair.

By the time we finished the deck of flashcards, Chase had answered most of them correctly, but I still got three questions out of him. He, of course, was entitled to two from me. Chase flipped through the channels.

"Okay. A deal's a deal." He groaned in response, but I ignored it. "Question one: how long have you known sign language?"

"I guess eight years or so."

"So Kyle . . ." I trailed off and Chase finished for me, "Wasn't always deaf? No."

"You hardly ever mention him."

He sighed. "There's not much to say; we aren't very

close. He has his friends and I have the guys." I didn't want to push him to talk about it, so I waited silently.

"Growing up, Kyle and I were super close. When he was ten and I was eight he was in an accident and lost his hearing. After that we both learned sign language, but he started hanging out with a different group of friends and sort of pushed me away."

"That must have been hard on both of you."

He nodded before turning toward me. "Okay. It's my turn now." *Crap, what is he going to ask?*

"Why did you agree to go to lunch with Tyler?" *What? That came out of nowhere.*

I twirled my hair around my finger. "I don't have many friends and he seemed nice."

"That's all?" He asked, his eyes searching my own for something.

I shrugged and he seemed to drop the matter. I could feel relief setting in, relief and confusion over Chase's interest. *Does it bother Chase that I went to lunch with Tyler?* Was it because of their team rivalries?

"Okay," I said. "Question two: will you tell me what's bothering you? I know you can't tell me specifics, but maybe just talking generally will help."

Chase ran a hand over his mouth and chin before resting his chin on his closed fist and looking toward the ground. The silence stretched before us until he spoke. "I've been distracted lately, and it's catching up to me."

"How so?" I asked in a quiet voice.

He let out a frustrated, almost pained, sound. "I didn't do enough to help someone and they ended up getting hurt." If I hadn't known better, I would have thought he was referring to me and my dad.

"I'm sure you did all that you could, Chase."

He put his head between his hands and leaned forward. I had never seen him like this, and it took everything in me not to reach out and comfort him.

"That's just it; I don't know that I did, and the 'what ifs' are haunting me. If only I had done x or y, maybe I could have changed the outcome."

I put my hand on his back, gently rubbing in wide circles. "Sometimes no matter how badly we want to, or how hard we try, we can't control the outcome. And sometimes, it really sucks."

He looked up at me, his blue eyes sorrowful; I could tell that he was acknowledging my own situation while sharing his pain. He turned and opened his arms, pulling me onto his lap and swallowing me into his arms. I closed my eyes and could hear his heart beating in his chest as he held me.

The feel of my phone buzzing in my pocket made me jump, and Chase chuckled as I pulled away from him to check the screen. There was a new text message.

Liam: Tennis tomorrow?

Haley: Game on.

My phone buzzed for another incoming text, this time from Knox.

Knox: Be subtle but kick his ass.

Huh? That was fast. Were Knox and Liam together?

Me: Got it. Are you with him now?

Knox: Yeah, but I gotta go. Be good.

Chase led me into his bedroom, and I slowly spun around, taking in his space. It was nice; not huge but cozy, with a large window overlooking the green strip. The full-sized bed had a dark walnut headboard, and a red-and-navy-striped comforter was pulled back revealing crisp white sheets beneath. Photos of a sports stadium, baseballs, and other sports-related items hung above the bed.

"Pictures by Theo?"

Chase smiled and nodded, his eyes intent as he watched me take it all in, hands tucked in his back pockets.

Across the room a wooden desk and chair had computer parts sprawled across the top.

"Did you have to murder C-3PO?"

Chase laughed. "Oh, you know, just a little Operation."

I stifled a grin at his cheesy pun on the classic board game and continued my perusal of his room. Above the desk, a bulletin board had lines of gibberish that I was guessing were computer code, an Anaheim Angels game schedule, and the photo strip from the boardwalk of me, Chase, and Theo. I smiled as I continued to scan the room, passing the closet door and dresser.

When I caught sight of what was tucked away in the corner, I stopped in my tracks. A stunning six-string guitar with an amber-honey colored center that faded to black sat against the wall.

"Oh, wow. This is a Gibson Hummingbird, right?"

Chase's eyes widened in surprise. "You know guitars?"

"A little bit. But, I've never seen one of these in person. It's beautiful."

"Thank you. The guys gave it to me as a joining-the-team gift." He smiled, his eyes shining. "Suffice it to say, I was excited."

I laughed, "Yeah, I should say so."

Chase lifted the guitar off its stand and held it out. "Do you want to give it a try?"

I shook my head, afraid to even touch the Gibson. "I'm really not that good. But, *you* have to play for me!" I fluttered my eyelashes playfully. "Please?"

Chase scratched his chin. "Hmmm. I don't know." He paused dramatically. "Okay, okay. On one condition."

"What's that?"

"You play first." I frowned at him. "Just one little song?" When I still didn't respond, he gave me a sinfully sweet smile. "Come on, Haley. You have to at least try out the guitar. You know you want to."

I huffed out a sigh, relenting. "Ugh, fine. You can put your stupid dimple away now. I'll do it."

For the first time all night, Chase seemed to forget his problems, erupting into genuine laughter. "No dimple. Got it."

I sat down in the desk chair and cradled the guitar in my arms. I strummed lightly on the strings and made a few tuning adjustments while I considered what to play. Since I didn't know what kind of music Chase liked, I decided to go with one of my favorites: a simple version of Fleetwood Mac's "Landslide."

I took a few deep breaths to calm my nerves and started to play, not looking up at him even once. Honestly, I was rather shocked that I had agreed, dimple or no. I'd played a few songs for my dad and Jessica, but I considered playing and singing a mostly solitary activity. Once I reached the bridge, I was able to forget my audience and lose myself in the song, my fingers moving over the strings on pure muscle memory.

After playing the last few notes, I stared down at the guitar, somehow both anxious and excited to see Chase's reaction.

Chase broke the silence. "Haley, that was fantastic."

I finally lifted my head and tried to fight the pink darkening my cheeks. "Thanks."

"Where did you learn to play?"

I laid the guitar across my lap and self-consciously tucked a stray piece of hair behind my ear. "Oh, um, you know me. I checked out a few DVDs and books from the library and taught myself." When I saw a look of astonishment cross his face, I shrugged. "It's not a big deal. I had a *lot* of free time."

"I disagree, Haley. It's one thing to teach yourself the chords, but it takes natural talent to play like that. I could feel your emotion seeping into every note."

I avoided making eye contact. "Thanks. Now it's your turn," I said, handing him the guitar.

He chuckled softly. "Okay, okay, I can take a hint."

Chase strummed a couple of random chords like he couldn't decide on a song before a small grin crossed his face. Unlike my decision to dodge eye contact, he stared right at me while he played, only occasionally glancing down at his hands. Not that he needed to watch what he was doing; he played with the ease of someone who'd been doing so for many years.

Entranced by the music and the captivating expression on his face, I really wished I recognized the song. *Is he singing the lyrics to me in his head?*

When he finished, I clapped. "I loved that song. What is it?"

"'Collide' by Howie Day. You don't know it?"

I shook my head and pulled my phone out of my pocket. "I'm going to download it right now, though." I quickly searched for the song in the iTunes Store and purchased it before laying my phone down on Chase's desk.

He reached behind his neck to ruffle his hair before saying, "Okay, I'm sure you know this one."

A couple of notes into Taylor Swift's "You Belong with Me," I smiled and started mouthing the words while he played. After just a few lines, he stopped abruptly and gave me a mischievous grin.

"I'm cashing in my second question now."

I looked at him suspiciously. "Okay . . ."

"Will you sing for me?"

My heart jumped into my throat. "What? No!"

"Please? You obviously know the words, and I heard you humming along with 'Landslide.' You have a pretty voice."

I hummed along? Dang it. I should have been paying more attention to what I was doing.

"I don't really feel comfortable singing in front of other people."

Chase's voice took on a pleading tone. "Not even me? I promise not to throw rotten fruit at you."

I couldn't help but laugh and reminded myself how sad Chase was earlier. Surely I could do this one little thing to cheer him up?

"Okay, fine. I can't believe you talked me into two things in one night. And what did I tell you about that dimple?"

Chase's smile grew, but he remained silent, re-starting the song. I began to sing quietly, hesitant to let him hear my voice. It's not that I thought I had a bad voice; I'd recorded myself singing along with the guitar a few times, and even I could admit that I sounded decent. But, I still felt incredibly awkward singing in front of Chase. What if he thought I was terrible?

Of course, Chase knew what he was doing when he selected my favorite Taylor Swift song. I couldn't help but get into it and have fun.

His grin was smug. "Now was that so painful?"

Not willing to admit how much I'd enjoyed singing along with him, I glared and said, "Torture."

He just shook his head. "Seriously though, you shouldn't be shy about singing in front of an audience.

Your voice is incredible. Is there anything you don't do well?"

Hoping to distract him from his effusive compliments, I tapped my finger against my lips and scrunched my forehead like I was thinking hard. "Oh, I have one. Video games."

"Okay, I'll agree with that one. I can't believe you've never even played *Super Mario World*."

"I know. I've been so deprived."

"You have." He yawned loudly before giving me a sheepish look. "I know it's not that late, but I'm exhausted. I think I'm going to take a quick shower and then hit the couch. You can stay in here and read or watch a movie on my laptop if you want."

He pulled a few items of clothing from his dresser before leaving the bedroom, shutting the door behind him. At the thought of Chase sleeping on the couch, I couldn't tell if I was more relieved or disappointed. *Does he not want to sleep with me? Maybe I should volunteer to sleep on the couch.*

Taking advantage of his absence, I locked the bedroom door and quickly changed into my pajamas—striped cotton shorts with a coordinating T-shirt. I paced the short length of the bedroom a few times, trying to decide what to do about the sleeping arrangements. It didn't seem fair to kick Chase out of his bed when he so clearly needed a good night's sleep.

A light knock on the door startled me out of my preoccupied thoughts, and I unlocked and opened the door to a freshly-showered Chase. His wet hair looked darker than usual and was sticking up like he'd forgotten to comb it. His scent hit me full-force and I had to bite my lip from groaning. *Could he be any more appealing?*

"Um, Haley, are you going to let me in?" His dimple winked at me, and I thought, *Yes, he could be.*

"Sorry," I stammered, before stepping away from the door.

He threw his clothes in the hamper and grabbed his phone off the nightstand. When he reached for his pillow, I forced myself to speak.

"You don't have to sleep on the couch."

When he turned to look at me, I continued, speaking quickly. "I mean, we've already shared a bed, and you're exhausted. There's no reason we can't both sleep in here." I hesitated. "Or I can take the couch."

"No way; you're not sleeping on the couch, Haley." He looked uncertain. "Are you sure? I don't mind sleeping out there."

"Yep. I'll just go brush my teeth," I replied, leaving the room before things had a chance to get any more awkward.

When I finally worked up the nerve to return to the bedroom, Chase was sitting on top of the covers against the headboard with his eyes closed. His arms were folded against his chest and one leg was crossed over the other at the ankle. The overhead light was off, the room softly illuminated by the bedside lamp. I made my way to the other side of the bed and slipped under the covers. I glanced toward Chase and was surprised to find him watching me.

"Are you sure you're ready for bed? I know it's not that late."

I gave him a small smile. "I'm sure. I've been trying to go to bed earlier so I'm not dragging too much when I go running with Knox at the unholy crack of dawn."

Chase snickered as he got up and pulled back the covers before climbing in bed. When he settled in facing me, I suddenly realized how much of a difference a full versus a queen bed made. In Chase's smaller bed, our faces were only inches apart. Even in the dim light, I could make out the contours of his strong jaw and the short golden hairs of his five o'clock shadow.

"I know you're a runner, but I'm still impressed that you can keep up with him, especially at that hour. Knox is a beast. I'm not sure he even needs sleep."

I laughed at Chase's apt description of my gruff room-mate. It did seem like Knox was on alert at all hours of night and day. He would have been an ideal candidate for the military, but I couldn't imagine him spending his life taking orders.

Since Chase seemed in the mood to chat, I racked my brain for a topic. When nothing came to mind, I decided to go with an open-ended question.

"Tell me something about you that I don't know."

Chase flipped onto his back and groaned playfully. "Haley, you should know by now that I'm not that interesting."

I scoffed. "Not true. You're a swimmer, you play guitar, and you love board games."

He chuckled. "Right. Nothing says 'cool' like *Parcheesi* and *Battleship*."

When he didn't say anything else, I tapped at the invisible watch on my wrist and said, "I'm waiting."

He stayed silent for what felt like minutes before finally turning back on his side. "Okay, I'll tell you a secret." His expression looked undecided, but then he quietly continued, "You're the only girl who has ever been in my bed."

What?

I tried to keep the shock off my face while I processed his statement, my pulse racing. I wasn't sure if I was more surprised by his admission or by the fact that he decided to tell me. *Why* did he tell me?

I didn't know if it was our close proximity, the almost-dark, or a momentary lapse of judgment, but I found myself asking a question that had crossed my mind so many times.

"Why don't you have a girlfriend?"

When he just blinked at me, I started rambling, "I mean, it definitely seems like you could if you wanted. I know Melissa likes you. And you're such a great guy. It's just surprising, that's all." When he still didn't respond, I continued, "And you owe me a question."

Chase's face became pensive. "I don't know. I've dated a little in the past, but I don't have much free time between classes and Zenith." His gazed at me, almost like he was trying to tell me something with his eyes. "I guess it would take the right girl."

Is he suggesting I could be that girl? Ugh, snap out of it, Haley.

He adjusted his pillow, snagging a strand of my hair in the process.

"Sorry," he said, gently stroking the hair he had pulled.

"It's fine," I smiled, hoping to reassure him that it really hadn't hurt.

"Your hair is so soft," Chase said as he gently ran his fingers through the strands. He paused and looked directly into my eyes. "Is this okay?"

I nodded, unable to say anything more. Before tonight, Chase had never initiated more than side hugs and that one long hug. But now, he'd pulled me onto his lap and was playing with my hair. I knew I was reading too much into a few innocent touches, but my thoughts kept returning to his comment about the "right girl." And I suddenly found myself wishing I could be that girl.

18

BACK & FORTH

THE LARGE IRON and glass door opened and Patrick smiled at Chase and me. "Welcome, Haley. Hello, Chase. Please come in."

I returned his smile and tentatively stepped over the threshold. Noting Patrick's khaki chinos, pink polo shirt, and boat shoes, I was thankful I had worn a dressier blouse with my dark skinny jeans and cork wedges. Patrick's mansion was as beautiful as I remembered, and I took a moment to gaze over the elegant interior.

When I noticed that my calendar listed Patrick on my schedule for today, I brushed it off, assuming that with the gala less than a week away, we would all meet up with him to prepare for the mission. I hadn't expected a meeting at his house, though, and I was surprised that Jackson or some of the others hadn't already arrived. *Maybe they're on their way*, I reassured myself.

Chase cleared his throat. "I'm going to head out. You have everything you need?"

Wait, what? Attempting to appear outwardly calm, I nodded, but I was freaking out on the inside. Couldn't one of the guys have warned me that I was going to spend the afternoon alone with Patrick? Outside our rare encounters at the office, I had barely even spoken to him. Somehow I didn't think being dropped off at the boss's house was typical for Zenith employees, but considering he was Jackson's uncle, clearly the normal rules didn't apply.

When we reached the kitchen, Patrick gestured to the counter where a tempting spread of sandwiches, salad, and fruit was laid out on simple but expensive-looking cream platters.

"Would you like some lunch?"

"Thank you. It looks delicious."

Even though I was too nervous to be particularly hungry, I piled my plate with food and followed Patrick outside to the patio.

"You have a lovely home, Mr. Ross."

"Thank you, Haley, but please call me Patrick. Half the guys on Jax's team just call me 'Uncle' as it is," he said with a warm chuckle, his relaxed demeanor putting me more at ease.

"I've noticed that. I guess you have known all of them a long time?"

"Some longer than others, but yes. I don't actually have any nephews of my own, but I doubt I'd be as close to any blood relatives as I am to Liam, Knox, and the rest."

"Isn't Jackson your nephew?"

Patrick's expression turned somber. "No, unfortunately Jax doesn't have any living relatives. When I adopted him, I told him he could call me 'Uncle Patrick' because I wanted him to feel like family, but I wasn't trying to replace his father."

"Wow, I had no idea."

"I'm sure you've discovered that there's a bit of tragedy

in all the guys' pasts. Which is undoubtedly one of the reasons they've so quickly embraced you as one of their own. You may not have realized this yet, but those six do not let people in. Ever. Zenith encourages strong team bonds, but they're an anomaly even within the organization."

Have they embraced me as one of their own? And why did Patrick feel the need to point it out?

He paused, taking a sip of his iced tea. "You're probably wondering why I'm telling you this..."

My cheeks pinkened, "It did cross my mind."

His smile was kind, fatherly even. "Even though Team Jaguar is just one of many teams under my direction, they are always my first priority. Don't tell anyone," he said with a wink. "And it has become clear over the past weeks that you, my dear, have become very important to them. Which means you're now important to me."

Surprised by the turn in conversation, I sat in silence and tried not to visibly react while he continued speaking.

"I don't want to overwhelm you, but I was hoping you would be willing to consider me a friend, a confidante even. I've been told that I'm a good listener, and I suspect that you may need someone to talk to now and then other than the rowdy boys constantly surrounding you."

Touched by his unexpected offer, I said, "Thank you. That's very kind of you."

Perhaps realizing we needed time to build trust and develop a rapport, Patrick lightened the mood, regaling me with stories of Jackson and Liam as teenagers. It was obvious that Patrick relished in his role in raising them. When he spoke of them with such pride and love, I found myself longing for the comfort of my own dad's presence.

After clearing the dishes, Patrick led me into his office overlooking the backyard. Built-in bookshelves covered one wall and a wooden desk that could double as a large dining table sat in the center of the room. He gestured toward a chair as he sat across the desk from me. I glanced at the bookshelves which were more for display than book storage; large decorative items were spaced among several stacks of books and even a few framed photographs that I was dying to get a closer look at.

He opened a folder, scanning the top page before turning back to me. "With the gala coming up next week, I do need to go over a few things with you."

"Okay."

"Typically, we don't allow employees to be involved in a mission unless they are official security personnel. But when Liam invited you as his guest, Jax and I decided to allow an exception because of your personal connection to the client. Now, I know you already received the confidentiality lecture when you started at Zenith, but I need to reiterate that your discretion is absolutely crucial."

He paused, smiling. "Thankfully, I know that you won't be tempted to post photos on Facebook or tweet about the evening. But, it's more than that. To everyone at the gala and anyone who might ask you about it later, you are merely attending as Liam's date. If prompted, you can admit to knowing the Zenith security on duty, but treat their presence as a coincidence. In short, consider it a social event and nothing more."

I nodded slowly, letting Patrick's words sink in. I tried not to dwell on his use of the word "date" and instead focused on his instructions. They seemed simple enough, but social events weren't exactly my forte. Hopefully the other guests would be so distracted by Liam's charming accent that they wouldn't bother paying attention to me.

Patrick flipped through the file and placed three

photographs in front of me. The first I instantly recognized as Gerald Douglas, but the others didn't look familiar.

Pointing to Douglas's photo, he said, "Since this event is hosted by Mr. Douglas, you will obviously see him there. If you are introduced to him, try to act as natural as possible. He'll be very busy, so I don't anticipate that you will have to endure more than a handshake."

Holding up the other two photos, he continued. "These men, Clive and Rob, are on Douglas's security team and will likely be there as part of his personal security. As Jax explained to you, they were the men seen chasing your father. I don't want you to worry about them, but be aware of your surroundings at all times. We still hope that they don't know about you, but you can't be too careful."

He returned the pages to the folder and leaned back in his chair. "Other than that, try to have a good time. Do you have any questions?"

When nothing came to mind, I replied, "Will I know which fork to use?"

Patrick laughed, "If all else fails, just watch the people around you." He stood and said, "Now that we have that out of the way, why don't we return to the kitchen? I believe there are cookies and lemonade waiting, if you'd like."

Patrick took a cookie and I filled a glass with lemonade before we sat at the kitchen table. I was amazed by how comfortable I was around him after just a couple of hours together. It wasn't long before I heard footsteps headed our way, but I couldn't see who approached without turning around.

"Liam," Patrick said, before I turned to follow his gaze.

Liam sauntered into the kitchen looking sharp in navy athletic shorts and a navy, turquoise, and red collared shirt. *These guys are going to be the death of me.*

"Uncle." Liam smiled; his voice had a warmth I hadn't heard before.

"Haley and I were just wrapping up. Are you taking her back to the loft?"

Liam's gray eyes sparkled. "Actually, if it's alright with you, I'd like to use the tennis courts. I promised Haley a lesson." He winked at me.

As before with Chase, I sensed that Patrick was watching my interactions with the guys, observing us. I wondered what he was thinking.

"Of course," Patrick said. "You know you don't have to ask."

Crap. I had completely forgotten about Liam's text last night. Even though Knox helped me with the basics, I still wasn't sure I was ready. I considered pretending that I didn't have the proper attire, but I had packed workout clothes in my bag in case I felt like going for a run. I really did want to learn how to play, I just wasn't sure Liam was the right teacher.

Patrick stood from the table and I followed suit. "I believe Chase left your bag in the mudroom. You're welcome to change in the downstairs guest room."

Liam remained in the kitchen while Patrick escorted me down the hall. This guestroom was as nice as the one I had stayed in previously, just with slightly different decor. After placing my bag at the door, Patrick said, "Thanks for a lovely afternoon, Haley."

"No, thank you, Patrick." I smiled, hoping he could tell how sincere I was. "Lunch was delicious and I'm really glad I had the opportunity to get to know you."

Once Patrick left, I quickly changed into my navy and cranberry athletic shorts and cranberry-colored V-neck T-shirt. I pulled my hair into a high ponytail and grabbed my sunglasses before meeting Liam at the front door.

He crossed his arms and leaned back on his heels, giving me his usual once-over. "Clearly I can't count on Theo to shop for proper tennis attire. Don't get me wrong; the shorts are nice, but we must find you a tennis skirt. Preferably a really short one."

I rolled my eyes and pushed past him and out the front door.

"No need to get huffy. You don't *have* to wear a skirt...I have a vivid imagination," he said.

I stopped in my tracks so suddenly that he bumped into the back of me. I spun around and glared at him. "You, Liam Carlyle, are incorrigible."

His grin grew slowly until it was an all-out devilish smirk. "Thank you."

Shaking my head, I started walking again toward the tennis courts I'd seen near Patrick's house. Liam casually flung an arm around my shoulder and asked, "So, Haley, are you ready to learn from the best?"

"I don't know, maybe we should alert the media instead. Apparently the world's best tennis player is hiding in San Jose. Move over Roger Federer."

Liam's laugh was contagious and I couldn't help but let out a giggle of my own. "Have I ever told you how much I adore your cheekiness?"

Apparently I was suddenly possessed by a coy teenage girl, because I found myself flirting back. "No . . . but, please do go on. What else about me do you adore?" *Did I really just say that?*

Liam moved in front of me, walking backwards while he spoke, his amusement obvious. "Brilliant. Ten minutes alone with me and I've corrupted you."

Holding up his hand, he started ticking off his fingers. "Your hair—especially when you wear it down. The barely-there freckles on your nose. Your mouth. Your legs."

I practically shouted, trying to interrupt him. "Okay, okay. I get the picture."

His grin was distinctly Cheshire-like. "You sure? I can keep going."

"Positive." I jogged ahead, relieved to find the courts empty. I didn't need any witnesses to what would inevitably be a serious stomping by Liam.

Liam walked to the opposite side of the court, his racket in one hand, several tennis balls in the other. He looked every inch the tennis pro as he shifted the balls in his hand before placing all but one in his pocket.

"Don't worry about scoring or rules; let's just hit the ball around for now. We can score later." A smirk passed his lips while I pointedly ignored his innuendo.

Liam bounced the ball on the ground in front of him before hitting it gracefully over the net. I returned it quickly, feeling edgy yet determined. We volleyed the ball back and forth for a while.

"Relax, gorgeous. This isn't the Wimbledon championships," Liam called out, smiling.

"I am relaxed," I practically barked back, but even I knew that was a lie.

When the ball returned to him, he quickly pocketed it before walking around the net toward my side. He stopped less than a foot away from me. "You have to relax," he said, drawing out the word while he grabbed my hips and swayed them from side to side. My skin burned beneath his touch as my hips loosened and he started swaying with me.

We stopped moving, but his hands remained in place as

he continued talking. "Quit thinking so much. You have the technique, but you need the finesse."

I was thankful I at least had my sunglasses to hide behind. "Um, thanks. I think."

"Anytime." He flashed me a smile that was dazzling. "You've got potential and you are fit." He eyed me from head to toe before drawing in a breath that hitched.

"I should hope so; I do workout."

He laughed. "Ahhh, such an American. To us Brits, 'fit' is a slang term for someone who is hot or attractive."

I blushed. Liam was really on a roll today.

"Now do you think you can loosen up and have some fun?" He tweaked my nose.

Not wanting him to discover how much his touch was distracting me, I opted for a bossy attitude. "Yes. Now get back on your side of the court and tell me how the scoring works so I can beat the pants off of you."

When his eyebrow raised above his sunglasses, I immediately cringed at my word choice. Fortunately, amazingly, Liam let the remark pass without comment and jogged back to his side before explaining the scoring while we hit the ball back and forth.

When he finally finished, I said, "Games, sets, matches. Got it." Thanks to my beginner's tennis lesson from Knox, I was prepared.

Liam served, his form elegant as he powerfully struck the ball. It came flying across the net and I returned it, feeling the power in his stroke when it met my racket. I had played once with Knox, and he was a powerful player, but Liam had the grace of a trained tennis player. He was light on his feet, quickly and efficiently covering the court.

Finally, the volley ended with Liam scoring the point. "Fifteen-love," Liam called out.

"Did you just call me 'love'?" I asked playfully, knowing full well it was the tennis term for "zero." *Geez, was there something in that lemonade?*

He chuckled, pausing before he served again. "Just stating the score, *gorgeous*. Would you prefer that I call you 'love'?"

Three games later, Liam remained in the lead, although I had held my own and even won a game in the set.

"Time out," Liam called.

"Everything okay?"

"Everything but that atrocious technique you're trying to pass as a backhand."

"What's wrong with it?" I shrugged my shoulders.

He came to my side of the court and stood parallel to me. "Watch and learn." He demonstrated a few backhand strokes as he explained the optimal way to employ it. Then he watched as I attempted a few.

"Better, but something is still off," he said, moving to stand behind me. He reached around and laid his hands over mine as we held the racket together. I could feel the full length of his muscular body behind me, his warmth radiating off him in waves. *Tennis. Tennis. Tennis.* I kept repeating the word to anchor myself in reality.

He brushed my ponytail to the side, his long fingers gently grazing my arm as he returned his hand to mine. And just when I didn't think he could get any closer, he hunched to mirror my own size.

With his face mere inches from mine, he said, "Ahhh, now I see," before he repositioned my left hand and then replaced his left hand over mine again. "Now let's try."

We swung together and I could feel the difference. When he stepped back from me, I immediately missed the feel of him. *No. No. No, Haley. You cannot get sucked in by Liam's charm.*

"Next time, don't let Knox give you tennis pointers; leave it to the master." Liam smirked.

My mouth involuntarily dropped open in shock before I could even attempt to protest. Liam placed a finger under my chin and gently lifted, forcing me to meet his eyes. "Don't even try to argue, it's written all over your beautiful face." His sincerity sucked the air right out of me, and I stood there staring back at him without moving.

We resumed play and once I had recovered my wits, I finally decided to ask how he knew about my secret tennis lesson.

"So, what makes you think Knox gave me pointers?"

"One: you may have some natural talent, but you were a little too knowledgeable for a complete novice." He returned the ball.

"Two: among the guys, Knox is the only one with passable tennis skills. Although I'm not sure whether it was his idea or yours." The ball flew across the net once more.

"And, three: it was a mere hunch, but your reaction confirmed it." *Next time, I'm having Knox work on my poker face,* I thought as the ball flew across the net once more.

"Since you're such the tennis pro would you care to make a wager?" He asked, a tantalizingly devious expression playing across his face.

"What did you have in mind?"

"If I win," he said, "I cash in on that dinner for two at the restaurant, or kitchen, of your choice."

"What about your trust-fund girlfriend?" I hit the ball back slightly harder than I intended.

Liam almost missed the shot but recovered in time to

return it. "Somebody's been keeping tabs on me," he said, his expression smug. "But if you'd done a better job, you'd know she's not my girlfriend."

"And if I win?" I asked.

"Not likely, but I'll humor you. What would you like?"

"If I win . . . I get to drive your car." I grinned, imagining what it would be like to not only beat Liam but get to drive his sports car.

"Do you even have a driver's license?"

"Of course—Jackson gave me one."

Liam laughed. "A *valid* driver's license, Haley."

"I know how to drive. We could go outside the city, where there are less cars."

"Since I assume it will be a moot point, I accept your wager."

"Game on."

Despite my best efforts, Liam trounced me. Of course, he gloated all the way back to Patrick's house. We cut through the back of the property, and just as we passed Patrick's pool, Liam had the nerve to say, "Bollocks. I should have wagered a swim with you in a bikini."

I didn't think, I just acted, shoving him into the pool fully clothed. When he came to the surface, sputtering, I said with a sweet smile, "You looked like you could use a cool down."

Game, set, match.

19

FIRECRACKER

I SHOULDN'T HAVE BEEN LAYING in bed in the middle of the afternoon. But after getting up early to run with Knox and then another self-defense lesson with Ethan, I'd already had a busy Sunday. And since I'd be joining the entire team at the beach in an hour, I seriously needed time to decompress.

Flipping through the music on my iPhone, I paused on "Collide" and pressed play. I'd probably listened to the song ten times since downloading it on Friday night. And, if I had to be honest, it wasn't just because I loved the song— and I really did. Mostly, I couldn't stop thinking about my entire evening with Chase. Playing his guitar and then singing for him had been surprisingly exhilarating, not to mention his own swoon-worthy performances.

And then, just when I'd thought things couldn't get any more intense between us, we'd spent the night practically wrapped around each other. It wasn't intentional; we started out on our own sides of the bed, not even touching. But when I woke up a few hours later, Chase had moved closer to me and our legs were intertwined. Afraid he would wake up and discover us like that, I shifted slightly, but that just caused him to pull me closer in his sleep.

So, I stayed that way—twisted in the sheets with him— and tried desperately to relax and fall back asleep. Instead, I lay awake for what felt like hours and felt Chase's every breath on my neck and every unintentional brush of his body against mine. As my blood pulsated through my veins, I didn't think I'd ever been so aware of my own heartbeat. It was the sweetest kind of torture, wanting so much to burrow into his strong embrace, but spending every second terrified of what would happen if I did.

I knew better, I really did. But that knowledge didn't stop me from fixating on what an amazing boyfriend he would be. Between his all-American good looks and adorable personality, he was quite possibly the perfect guy. And let's not forget those sky-blue eyes and that dimple that could melt hearts with just one smile.

I buried my head under my pillow. *Haley, you are so screwed.*

Knowing I would obsess over how to act around him in front of the rest of the guys if I stayed in bed, I forced myself to get up and change clothes. Thankful that the temperature was cool enough to forgo a swimsuit, I slipped into a pair of denim shorts and flowy turquoise top. I threw a book and sweater in my tote before re-doing my braid and adding a swipe of pink lip gloss.

"Haley!" I heard Theo's voice carry down the hall. "It's time to go!"

When I reached the living room, Penny immediately trotted over to me and sat, looking up at me expectantly, her tail wagging. I reached down and scratched behind her ears, "Hello, Penny. I've missed you."

Jackson walked over. "You must have made an impression on her at the party. She's usually not quite so friendly with new people."

Theo laughed, "Penny's probably just happy to have another girl around."

Jackson scanned the loft. "What happened to Ethan? Wasn't he here earlier for Haley's self-defense lesson?"

Theo snorted, "I'm pretty sure he had to go let off some steam after that."

Knox smacked him in the shoulder. "Shut up, Theo." Turning to me, he said, "Ready to go?"

As we headed out, I realized that Jackson made a valid point. Why didn't Ethan just hang out at the loft after the lesson? It's not like he would have gone all the way home just to come back to the beach. From what I knew, his place was closer to the office than to the loft; he would be heading in the complete opposite direction of the beach.

When we reached the Jeep, Theo groaned. "Really, Jackson? You just had to take the top off?" He smoothed his hand over his perfectly-styled hair. "I don't know why I even try," he sighed dramatically.

"Deal with it, freckles. We're going to the beach; no one cares about your hair. Plus, Haley likes the top down."

All three sets of eyes swung to me and I shrugged. "What? It's fun. Like a rugged convertible."

Jackson opened the back door and Penny jumped in, settling on the seat next to Theo. I climbed in after her, happy to sit in the back with my furry friend.

A few miles outside of town, Theo turned to me. "I can't believe you haven't been to the beach yet. We're terrible tour guides."

"Well, it's not like I haven't *seen* the beach."

He shook his head, "Still, there's no excuse. You know, you can ask me when you want to go somewhere."

"It's not a big deal. I know you guys are busy."

Jackson caught my eye in the rearview mirror. "Theo's right, Haley. You don't have to be so accommodating all the time."

He pulled into a dirt parking area on the side of the road with a few other vehicles, thankfully cutting off the conversation. I looked around but didn't see any signs. How did anyone know there was a public beach here?

We parked next to Chase's SUV where he, Ethan, and Liam were pulling a cooler and some bags out of the trunk. After unloading from Jackson's Jeep, Knox and Jackson grabbed a few bags from the trunk and headed toward what looked like the beginnings of a trail. I followed behind, Penny and Theo at my side.

We took the path over railroad tracks and down a hill until we reached the sand. The beach was nestled between rocky cliffs, making it feel surprisingly secluded. There were maybe fifteen other people there: a family with children making sandcastles, a couple groups of co-eds, and several surfers in the distance. Numerous pelicans dotted the cliffs, occasionally diving into the water or flying overhead.

While I checked out the scenery, the guys were busy staking a claim on our portion of the beach. Several grabbed beers from the cooler and Chase set up some game that looked like a mini trampoline with balls the size of an over-sized grapefruit. *Okaaay.*

I walked over to Jackson. "Anything I can help with?"

"I think we're good for now." He smiled. "Want to play a game?"

Theo sang out, "Yeah, Haley. You can be on my team."

When Knox scowled behind Theo's back, I knew he was thinking about Theo's injury. It had been a week since

Theo mysteriously injured himself on a work assignment, and the stitches wouldn't heal for at least another week or so.

"Theodore." I gave him my best *you're in trouble* look and placed my hands on my hips.

"Yes, Haley." He batted his eyelashes innocently.

"Do you want to climb El Gigante or not?"

He blew out a breath. "Fine. I'll sit this one out."

"I'll hang out with you—we can watch and commentate."

He pointed a finger at me. "No way; you're playing. I'll be the ref."

"I really don't mind. I'm not even sure what kind of game that is."

The rest of the guys walked up, and I found myself in the middle of a huddle of six super hot guys. I saw at least one, if not more, of them on a daily basis, but it had been awhile since we were all together. I blinked, still stunned by each and every one of them. Would the butterflies they induced ever go away? *I sure hope not.*

Jackson spoke up. "Chase set up Spikeball. Everyone in?"

The guys nodded in agreement and he continued talking. "Okay, teams of two: Chase you're with me. Knox, you and Liam can be a team. Haley, you and Ethan together. Good?"

I leaned over to Ethan. "Sorry you're stuck with me. I have no clue what Spikeball is."

He chuckled. "Don't worry, we'll let the other teams go first so you can see how it works." That made me feel a little better. "Plus, we can learn their strengths and weaknesses before our first go at them." *Even better.*

Theo quickly explained the rules and then asked if there were any questions.

"Seems pretty straight-forward, almost like volleyball crossed with four square," I said.

Chase interjected. "You know about four square, Haley?"

"Yeah, Jess and I had a pretty serious obsession with two square at one point. Although I'm sure four square was even better; I only got to hear about that through Jess—she played with kids at school. I can't wait to tell her about Spikeball though; this is like four square on steroids."

I bit my tongue before I almost blew my cover on the secret emails with Jess. Since the first contact, I wavered in whether I should tell the guys. I guessed I relished having it as my little secret and worried they would tell me it was a bad idea or unsafe. Sometimes, I hoped it would convince them to lighten up on their "protection" schedule; it was getting to be ridiculous. Not that I didn't like hanging out with them, but I clearly wasn't in any danger, and I hated feeling like an inconvenience or even worse, an obligation.

Theo sat on one of the coolers to watch as Chase and Jackson faced off against Knox and Liam. Theo called the game like a TV sports commentator, even giving the guys funny nicknames and changing the inflection of his voice.

Ethan and I sat on a towel with Penny sprawled out next to me. I immediately began stroking her plush golden coat; she was such a sweet and well-behaved dog.

"You're so pretty, Penny." I cooed to Jackson's beautiful dog before turning to Ethan. "Why 'Penny'?"

Ethan answered, his focus still on the game. "It's a nod to Moneypenny from James Bond." *Interesting,* another item for my mental file on Jackson. At least he hadn't selected one of the more ridiculous Bond-girl names for his dog. I'd have to ask whether he preferred the movies or the novels; I had a hunch it was the latter.

We watched the game in companionable silence while I took notes on our opponents and the game. Knox and Liam made a good team, the strength of Knox balanced with the finesse of Liam. And Jackson and Chase were formidable opponents, Jackson playing a relaxed but focused game while Chase was surprisingly energetic.

"Do you have any pets, Ethan?" I asked, realizing I had never been to his house, or Jackson's, for that matter.

"No, I don't think my Aunt Jules would approve."

"You live with your aunt?" Knox and Theo lived together, and Chase lived with his brother, Kyle, but for some reason I always pictured Ethan living alone.

"Sort of. I live in the guest house over her garage."

"I'm surprised you don't live alone or with one of the guys."

"Yeah, Chase and I are talking about getting an apartment after Kyle graduates next May. For now, my aunt's house is a good location and the price can't be beat." His jaw dropped as one of the guys dove for the ball and recovered it in an impressive move. "Besides, I try to help my aunt when I can; she practically raised me."

When Knox and Liam erupted into loud cheers and started high-fiving, Ethan stood and extended a hand to help me up. I brushed my hands together and walked with him in the direction of the game. Chase and Jackson grabbed drinks before heading over to the towel to sit with Penny.

"Alright," Theo called out, "next up Haley and Ethan versus Knox and Liam."

"Take 'em down, Haley," Chase called, making me grin in response.

Liam served first and the ball quickly bounced off the net and into the air. Knowing that Ethan and I had up to three hits to get it back on Knox and Liam's turf, I jumped forward to strike. Watching the game, the guys had made it look easy, but playing it, I realized how much strategy and energy was actually involved.

By the end of the game I was laughing and breathless as my braid bounced around my shoulders. Thanks to a few lucky shots, Ethan and I had won.

We smiled at each other as he raised his hand for a high-five. "Way to go!"

"Thanks, E." I slapped his hand.

"And now," Theo said in a dramatic announcer-type voice, "It's time for the showdown. On one side, we have our fearless leader and the golden boy versus the Kung Fu fighter and the firecracker. Who will be the winner in this epic battle?"

I giggled at Theo's dramatics but quickly focused on the game at hand. There was no way I was losing this round, and the determined look in Ethan's eyes told me he felt the same.

I danced around the net, focusing on the game and laughing occasionally. I couldn't imagine a more perfect day on the beach, and Spikeball was quickly becoming my new favorite game.

Although Chase and Jackson started out strong, Ethan and I quickly caught up to them. The game was neck-and-neck, neither team able to break away from the other. With a series of "game points" and attempts to score a two-point lead, we were just one point away from the win.

We volleyed the ball back and forth in a seemingly endless loop before Jackson made a crazy shot. As the ball flew into the air, curving away from the net, I was determined to return it and win the game. I dove for the ball and thrust my hand under it, hoping by sheer force of will to return it to Ethan or the net in time.

Watching the ball bounce off my hand, I almost collided with Jackson before falling in the sand. The wind was knocked out of me, but I didn't care—the ball hit the net and then bounced to the ground, earning Ethan and I the winning point.

Ethan led out a loud cheer and hauled me up from the ground before throwing me over his shoulder. Breathless, I laughed and told him to put me down, but he only gripped my legs tighter. When I reached his sides to tickle him, he finally relented and set me on the ground.

Liam came up to us and nodded to Ethan. Before I knew it, Liam had grabbed my wrists and Ethan my ankles and they were carrying me over toward the ocean.

"No!" I cried.

"But I thought you wanted to go swimming in the ocean?" Ethan asked, knowing full well that I meant in a bathing suit when it was warmer out.

"Yeah, Haley," Liam taunted. "I know how much you love swimming . . . and hate the thought of a bikini."

Are they seriously going to go through with this? I wasn't going to let them get away with it, and I started kicking and writhing furiously. When I realized their grip was too tight to combat, I decided to call in the big guns.

"Knox!" I shouted in a playful cry for help, knowing he would bail me out of anything.

"Guys!" Knox barked before he quickly jogged over to us. They started swinging me, acting like they were going to throw me in. We were close to the water, but I felt a little better knowing Knox was nearby; he wouldn't let anything happen to me.

Liam said, "Fine, you want her Knox? You got her."

Liam and Ethan released me and I flew into the air, bracing for impact. But before I could hit the ground, Knox caught me in his arms and let out a whoosh of air. I felt like my heart stopped in that moment and he clutched me closer to him, reassuring me that everything was okay. Knox looked down at me quickly, his eyes scanning my face as if to confirm I was alright, before shooting his laser-like gaze at Liam and Ethan.

"We were just having a little fun," Ethan responded somewhat sheepishly while Knox gently helped me stand.

"Come on, dumb and dumber," he said as he looked at Ethan and Liam and hooked an arm around my shoulder, "Let's eat."

We joined Jackson, Chase, and Theo by the fire pit and spread out on the towels on the sand. There was a small fire burning, and as the sun dipped lower in the sky, I was thankful for the warmth. Flanked by Jackson and Knox, I waited for Liam to hand me a sandwich from the cooler. I opened the parchment wrapping to reveal what I figured would be a ham and cheese sandwich. I should have known better since Liam brought the food.

"Grilled chicken with bacon, lettuce, tomato, and avocado on toasted ciabatta," Liam said before I could even ask.

"Wow. Thanks, this looks amazing."

"Want a drink, Haley?" Theo asked leaning over one of the coolers.

"Sure, I'll take a water."

Sitting around the fire, we ate our sandwiches as the sun set over the beach.

Jackson gestured to the two surfers still in the water. "I don't think I've seen them around before. They're not bad."

Right after he spoke, one of them stood up on his board for just a few seconds before wiping out. The guys all chuckled.

"Okay, well maybe not so good either," he continued with a smile.

"Do all of you surf?" I asked.

Knox scoffed with a playful grin, "Are you kidding? Can you see *Theodore* on a surfboard?"

"Hey!" Theo threw a potato chip at Knox. "Haley can call me Theodore all she wants, but you know it's off limits to the rest of you."

"Whatever you say, Theodore," Liam said in a high-pitched, chipmunk-like voice.

The guys laughed while Theo feigned annoyance. "Anyway, it's not like I couldn't surf if I wanted to. I just prefer more sophisticated activities."

Liam interjected, "I agree. Who wants to spend all of their free time swallowing freezing cold salt water? Oh right, Jackson does."

Chase spoke up. "You and Theo are just jealous because you can't pull off a wetsuit like the rest of us."

Knox, Jackson, and Ethan all bust up laughing, and my jaw dropped in shock. Did Chase really just say that? I'd never heard him say anything remotely insulting to one of the guys, even teasingly.

Probably hoping to change the subject, Chase dug in one of the bags for something and revealed graham crackers, chocolate bars, and marshmallows. "Who wants s'mores?"

My hand shot in the air. "ME!" Eliciting a chuckle from Knox.

Chase distributed the s'more supplies, and we stood around the fire roasting marshmallows. Once my marshmallow was sufficiently roasted, I quickly sandwiched it between my graham crackers to fuse the flavors together. When I bit into the s'more, it tasted so good I instinctively closed my eyes and couldn't help but moan.

I opened my eyes and realized Knox was staring at me, his emerald green eyes striking in the light of the fire. He looked even more intense than normal, and I could see his hands clutching his thighs. *What did I do now?!*

The fire had consumed several logs, and the stack shifted as it started to break apart. When the air hit it, the fire suddenly flared. My vision blurred, and I started panting as images of the house fire flashed in my mind. I could feel the panic building within me while I remained frozen to the spot, anchored in a sea of memories.

I could see the house burning in front of me and feel the despair at wondering where my dad was. The smells, the heat, the sounds flooded my senses. My body broke out in a cold sweat, and I felt powerless.

When a hand touched my shoulder, I flinched and saw Jackson's eyes looking at me, filled with concern. He grasped my bicep and pulled me to my feet before leading me away from the fire. With my back to the fire, Jackson and I sat down facing each other on the sand before Penny placed her head in my lap. Penny's calm presence was reassuring, and I could already feel my heartbeat slowing.

"Do you want to talk to me about what just happened?" Jackson's voice was uncharacteristically soft.

I slowly ran my hands through Penny's soft fur while I considered what to say. Although I was starting to feel more comfortable around Jackson, he was still the last of the guys I would normally confide in.

When I didn't respond after a few long moments, he pressed. "Did you have a flashback of the fire?"

Finally looking up at him, I nodded. "I didn't think

about it at first, but when the fire shifted, it's like I was suddenly back there." Away from the warmth of the fire and still recovering from the shock, I shivered. "It's fine. I'm fine. I just wasn't expecting it, that's all."

Jackson took one of my hands and held it between both of his. "You don't have to right now, but I want you to know that I'm here if you want to talk about it. About everything that happened. I know from experience that it helps to unload."

Agreeing that I wasn't ready to go there with him, I just said a simple, "Thanks," before withdrawing my hand and standing up.

When we returned to the group, Ethan was dumping sand over the coals of the fire and everything had been packed up. Jackson grabbed a cooler with Liam, while Chase and Theo carried various items.

When I tried to pick up a bag, Knox said, "Oh no you don't," before turning his back to me. "Hop on!"

I didn't need to be told twice. I jumped up on his back and immediately felt his arms hook around my legs. With my arms over his broad shoulders, I bounced gently as Knox carried me up the sandy hill and back to the parking lot. Worn out from the events of the day, I closed my eyes and leaned my cheek against his shoulder. I let out a contented sigh; Knox always made everything better.

UNWANTED ATTENTION

I GLANCED down at my phone, hitting send on the text message before Melissa could sneak up on me and ask who I was texting.

Me: Good luck on your Spanish exam today! :)

Chase: Gracias, Haley! :)

Melissa finding out about the occasional text with Chase was the least of my concerns. But I knew if she ever discovered how close we were, especially our sleepovers, she would kill me. *When did my life become so complicated?*

Forcing myself to focus on the job at hand, I surveyed the mountain of paperwork in front of me. After easing into my job at Zenith, Melissa had been giving me more responsibility. I enjoyed the challenge and felt like I was coming closer to actually earning my over-inflated pay. And it felt good to know that I had a pretty sizeable stash of money in the safe in my room.

The morning passed by quickly and before I knew it, Melissa popped her head into my cubicle.

"Ready for lunch?"

It was only Monday, but I was looking forward to a

break from the office, even if it was for a short lunch at the sidewalk café downstairs. After selecting our food and checking out, we carried our trays to an empty table.

"So, Haley . . . do anything fun this weekend?"

"Nothing much," I said, cringing at my own lie, "Just spent some time at the beach." *And talking with Patrick Ross, and playing an intense game of tennis with Liam, and sleeping in a bed with the guy you like, but yeah . . . nothing much.*

"Sounds nice," she said, taking a bite of her sandwich.

While Melissa chewed, I decided to be proactive about the course of the conversation and shift the focus off of me. "What about you?"

"Let's see," she tapped a perfectly manicured finger on the table, "Friday was dinner and drinks; Saturday I got a mani-pedi with a couple girlfriends; and, Sunday I caught up on sleep and laundry."

"Sounds like a busy weekend."

She giggled, "It was pretty tame, actually. I try to hit up a club or party most weekends. Speaking of, you still need to come out with me sometime. You're way too much of a homebody, chica."

"Sure," I replied non-committally. Hopefully she would forget about her suggestion for a while, or at least until I had more freedom from the guys.

"Gotta live it up, especially with all the cute college guys around here. I mean, I would totally take advantage of the hot Zenith guys, but you know . . . they're kinda unattainable." As usual, she was speaking fast and changing gears even faster, so I was completely taken by surprise by her next question. "So do you think you want to go to college?"

I shrugged. I had no idea what I wanted to do, but I

really hadn't let myself think about it, at least until I found my dad; until then, I was stuck in a sort of limbo.

"You're way too smart for your job, Haley." She took a sip of her drink. "You know that Zenith has a program where they'll pay for your education if you join a team and commit to working a certain number of years for the company, right?"

"Really?"

"Don't those guys on Team Jaguar tell you anything?" She rolled her eyes playfully. "Anyway, I'm not security team material, so I work and go to school part-time. I started about a year ago and take online and evening classes. Before I moved here, I took two years at my community college, so hopefully I'll finish in two more years."

"Wow, that's awesome. What are you studying?"

"Legal studies."

"Impressive. Do you want to go to law school?"

"Probably, but I'm just trying to survive undergrad first." She smiled. "What about you; what would you study?"

"Astronomy," I answered without hesitation.

She raised an eyebrow. "So why aren't you?"

How was I supposed to answer when I couldn't possibly explain my situation—no legal identification, lack of proof of my homeschool education or graduation, and a missing father. Most of the time, our conversations were short enough that I avoided difficult topics like this. Fortunately, I was saved from answering when Tyler walked up to our table, his friendly smile as brilliant as ever.

"Hello, Haley. Melissa," he said, his eyes lingering on me. "Have a nice weekend?"

We both nodded and Melissa chatted away, her bubbly personality on full display. I caught Tyler sneaking glances at me, almost urging me to join the conversation, and by the pleased expression on Melissa's face, she was taking notes on his behavior.

I hoped Tyler didn't think I was being rude; it's just that while I was relatively comfortable around him when it was just the two of us, I felt awkward and unsure of myself with Melissa in the mix. I'd never told her about my lunch with Tyler, and I really didn't want her getting ideas about the two of us. *Too late for that.*

After a few minutes, Tyler told us to enjoy our lunch and he left looking slightly disappointed. Should I have asked him to join us? Ugh, I was so bad at this whole being social thing.

Melissa whisper-yelled, "OMG, Haley. He's totally into you."

"Nah, he's just a friend."

"He doesn't look at you like he wants to be just friends. He wanted to ask you out, and you should say yes."

"I can't."

"Why not?! He's hot, you're hot." She paused and eyed me as she assessed the situation. "Wait . . . are you dating someone, say one of the delectable members of Team Jaguar?"

I shook my head, more than ready for this conversation to end.

"So what's the problem?"

I hesitated as I debated the best way to answer without inviting more questions and finally settled on, "It's complicated."

She rolled her eyes playfully. "Whatever. If you're interested in Tyler, just go for it."

After a few bites in silence, Melissa spoke again. "Since you seem to have the inside track on Team Jaguar and now

Team Falcon," she grinned, "Can I ask you something?"
Uh oh.

Although I seriously wanted to say "no," I found myself nodding instead.

"So, I kind of have this theory."

"Okay . . ." I said, drawing the word out, seriously dreading whatever she was going to say next.

She leaned across the small table like whatever she was about to share was the biggest secret on the planet. Melissa spoke in a lowered voice. "Don't you ever wonder what Zenith really does?" *All the time.*

I kept my face blank. "What do you mean?"

"Well, I've worked here long enough to think it's more than just private security." She waited, for what I wasn't sure—gauging my reaction or dramatic impact perhaps.

"Mhmm." I said, encouraging her to continue. This was the closest I had come to getting more information on how the private investigation side of things came into play.

"Have you ever noticed that some of the teams, like Team Jaguar and Team Falcon, have nicer cars than the rest of the office?" I nodded, still wondering where this was going. "And it's kind of surprising considering how young they are. Take Ethan; he's like twenty-one or two and drives a $60,000 car. And Scott, the leader of Team Falcon, has a condo that has to be worth a million dollars. Where are they getting the money for this stuff?"

Assuming it was a rhetorical question with a Melissa-approved answer lined up, I simply shrugged my shoulders. I knew they were paying me an above-average salary; perhaps that wasn't the case for the rest of the Zenith employees apart from Team Jaguar and Team Falcon.

"And," she continued, "have you heard about their secret gear room? I've only heard rumors, but it's supposed to be some military-grade, kick ass high-security place with a super-tech armored car fleet. Which, if you ask me, seems like overkill for a regular private security firm." How she had managed to spit all that out so quickly was baffling.

"So, Sherlock, what's your theory? Some kind of off-the-books government contractor?"

"How boring would that be?" Melissa shook her head and rolled her eyes. "No. I think they run illegal operations with a sinister bent. Like super hot mafia that look more like models than assassins."

While I suspected there was more to Zenith than private security, I couldn't help but giggle at her earnestness. "You're kidding, right? You make them sound like James Bond's evil twins or something." Although if you'd asked me a few weeks ago, I had some pretty similar thoughts, minus the evil part. And I was still no closer to figuring out what was really going on behind the scenes.

She stared at me, dead serious. "No, Haley. And I'm pretty sure there are some cases that they take off-the-books." I couldn't admit to her that she was right—my dad's case had been as far off the record as possible. But I still didn't want to believe that the guys were involved in anything sinister.

Melissa looked down at her phone that dinged. "Crap. We need to get back. But think about what I said; I bet you'll start to see things that make you wonder."

* * *

"Hiya, Mary. Ready for the meeting?" Theo's cheerful voice broke my concentration on the report in front of me. Catching a glimpse of the time, I gasped and quickly grabbed a legal pad and pen before standing up to follow Theo.

Walking by Melissa's empty cubicle, I sighed in relief. After her comments at lunch, I really didn't want her to see me sneaking off with Theo for a meeting with Team Jaguar. I was sure she'd have a field day with that one.

When we entered the elevator to go up to the sixth floor, I gave Theo a puzzled look. "Mary?"

He grinned, "You totally have a sassy Mary Poppins vibe going on today with your hair pulled back and that black skirt, white ruffled top, and red belt. Add a hat and I bet you'd start a new trend."

Without thinking, I laughed and sang a couple lines of "A Spoonful of Sugar."

Theo's jaw dropped open then closed then opened again, imitating a fish, apparently. "Haley, what . . . how . . . why haven't you—"

"Oh look, we're here," I interrupted, rushing out of the elevator and down the hall to the conference room.

I hurried into the room and took the first available seat, next to Knox.

Looking over my shoulder, he raised an eyebrow and said, "Where's the fire, Haley?"

"Oh, you know me. I hate to be late," I replied with a nonchalant shrug and leaned past Knox to say a quick hello to Jackson, Ethan, and Chase.

Theo plopped into the seat on the other side of me and leaned in close, whispering, "We're going to have a chat about that voice of yours later, Miss Poppins."

I offered my most innocent look in response. "No idea what you're talking about."

Hearing unfamiliar male voices coming from the hall, I looked up to see three guys I didn't recognize entering the room followed by one girl a few years older than me . . . and Tyler.

Oh, crap. Team Falcon must be the other team working the gala.

Unlike the rest of Team Falcon, who all sat down and continued talking among themselves, Tyler greeted the Jaguar guys with a pleasant "hello." When his eyes met mine, his expression turned startled for a moment. "Oh, hey, Haley. Twice in one day; it must be my lucky day."

Feeling my face begin to pinken at the sudden attention from all the eyes in the room, I simply smiled back at him. Thankfully, Liam and Patrick chose that moment to make an appearance, and Liam winked at me as he slid in the seat next to Theo.

Patrick shut the door and remained standing at the front of the room. "Oh, good. You're all here. I know that Jackson and Scott have both gone over the mission specs in detail with your separate teams. But, as you know, I always like to have a joint meeting when multiple teams are involved to make sure we're all on the same page."

Honestly, I was surprised that Patrick had included me in this meeting, especially with the other team in attendance. Although I was going as Liam's date and knew more about the mission than I would have absent my connection to Gerard Douglas, Team Falcon didn't know that. And considering the puzzled looks several of them had thrown me, I guessed they were confused by my presence.

As Patrick went over some of the more technical aspects of the teams' responsibilities, I couldn't help but take a closer look at Team Falcon. For once, Melissa hadn't exaggerated one bit. *Holy hotness, indeed.* Of course, I was partial to *my* guys, but the Falcon guys definitely gave them a run for their money.

Hearing my name, my attention snapped back to the front. "Haley will be attending the gala as Liam's date." At Patrick's words, I forced myself to stare straight ahead and not watch for reactions—including Tyler's—to Patrick's use of "date." He continued, "Theo will be posing as Kara's escort for the evening. Those four get to have fun and wear costumes, but the rest of you need to be in black suits, white dress shirts, and black ties. Even if you're assigned to the control room, you should be prepared to work the party, if needed. Chase is off the hook since he's running tech from the suite."

"Excuse me, Patrick," one of the members of Team Falcon spoke up. Between his sandy brown hair, square jaw line, and striking blue eyes, he was classically handsome with a rugged twist. "No offense to Haley," his attention turned to me, "but why is she here? We all know that Liam always takes a date to these events, but it's usually some clueless socialite. And now we have an administrative assistant in our confidential mission meeting? What—"

"Cool it, Scott," Jackson interrupted. Although he was reclining comfortably in his chair, I'd never seen his expression so severe. "We're just covering the basics in this meeting, and as a Zenith employee, Haley is under a strict NDA. You have nothing to worry about."

Scott smirked. "So it has nothing to do with the fact that's she's dating Liam, or is she shacking up with Theo and Knox? I can't keep track."

Shocked by his statement, I swallowed my gasp and watched Knox rise to his feet with extreme slowness. He leaned over the table, his figure imposing and his face ferocious. "I suggest you stop there, Burke. You know that I refuse to be involved in the ridiculous rivalry between our teams. But, if you continue to speak about Haley in that way, you will regret it."

Patrick cleared his throat. "Look, Scott, I should have notified you that Haley would be attending today's meeting. But I approved Jackson's request, and I stand by that. If you have anything else to say on the issue, please make an appointment with my assistant."

Never in my life had I wished so fervently to disappear. I could feel all the eyes in the room trained on me, some in curiosity or annoyance, perhaps, others in concern, but I kept my head down and stared at my fingernails, suddenly the most fascinating sight in the world. Out of the corner of my eye, I could tell that Knox was still frozen in place; what he was waiting for, I didn't know.

"Haley," at the sound of Scott's voice saying my name, I hesitantly looked up. "I apologize. My comments were uncalled for."

Wholly unable to speak in that moment, I simply nodded.

Knox finally sat back down but crossed his arms over his chest, and I could have sworn I actually heard his teeth grinding.

While Patrick went over the list of public figures who were expected to attend the gala, I found myself scrutinizing Scott's reaction to my presence. Honestly, everything they'd discussed so far was pretty mundane. What sensitive information was he so concerned about me hearing? Or was Patrick purposely sticking to the unclassified stuff while I was in the room? There had to be more going on than met the eye, but I couldn't make sense of it. Running security at a charity gala didn't seem particularly mafia-like, but maybe there was something to Melissa's outrageous theory. Who knew what kind of illicit activities the Zenith teams could be running behind the scenes of the legitimate company. *Ugh, Haley, stop being paranoid.*

Wait, did Patrick just list Bill Gates? Holy crap!

Patrick continued talking while my mind chewed on that detail. "So, everyone has the schedule and should know their role. Hunter, can you coordinate gear and ensure everything is accounted for at the end of the night?"

"No problem."

"Any further questions before we wrap up?" Patrick asked the room.

One of the Team Falcon guys raised his hand and Patrick nodded at him, indicating he should speak. "Yes, Logan?"

A lean, but definitely fit, guy with dark brown hair and olive skin spoke. Despite his five o'clock shadow and dark eyebrows, he looked pretty young.

"How will credit work for this assignment since we're combining two full teams?" *Credit?*

Patrick tapped his fingers on the table. "Same as usual. Please remember," Patrick said, glancing around the room, "that for this event, you are one team. There is no Team Falcon or Team Jaguar, simply Zenith."

Everyone nodded, but even I could sense the coiled tension in the room.

"Yes, Scott?" Patrick said, turning slightly to face Scott.

"Have you made your decision on the chain of decision?"

Patrick nodded. "Yes, thank you for reminding me. Jackson will have final say. And on that note, I think we're finished." Patrick said as he rose from his seat. Everyone else followed suit, erupting into conversation while most of Team Falcon filed out of the room.

"Haley, may I speak to you for a second?" I looked up to

see Tyler watching me with worry in his eyes. *Oh, geez. Could this day get any more awkward?*

"Of course."

He glanced at Jackson and Knox before saying quietly, "I'm really sorry about what Scott said. I hope you won't hold it against me."

"Thanks, Tyler. But, it's fine, really." I forced a small smile.

"Okay, well, I'll see you around."

Once Tyler had left the room, I looked up to see all of the Jaguar guys staring at me. Desperate to get their attention away from the embarrassment surrounding me, I said, "So, who's up for Taco Tuesday next week?"

JAZZED UP

"Oh, Haley," Theo sang out, waving a flyer in the air as he entered the living room.

I could hear the paper fluttering in the air but studiously ignored him, pretending extreme absorption in my latest book. Not that it wasn't an interesting read, but I knew what Theo wanted, and I wasn't sure I was willing to agree.

"You don't seriously think you can ignore me, right?" Theo said as he plopped down on the couch next to me.

I felt a smirk threatening to betray me, but I held firm and remained focused on the book. A moment later, I snuck a peek at Theo and found him acting disinterested, smiling to himself and humming a tune. Sometimes he was just too cute for his own good. *Strike that, for my own good.* Theo could talk me into almost anything.

Theo leaned closer to me, lightly nudging me in the shoulder with his own. "Whatcha reading, pumpkin?"

Smiling, I held up the front of the book for his inspection and continued to read, or at least pretend to, while he scanned the cover.

"Ahh, yes. What an interesting read *Guns, Germs, and Steel* is," he said in a slightly sarcastic tone. "That must be another one of Jackson's picks."

I nodded and closed the cover, knowing full well Theo had no intentions of leaving me alone. "What's up?"

"You know my friend Drew, the one you met last Friday outside Madame Walska's?"

"Yeah . . ." Oh, I knew Drew, and I knew where this was headed.

"His band is playing at that jazz club tonight, and I really want you to go with me."

I twisted a piece of hair between my fingers as I pursed my lips and remained silent.

"Come on, you need to let loose. And it will be fun, I promise." He inclined his head and looked up at me, his hazel-green eyes wide. "Pretty please?"

After a moment's pause, I finally relented. "Okay." I didn't have a legitimate reason not to. Plus, I knew if I didn't go Theo couldn't either since he had to babysit me tonight. I loved spending time with the guys, but I hated the thought constantly lingering in the back of my mind that they only hung out with me because they had to.

Theo practically jumped off the couch, but then quickly groaned, grabbing his side lightly. "Argh, I can't wait until my fracking injury is healed."

"Only a few more days, right?" I said hopefully.

"Yeah, it's just uncomfortable; the skin is tight. Fortunately, I should be all better by the gala."

I got up from the couch, glancing at the clock in the kitchen.

"Can you be ready in an hour?" Theo asked.

I laughed as I headed down the hall to my bedroom. "Yeah, that shouldn't be a problem."

Once I reached my room, I pulled out the laptop and opened my email. Jessica had been pestering me for more information, pictures even, on the guys while sharing tidbits from her own life. Ever the boy-crazy friend, she had included links to YouTube videos with hair and makeup tips "just in case."

I smiled to myself as I opened the links from her latest email. I loved one of the loose updos she had sent and hoped I wasn't being overly-ambitious. While scanning my limited clothing options, my phone buzzed on my night-stand, alerting me of an incoming text message. I set my outfit on the bed before swiping the screen to read the message.

Liam: What are you up to tonight?

Me: Getting ready. Theo's dragging me to a jazz club.

Liam: The one in Santa Cruz?

Me: I think so. His friend Drew invited us to hear his band play.

Liam: What time are you going?

Me: Heading out in an hour or so.

Liam didn't respond again, so I started getting ready, wondering if he had gotten busy or just didn't have any more to say.

After washing my face and applying moisturizer, I dug through the makeup Theo and I had picked up when we were out costume shopping. When I found the black eyeliner, I shrugged. Tonight was as good as any to attempt it. Leaning close to the mirror, I carefully drew a line along the edge of my upper lashes before gently tracing the lower water line. I added a heavy coat of black mascara and then stood back to inspect myself.

I had to admit that I was pretty pleased with the results. My eyes looked more piercing and the eyeliner created an illusion of even longer and thicker lashes. I grabbed a hair band and bobby pins before heading back to my room.

Sitting cross-legged on the floor in front of the full length mirror, I had the laptop to one side and my hair supplies to the other. I watched the video twice before attempting it myself. When I was finally finished, I was surprised by how close it actually looked to the example in the video. My hair was shiny and mostly swept back, with several loose curls hanging near my face. It was romantic and seductive all at once, and the dangly earrings I selected drew attention to my collarbone and neck.

I stood in front of the mirror, studying my reflection. Tight black jeans, a fitted black V-neck top, and black heels —my outfit was still the simple, classic style that I favored, but it was sexier than normal. And my hair and makeup were definitely stepping out for me, especially with the dark berry lipstick I dabbed on my lips. I honestly wasn't sure whether I had selected this look to blend in or stand out.

Since I had no clue what people wore to jazz clubs, I began to wonder if I would look silly when Theo knocked on my door.

"Ready, songbird?"

I grabbed my phone and shoved it, some money, and my (fake) ID in my back pocket before opening the door. I knew Theo would give me an honest assessment and I trusted his opinion.

His eyes bugged out, and his jaw snapped open before he spoke. "Holy shiitake, Haley. Maybe I should let you get ready on your own more often."

I couldn't help laughing at his reaction; I guessed he approved.

He stuck his head around the corner into the room. "Is Max hiding in there? Your hair looks amazing."

* * *

THEO USHERED me into the club, his hand on the small of my back. Fast-paced, upbeat music filled the space along with chatter. We walked past the bar toward a lower section closer to the stage and dance floor. There were a number of people in the club, but the smaller tables and alcoves created an intimate atmosphere. Before we could select one of the empty round tables, someone called Theo's name.

"Alyssa!" Theo said as he hugged a girl in a red-and-white polka dot dress.

Theo slung an arm around my shoulders. "Alyssa, this is Haley."

She gave me a genuine smile, "It's nice to meet you, Haley. We have a table over there," she said, leading us to a larger alcove surrounded by Theo's friends. Some looked familiar from his birthday party, and I was relieved when I realized Kenzi was absent. They each introduced themselves after Theo presented me to the group. We sat down to enjoy the show; there was a band on stage with a trumpet, saxophone, drums, and bass. The singer was amazing, belting out tunes like they poured from her soul.

When Devin—the friendly guy who brought me a vodka cranberry at Theo's party—approached from the bar, he set a handful of drinks on the table before turning to me. "Haley. What a pleasant surprise."

He grinned, and I sensed Theo's attention on us. Devin, like the rest of Theo's group, was dressed in a glamorous retro outfit. I glanced around at the other patrons, noticing that many wore jeans or dresses and my outfit seemed to fit right in, striking the right balance between dressy and fun.

As Theo talked with his friends, Devin held out a hand to me. "Care to dance?"

Hesitantly, I glanced over at Theo, wondering if he would give me an out. But he just shot me a reassuring smile before I placed my hand in Devin's and let him lead me to the dance floor. *What the heck am I doing?*

With the gala less than a week away, I had to admit this was a good time to practice my non-existent dancing skills. But that thought didn't calm my nerves as Devin placed one hand on the small of my back.

"Have you ever swing danced?"

I shook my head while I tried to ignore everyone else, hoping I wouldn't look like an idiot or fall flat on my face. But as the music played, Devin led me around the floor like an expert.

"But you have." I finally said, feeling confident enough to attempt talking while dancing.

He chuckled. "Yeah, at least once a week. Theo often comes . . . when he can get away from work and school."

I wasn't surprised. I had seen Theo dancing around the loft a number of times and he had moves. The first song ended, leading into another. Other than feeling awkward about the intimacy of dancing with Devin, I was actually enjoying myself. I wished Theo was out there, too; it was probably killing him to have to sit on the sidelines.

When Devin spun me around, he released my hand for a second, and before I could turn back to him, I landed in someone's arms. The air whooshed out of me when I realized Liam had caught me; I shook my head and blinked a few times to make sure I wasn't imagining things.

"Hello, gorgeous." Liam said, practically licking his lips.

Devin appeared at our side, and his eyes darkened as he looked at Liam before glancing at me. "Haley?"

Before I could respond, Liam said, "Sorry, she's taken."

"Hey there, Casanova," I said playfully while pointedly

looking at Liam, hoping to defuse the situation. "What makes you think you can just sweep me off my feet?"

"It's called cutting in. And I just did." Before Devin could respond, Liam spun us around a few times, putting distance between us and Devin as other dancers filled the gap. I shot a worried glance back and Devin, but fortunately another girl had approached him and they were dancing.

Alone with Liam, he said, "So you think I'm a Casanova, huh?"

I glared back at him. "No, I think you're kind of rude."

"Oh come on, Haley." He tilted his head down to look at me, his gray eyes sparkling. "You know better; cutting in is completely acceptable."

He spun me around and then pulled me back firmly into his embrace. "Although, I can't blame him for being mad. I wouldn't give you up without a fight either."

I gave him a dirty look, and he grinned in response. "Come on, sweet cheeks, you're not really mad at me. Stop scowling and dance."

I danced a few more songs, several with Devin and a couple with Liam. Other girls watched Liam, and I couldn't blame them; he looked fantastic in his dark slacks and button-down shirt. Perfect hair, chiseled face, lean body; he was magnetic.

Back in Liam's arms, I noticed again how he was light on his feet, adept at leading, and he fit right in. I don't know why it surprised me that both he and Theo would fit in so well at a jazz club, but it did. Out of the group, they often seemed at opposite ends of the spectrum; apparently not.

"Haley?"

"Yeah . . ."

"How do you define dancing?" Liam paused. "Because based on what I see, you can dance just fine. Although I guess your excuse for not going to the gala was better than 'I have to wash my hair.'"

My head snapped up. "No, I meant it. I've never danced like this . . . with a guy." I finished more quietly.

"Have you danced like this with a girl?" Liam asked, his eyebrow raised.

"Um, no." I laughed. Since he had opened up the gala can of worms, I so wanted to ask him why he invited me. And for some reason, I felt bold enough to.

"Liam. Why did you invite me to the gala?"

"Honestly?"

"Hmm . . . what do you think?"

"Mostly, I thought you should be there because it's our best lead on your dad, and I thought you deserved to be included. Selfishly, I wanted you there with me, having fun."

I still had my doubts that he wasn't just stuck babysitting me, but his answer seemed genuine.

Our pace slowed to match the music as a new song began, the singer's voice adopting a sultry, sensual tone. Liam held me closer; smelling his cologne as he held me in his arms was doing funny things to my head. It was like gravity pulled me closer until my cheek leaned against his chest. *How did that happen?*

When the song ended, I turned for the table. Liam's charm was intoxicating me. He made me feel bold, confident, sexy, beautiful—like the only other person in the room. I needed to back away before I did something I would regret.

Liam gently clasped my wrist, pulling me back. "Where do you think you're going?"

The idea of sitting down was more and more tempting

thanks to a longer-than-normal run with Knox and now the dancing.

"I should check in with Theo; I don't want him to worry about me. Plus, I need a break." I fanned myself, feeling warm and thankful my hair was up.

"I could use a drink. Do you want anything?"

"Just a water, thanks."

As I approached the table, I realized I shouldn't have been worried about Theo. Surrounded by his friends, he was the life of the party, chatting merrily as he sipped on a cocktail. Was this what his life had been like before I came along? Was this what it would be like after I left?

"Haley!" Theo called out. "Having fun? Come grab a seat." He patted the space on the banquette next to him. I nodded and realized as I sat next to him that he had a clear shot of the dance floor.

He leaned closer. "Where did Liam run off to?" He asked, letting me know he had been keeping an eye on me.

"The bar. He should be over soon." I bit my lip.

"What's bothering that pretty head of yours?" Theo asked, his tone light.

"I hope you aren't mad that Liam came. He asked me what I was doing tonight and I told him, but I didn't realize he was going to show up."

Theo laughed. "I'm always glad to see any of the guys, especially Liam. Our schedules don't always overlap, and he loves jazz as much or more than I do."

Although there was a lot of energy in the club, it still had a relaxed, carefree vibe to it. Shortly after Liam arrived with our drinks, Drew's band was announced and came on stage. They were amazing and the crowd clearly loved them.

Out of the corner of my eye, I saw that Kenzi had

entered the club and was strutting toward us. *Ugh, of course she looks perfect*, I thought. She had on a retro-style dress with a sweetheart neckline and a full skirt. Her hair was pulled to one shoulder to show off her halter top that was tied in a bow. I glanced over at Theo to see if he had noticed her entrance, but he was focused on the stage.

I braced myself for the encounter with Kenzi but was distracted when Liam slipped an arm around the back of the banquette, bringing us even closer than we already were. He gently fingered one of my tendrils and leaned into me. When he spoke, his voice was loud enough for me to hear him over the music, but soft enough that no one else could listen in.

"You are enchanting; this hairstyle is officially my favorite."

I continued staring at the stage, hoping everyone would attribute my flushed complexion to the warmth of the club and not Liam's whisperings. Meanwhile, Kenzi hugged several people on the opposite side of the table and was edging closer to Theo. After our little run-in at his birthday, I realized that I didn't trust Kenzi, but I also didn't really know her.

"Hey, Kenzi." I smiled politely as she approached.

"Hi, Haley," she responded as she hugged Theo and then placed a quick kiss on his cheek.

"I'm going to get a drink. Want to come with me, Theo?" Kenzi asked, oozing sexuality.

"Sure. Haley, you okay here?"

I nodded and they headed to the bar, Kenzi holding Theo's forearm. I wanted to be nice to Kenzi, for Theo's sake, but I just did not like her. I didn't want her there, holding onto Theo's arm and hanging on his every word.

Liam's voice startled me from my thoughts. "Come on, gorgeous, let's dance."

Apparently I was a glutton for punishment because I willingly allowed him to lead me to the dance floor. He held my hand, pulling me behind him into the crowd and giving me a nice view of his backside. Of course, he turned his head at that moment, and I flicked my eyes up from his butt to his face. His confident smirk told me that I was busted, but he didn't say anything as he pulled me to face him in his arms.

Despite feeling a little tired, I was actually having fun. *With Liam.* I tried not to linger too long on that thought. After a while, in need of a break and a bathroom, I motioned to Liam and told him I'd be back.

Walking down the dim hallway to the restroom, I felt almost giddy. I had pushed past my comfort zone more than once tonight. Jessica would be proud, probably a little surprised even. Heck, I was even surprised by my boldness.

Amazingly there was no line for the restroom, and I quickly washed my hands, checking my makeup in the somewhat distorted mirror. My skin had a rosy glow to it, and although my hair was a bit looser than when we left the house, it was holding up remarkably well.

I returned to the hall once more, the music blanketing the area with its sound. A large guy approached the men's bathroom. "Hey there."

I looked down to the ground, hoping he wasn't referring to me. We were all alone in the hall, but I figured he was probably a little buzzed but harmless. I continued walking back to the club, but he advanced toward me, passing the entrance to the men's bathroom. I could feel myself tensing up, mentally urging myself to just ignore him and walk by quickly.

He stuck his arm out in front of me, blocking my path. "I said, 'hey,'" he repeated.

"Um, hello." I responded, attempting to duck under his arm.

He leaned forward, getting closer. "Where you going?"

In another time and place, I might have found him attractive, with his shaggy black hair and crooked smile. But, alone with him in the dark hallway, his proximity was unnerving. Crossing my fingers that he would be reasonable, I politely said, "My friends are waiting; please let me by."

"I was just trying to get to know you, Miss Popular. Why don't you stay? I'll be your friend." He slurred the last sentence.

"Maybe some other time." I attempted to go around him, but he placed both of his arms beside my head and angled in. He reeked of alcohol, and I turned my face away to create a little more space between us. He ran a hand down the side of my face, tracing down my neck and collarbone before resting his large hands on my waist.

I shivered from the unwanted contact before ramming my knee into his groin.

He instinctively reached to cover it as he groaned. "What the hell, bitch?"

I lunged away, but he grabbed my forearm and roughly pulled me back to him. Trying not to panic, I shifted to make my next move.

Clutched against him, I stomped on his instep before jabbing my elbow into his solar plexus. This wasn't practice with Ethan, and I wasn't holding back. When he stumbled backwards, I quickly darted away, eager to put distance between us.

"Bloody hell," said a voice that could only be Liam's.

When I looked up, Liam was quickly approaching from the end of the hallway and reached out for me, eyes blazing as he glared at the crumpled figure behind me. He quickly folded me into his arms and ushered me back into the club.

"Haley, are you okay?" Liam said, his eyes full of concern.

I took a deep breath and nodded.

"It looked like you did a number on him, but if he touched you, I swear I will go and teach that rat arsed bastard a lesson he won't forget." Liam's jaw clenched, and for a moment, I seriously worried that he was headed back to the hallway. I just wanted him to stay with me and make me feel safe again.

Theo rushed over to us. "Haley, what's going on? Are you okay?"

Still in shock, I realized I was shaking as Theo wrapped me into a big hug. He pulled away and brushed a lock of hair behind my ear, staring into my eyes. "It's okay. It will be okay." His tone was calm and soothing. "Let's get you home."

I caught sight of Kenzi scowling in the background, but I couldn't really think about anything but getting out of there.

Liam opened the passenger door of his cobalt sportscar and I slid in, quickly wrapping my arms around myself. I was trying not to completely freak out, but I had never been in a situation like that before. I should have reacted more quickly, should never have let my guard down. After almost a lifetime of living on edge, I had become complacent in just a month. Liam reached over and took my hand, gently rubbing circles on the skin near my thumb.

By the time we made it back to the loft, I had calmed down some. Liam opened my door and wrapped his arm around me as we walked up to the house with Theo close behind. I was more than ready for bed, but I felt Liam's arm tense around me, and I noticed Knox sitting in my favorite arm chair, sipping a drink and reading a book. If Knox found out about the incident, he was going to be pissed.

"Have fun?" Knox asked as he set his book aside and took another sip of his drink.

Theo piped up. "Yeah. We went to hear Drew's band at the jazz club. They were awesome." He was putting on a good show, but I wasn't sure Knox was buying it. We were all still a little on edge after the way the night ended.

"Did something happen?" Knox looked from me, to Liam, to Theo expecting an answer.

Liam answered. "There was a slight incident, no big deal."

Knox stood from his chair and crossed his arms over his chest. The shift in the room was making me nervous. He was going to flip out if he knew what happened—of all the guys, Knox was the most protective. "An incident?"

Theo stepped from toe to toe. "Yeah. Just some guy, tried to get too friendly, Haley was a badass and showed him what happens when you don't act like a gentleman. Now let's go to bed." He finished quickly as he started walking toward the stairs and then stopped.

Knox's silence was deadly as he glared at Liam and Theo. I wanted to hide behind one of them.

Liam was finally brave enough to speak. "Look, Knox. Haley's fine, perhaps a little shaken, but she did an excellent job of defending herself. And there was no way Theo or I would let anything happen to her."

The silence in the room stretched on before Knox growled, "It shouldn't have happened in the first place. Why did you leave her alone?"

"I've never had an issue at that club. Besides, she had to use the restroom and there's usually a line so I figured she'd be fine. Did you want me to hold her hand all the way to the stall?"

Knox glowered at Liam and the tension in the room was palpable. It was rare to see any of the guys argue, and I hated that I was the cause of it. And I was getting annoyed. It was bad enough that I often suspected that they talked about me behind my back, but now they were acting as if I wasn't even in the room.

"I wish you'd stop talking about me like I'm not standing here," I blurted out.

I saw Theo's eyes bug out while Knox and Liam turned to look at me. "Although I guess I shouldn't let it bother me. It's not the first time you guys have decided something *for me* without consulting me."

I drew in deep breath. "Haley, would you like to come to Santa Cruz? No? That's okay, we'll just drug and kidnap you. Haley, would you like to be protected twenty-four-seven since we don't trust you to be alone? No? Too bad, it's not your decision."

All three stared at me in shock. Even I was a little surprised at myself, but I was tired of smothering these feelings.

"I am beyond grateful to you guys for all that you've done for me. But you can't protect me forever. And someday, hopefully, I'll actually find my dad. Then I'll no longer be your obligation."

"Haley . . ." Theo said, a pained look in his eyes. But I shook my head and ignored the looks from Liam and Knox as I stalked down the hall to my bedroom and shut the door with a soft click.

AS YOU WISH

Knox and Jackson were in the front seat of Knox's truck talking amongst themselves, and I couldn't be more relieved that they were practically ignoring me. I had no idea where we were going, and I didn't really care either. After the post-jazz club scene at the loft last night, I just wasn't in the mood. Honestly, I would have happily stayed in bed all day if Knox hadn't insisted that I come along. And it's not like I had a choice . . . I wasn't allowed to stay at "home" alone anyway.

I sighed inwardly, trying to reign in the unnecessary bitterness. Obviously, things could be much, much worse. And I should probably try to be nice to Knox after the way I went off on him, Liam, and Theo then stormed out. He seemed almost hurt when I bailed on him for our daily run this morning. And I didn't really blame him. I was acting like an ungrateful brat...even though everything I said was true.

"No input, Haley?" Jackson asked from the front seat.

Umm . . . "What?"

"We were taking bets on what crazy costume Theo has planned for Friday night. In his typical dramatic fashion, he's keeping it a secret. I'm guessing James Bond and Knox is going with Heathcliff."

I laughed. "Heathcliff, really? But, I'm not surprised you guessed James Bond, Jackson, since you named your dog after a Bond character."

"Yeah, well, who wouldn't want to be James Bond? Ignoring the gadgets, cars, and perks of his job, he's a realistic badass—no superpowers or freak accidents needed."

"Yeah, apart from his lack of any relationship of substance and alcohol consumption that borders on excessive, I'd agree." I chimed in quickly to a chorus of laughter from Knox.

"Man, most girls would be distracted by the flashy cars, the good looks, the accent. Not Haley," Knox said.

"I didn't say those things weren't appealing." I smirked.

"Okay, admittedly, he's not perfect. But you should cut him some slack—he has a painful past, an intense job, and can't have a complicated personal life." Jackson interjected, speaking in a tone that almost sounded like he identified with the character on a deeper level. He continued in a lighter tone. "You should read the books if you haven't; they show more insight into Bond's thoughts." I snickered to myself. I'd guessed Jackson was a fan of the books over the movies.

After a few moments silence, sensing we had exhausted the topic of Bond for the moment, I switched gears back to Theo's costume. "Oooh, how about Sherlock Holmes? I think Theo could totally pull off the classic Holmes look."

"That's a good one, although I can't see Kara agreeing to go as Dr. Watson. She's not exactly the sidekick type."

Unable to pass up the opportunity to learn more about Theo's date, I asked, "What type is she?"

Knox chuckled, joining the conversation again. "She's more of the kicking ass and taking names type. She has to be in order to hold her own surrounded by the Neanderthals on her team. I'm still shocked they let her join."

"Why, because she's a girl?" My tone intimated that the idea bothered me. I didn't even know her, but I was suddenly on Kara's side. Why couldn't she be just as good at private security—and whatever else they did—as the guys on her team?

Knox glanced at me in the rear-view mirror, his amusement obvious. "Simmer down, tiger. Everything I've seen of Kara suggests that she's perfectly capable. It has more to do with the guys on the team, specifically Scott. It seems like he would constantly butt heads with Kara, given their similarly dominant personalities."

"Oh. Well, I guess I see your point. While Tyler is always really nice, my one experience with Scott was distinctly unpleasant. I'd probably butt heads with him too."

Jackson and Knox both laughed, and I heard Knox mutter, "no doubt" under his breath.

We pulled into the gravel parking lot of The Buttery and I leapt out of the car. Ethan and Theo had talked this place up so much, I couldn't wait to experience it for myself. Enveloped by warmth and the smell of freshly baked treats, I tried not to feel overwhelmed by the small space that was crowded with noise and people. Most of the small wooden tables were full, which didn't surprise me considering how good the food looked and smelled.

I stood transfixed in front of the beautiful baked goods: cookies piled high, amazing cakes, delicate pastries. Knox tutted playfully and pulled lightly at my wrist.

"Come on, Haley. Let's get some lunch before skipping straight to dessert."

"Okay," I relented, "but I'm not leaving here without at least one dessert."

We joined the line on the opposite side of the small café, and Jackson handed me a menu. As I perused the options, my phone vibrated in my cross-body purse. I pulled it out and noticed a new text message.

Chase: Hola, chica bonita! Thanks to you, I got an A on my Spanish exam.

Me: Excelente! That's great news, Chase. And you deserved it.

After agonizing over the seemingly endless choices of sandwiches, salads, and soups, I finally selected just in time to step up to the counter and order. Jackson paid and grabbed our number before we headed to a table that had just opened up.

After we finished our delicious lunch, I picked up dessert and rejoined Knox and Jackson at the table.

"Not that I'm complaining, considering this delectable cupcake I'm eating, but shouldn't you two be at work? Especially you, Jackson. It *is* a Wednesday. In the middle of the day."

"What?" Jackson said, feigning indignance. "I'm not allowed to take a day off now and then?"

"I don't know, are you? Do the mice play when the boss is away?"

"Hey, now," Knox interrupted. "We don't use the 'b' word around here. Jax is our fearless leader, but he's not now, nor will he ever be, my boss."

Jackson scoffed at Knox. "Call me whatever you like, but I still get to tell you what to do. Deal with it." He turned back to me, swiping a curly lock of black hair off his forehead, "Anyway, I do spend more time in the office than the other guys. But I work remotely sometimes, and I take a day off now and then."

Knox grinned, "And when he says 'a day off,' what he really means is that he's checking his phone twenty times an hour. Just wait for it."

Jackson shook his head good-naturedly. "Don't let Knox fool you. He's equally committed to his job; he's just sneakier about it."

"Well, given how committed you both are to your jobs, what did I do to deserve the honor of your company? It seems like you'd have better things to do on your rare day off than take me to lunch."

"Who said we were just taking you to lunch?" Knox replied.

I sighed. "Regardless, you know I really don't need one, much less two, babysitters. I mean, surely I could at least stay at the loft by myself."

Jackson and Knox exchanged a look before Jackson said, "Haley, why don't we table this discussion until after the gala? I know that you're frustrated, but we still don't know what Douglas is up to. I promise we'll re-visit the issue in the next couple of weeks."

I didn't want to agree, but I didn't have a good reason not to. The gala was just two days away, and I found myself hoping that something, anything, would happen that night to shed light on the situation.

"Okay, but I'm holding you to that promise."

"Understood." Jackson fiddled with his coffee mug before directing his cerulean gaze back to me. "Speaking of the gala, I wanted to ask you if you've thought any more about skipping it."

I started to interrupt, but he held up his hand. "Just hear me out for a minute. Even though I technically approved your attendance, I still think it would be best if you didn't go. Beyond the possibility that one of Douglas's men will recognize you, this is a very public event." His voice started to strain with agitation. "There will be press there; your picture could end up in the paper." He stopped for a moment, adjusting his polo shirt as if it was strangling him. "I just don't think it's worth the risk."

He looked at me expectantly, and I honestly didn't know how to respond. It seemed like he was sincerely worried about me, but maybe it was my imagination. He probably just didn't want to clean up another one of my messes, didn't want his team distracted by my presence.

After a long moment of silence, Knox spoke, his gruff voice unusually soft. "Jax does have a point, Haley. You don't need to be there, and Liam would understand. We'll leave the decision up to you, but you shouldn't feel pressured to go when it's honestly not in your best interest."

I smiled then, warmed by his concern. "Thank you, but I really do want to go. I've obviously never even been to a school dance, so it's not like I can pass up this opportunity. I promise to try my best to blend in and stay out of the spotlight. I can't imagine the press being interested in me anyway; I'm sure there will be plenty of more newsworthy attendees."

Jackson shook his head with a loud sigh. "As you wish."

Laughing, I replied, "Why, Jackson, I didn't peg you as a fan of *The Princess Bride*."

He shrugged. "I may have seen it once or twice."

I figured after a quick lunch, it would be back to work for Knox, at least. But as the clustered shops and homes of

Santa Cruz faded into ocean and farmland, that was looking less and less likely. Driving north on Highway 1, the road signs indicated that we were heading toward Half Moon Bay.

I chewed my lip. "Where are we going?"

"You'll see," Knox responded, and I saw him look at me in the rear-view mirror, the corner of his mouth twisting up as if he was suppressing a secret. *Was that an undercurrent of excitement?* Knox so rarely got excited about anything, wherever we were going, it must be big.

"You're not kidnapping me again, are you?" I shot him a playful glare.

"Just for the afternoon. I promise you'll be back to the loft by dinner."

Sensing I wouldn't get any more answers out of them, I focused on the passing scenery as we made our way up the coast. With the ocean to our left, the road was windy and snaked around corners and past precipices that I dared not look over.

My phone vibrated in my purse, distracting me from the breathtaking scenery.

Theo: What does a skeleton say before dinner?

No clue, I thought, as I racked my brain for clever responses.

Me: Dig in?

Theo: Bone appetit!

Me: Ha ha ha. So cheesy.

Wanting to smooth over any hurt feelings from last night, I decided to try and keep things light.

Me: Speaking of food—guess where I had lunch today.

Theo: Hmmm . . . Walnut Avenue Café?

Me: The Buttery!

Theo: Finally. I'm so jealous.

Me: You should be. You were right—it was delicious and my cupcake was amazing.

Theo: Haven't you figured it out by now? I'm always right!

When I put my phone away, I was surprised to realize I had a smile on my face. Theo just had that way about him—he could always cheer me up. And, as much as I started the day wanting to avoid all the guys, Knox and Jackson had gone a long way toward putting me at ease again. For being the two most intense guys on the team, they'd been remarkably laid-back, playful even. Although Jackson was still slightly standoffish with me, I felt like we were slowly warming up to each other.

When Knox turned off the main highway onto a smaller road, we were surrounded by farmland, and I wondered what on earth we were doing. When he parked in a large gravel parking lot, I was still in the dark as to their plans.

Jackson and Knox got out of the truck while I remained in the back seat, until Jackson called to me. "Come on, Haley."

"I'll just wait in the car."

Knox shoved his hands in the pockets of his jeans. "That's fine. We'll just be over in the pumpkin patch. I guess we can pick one for you."

After a second, what Knox said sunk in and I shook my head as if to clear it. "Wait. Did you say pumpkin patch?"

"I did indeed." His green eyes sparkled.

"You guys brought me to a pumpkin patch?" I said again with a mixture of enthusiasm and disbelief, still not quite comprehending that was the case despite the landscape and the sign that had a huge pumpkin painted on it. I scrambled to get out of the truck, practically tripping over myself.

As we walked through a large gate, an employee greeted

us before letting us loose on the farm. It was the perfect fall day, cool but sunny, and the clear sky was an amazing shade of blue. A variety of pumpkins in all shapes, colors, and sizes were stacked in large piles bordered by bales of hay.

Fields of corn and a wooded area enveloped us. The scene was idyllic; it blew the pumpkin farms near Coleville out of the water. The thought made me miss my dad and wonder what he was up to at the moment. Before I could dwell too long on it, Knox grabbed my wrist and pulled me in the direction of the trees.

"Labyrinth first, then pumpkins."

Knox, Jackson, and I followed the signs past the pumpkin patch and through a wooded area. When we emerged on the other side, we found ourselves in the middle of a large field that had been ploughed. Having expected a maze that would be knee height at most, I was completely unprepared for the fortress of hay that stood before me. *Whoa.*

Walls of hay that had to be eight feet tall loomed over the landscape and dominated the entire clearing. The smell of hay permeated the air, reinforcing the feeling of fall. I was so excited, I was bouncing on my toes while a wide grin stretched across my face. I could feel Knox's eyes on me and looked back at him, surprised at the warmth of his own smile.

"I guess this was a good choice?" Knox said.

"Yes! Thank you, it's amazing!" I said, launching myself at him then wrapping my arms around his torso. I could feel the rumble of his laughter as his chest shook beneath my cheek and he squeezed me in return.

Jackson darted into the maze calling out, "Last one to the finish buys ice cream."

Never one to turn down a challenge, I charged into the

maze behind him with Knox in close pursuit. Jackson was quickly out of sight, and Knox and I were separated when the maze opened into several paths. I jogged through the maze, but when I hit a dead end with a knight in armor, I knew I'd have to pick up the pace to have any chance of beating Jackson and Knox.

I took a right turn and the walls curved; I found myself spiraling toward what I guessed was the center of the maze. Groaning, I stopped for a moment and debated turning back the way I had come, but decided to push forward. Surging forward once again, I finally wound back out of the spiral, nearing an intersection. Still jogging while looking to my left at another knight on display, I narrowly avoided colliding with Jackson coming from the opposite direction.

I could hear Knox, even over the bales of hay. "Better hurry, I can practically taste the finish line!"

Under my breath I muttered, "crap," as Jackson shot me a challenging smirk before jogging in the direction of Knox's voice. Determined to not come in last, I raced ahead and almost caught up with Jackson before he shot ahead in a burst of speed. I started sprinting and attempted to pass him, but the walls were too narrow.

When we suddenly burst out of the end of the maze, Jackson and I were both laughing, and he barely seemed winded as he beat me to the finish. Knox was leaning back on the bales of hay, relaxing like he had been there for hours.

I couldn't help smiling as I said, "Ice cream is on me. No arguments."

"As you wish," Jackson responded, the corners of his lips curving into a grin.

Browsing the impressive display of pumpkins, I still couldn't believe how thoughtful Knox and Jackson had been. I only briefly mentioned my pumpkin patch memories at our Taco Tuesday dinner. And yet, they had both taken the day off to spend it with me, doing something they knew I would love, once again making the idea of leaving them incomprehensible.

23

QUEEN OF HEARTS

I CLOSED my eyes as Max combed, twisted, and pinned my hair. I couldn't see what she was doing, but she had a light touch, and I found her presence calming as we prepared for the gala. My stomach had been a ball of nerves all day. Not only was I attending a costume gala with Liam as some sort of pseudo-date, it was hosted by the man responsible for my dad's disappearance.

Gerald Douglas. I tried to stayed calm at the thought of him, feeling marginally better by the fact that his wallet would definitely be taking a hit from Zenith's services tonight. Team Jaguar's suite at The Corinthian alone had to have cost a pretty penny judging by the high-end furnishings of the bedroom I was in. With its own (quite large) private bathroom, it was one of two bedrooms attached to a living room and kitchen.

Theo and the rest of the guys were busy getting ready for the gala, and I hadn't seen them since lunch. I knew that Chase was nearby, setting up his tech gear in the other room of the suite while his counterpart from Team Falcon did the same in the control room. Was this what most of their

Zenith assignments were—elegant parties that seemed more like play than work? I knew my perspective was skewed since I wasn't actually working the event, but this was definitely not your normal job.

Max's voice called me back to the present. "You okay, Haley?"

I opened my eyes and forced a smile. "Yeah," I paused, fingering the delicate edge of the silk floral dressing gown I was wearing. "I've just never been to anything like this and I'm kind of nervous."

She nodded her head. "Totally understandable. Sometimes I do hair for weddings. You should see the brides—some are calm and collected, but others totally flip out. Don't worry; you're going to look fantastic, and I'm sure you'll have fun."

She held a bobby pin between her lips as she said, "You have to! You're going to a costume ball for crying out loud." I couldn't help but laugh and felt myself relax ever so slightly.

When Max finished, I still hadn't seen my hair, but there was no time as the makeup artist was already fluttering around me. Having never worn much makeup, and having never met the guy currently unpacking his absurdly large wheeled makeup case, I sincerely hoped I wouldn't look like a clown. He was beautiful (definitely not a word I usually associated with men) with tan skin, rich wavy brown hair, and a slim but fit build.

"Hi, Haley," he held out his hand, "I'm Mateo." I shook his hand, noticing how incredibly soft his skin was.

"Wow, I've never seen so much makeup. I had no idea . . ." I trailed off, fascinated by his collection of powders, brushes, pencils, and lipsticks. He was definitely an artist, and it made me miss my sketch books and art supplies that had gone up in smoke.

Mateo flashed his brilliant white teeth at me and dug into his supplies. "You're so naturally pretty, I can't imagine you wear much makeup. But don't worry, you're in good hands."

Mateo stood back as if he was evaluating me before glancing at his phone. Then he quickly set to work, grabbing brushes and creams and asking me to close or open my eyes at random. I closed my mouth and breathed through my nose while he stood in front of me. Although his cologne was pleasant, I felt slightly awkward and was afraid if I opened my mouth I would be breathing on him. *What is the protocol for getting your makeup done?*

"What's your usual makeup routine?"

"I don't have much practice, so I usually stick to the basics—mascara and lip gloss."

"Can't go wrong with those." I could hear the smile in Mateo's voice, and I felt a few gentle brush strokes along my cheek. "But sometimes it's fun to be a little flashy. And you are definitely going to turn heads tonight, although I'm sure that's a pretty common occurrence for you."

It was hard to tell how much time had passed, but after he applied lipstick to my lips, he had me open my eyes so he could line them and add mascara before he stood back again.

"Perfection." He smiled, clearly pleased with his work.

Mateo handed me a bottle of lip gloss for later and wished me a fun evening before leaving me alone in the room. I was dying to see what Max and Mateo had done to me and crossed my fingers that I would love it.

Standing in front of the mirror, I was speechless. I looked

like myself, yet I was astonished at how glamorous I appeared. The makeup was dramatic but tasteful. And my hair . . . *Wow.* Half my hair was pulled back, leaving the rest cascading down my back in curls. An assortment of twists and braids kept the hair out of my face apart from a few tendrils.

I admired my costume once again before walking to the large window to watch the sun set over the skyline. It wasn't quite time to get dressed, and I needed to compose my thoughts before the evening ahead. Running my fingers over my sapphire silk bustier, I couldn't believe the effort Theo had gone to for me. More than that, I couldn't believe this was my life; it felt more like a dream.

A few minutes later, there was a muted knock on the door before Theo's muffled voice called, "Can I come in?"

The door opened, and I glanced over my shoulder as Theo entered the room, standing tall in his perfectly fitted tuxedo with a white shirt, cufflinks, and black bow tie. His hair was combed to the side and gelled into a wavy style. Ever stylish, Theo had outdone himself. I had never seen him look so handsome, sexy, even. I snapped my jaw shut as I stood facing him. If I hadn't been so distracted by his appearance, I probably would have been concerned by his own silence.

"Wow, Haley," he half-whispered, "you . . ."

His eyes moved over me like a soft caress, skimming me from head to toe then back up again. When he met my eyes, he was still somewhat quiet. "You . . . just. Wow," he exhaled.

At the sound of my phone alarm buzzing, Theo seemed to snap out of his trance. He shook his head as if to clear it and came closer, holding my hands in his.

"Right. I have to meet up with Kara, a.k.a. Daisy Buchanan, but I wanted to wish you luck."

I smiled. "I should have known you'd choose something classic and glamorous. You are the perfect Jay Gatsby."

"Thanks! Now it's time for the finishing touch," he said as he pulled a velvet pouch from his pocket.

"Really?" I smiled. "Theo, how could you possibly give me anything more? Thank you for a wonderful day; all of this is beyond my wildest dreams."

Theo smiled, looking genuinely pleased by my comment, his eyes sparkling. He revealed a beautiful and delicately fashioned gold diadem and placed it in my hair before stepping back.

"There."

"Sincerely, Theo. Thank you."

Just when I thought my life couldn't be any closer to a fairy tale, he gently lifted my hand to his lips. "My pleasure, my lady." He bowed gallantly at the waist. "Now I better get going. See you downstairs."

I carefully pulled the sapphire-colored dress off the bed and slipped into it. The silky bustier gave me structure and support, and the velvety dress felt sensual as it conformed to my curves. I looked down, concerned by the low neckline of the dress combined with the lifting effect of my undergarments. *Too much?* I hoped not because it was too late now.

With my shoes on and purse in hand, I stood to face the mirror and admired the stranger standing before me. The costume was even better than I remembered between the bell sleeves and the way it draped on my shoulders. The gold diadem was the perfect finishing touch, complementing both the beading along the neckline and the embellished belt. Tonight I wasn't Haley Jones, a girl who had never been kissed and was struggling to find her place in the world; I was Lady Guinevere, the queen of men's hearts and ruler of a kingdom.

Not normally one for selfies, I quickly held up my phone wanting to capture the moment for myself and Jessica. *She is going to flip.* Smiling at the thought of Jessica, I knew she would be blown away by the hair, makeup, and the dress. I certainly was. I took a deep breath, knowing it was almost time to leave.

I quietly entered the hallway and glanced around, all the while trying to smother the nervous butterflies threatening to overtake me. Through the open door to my right, I could see Chase sitting at a table surrounded by computers, tech gear, and talking into a headset. He glanced my way and then did a double take before his jaw dropped. I waved sheepishly, smiling quickly before proceeding to the living room. I could get used to dressing like this; I loved the way my skirt lightly swished about my legs as I moved.

At the end of the hall, Liam stood with his back to me; a cape the same color as my dress hung from his shoulders and black leather riding boots covered his legs. When Liam turned to face me, I felt his eyes drink me in as he walked toward me in his silver chainmail with a broad leather belt and black pants.

"You look ravishing," Liam said, his lips spreading into a wide grin.

"Thank you; you make an excellent Sir Lancelot." I didn't dare tell him how good I really thought he looked. "Where's your sword? Wouldn't a knight carry one?"

"All of my weapons are concealed this evening."

When I heard someone clear his throat angrily, I turned and felt my heart rate escalate at the sight of Knox. He stood facing me, his broad shoulders filling out an impeccably tailored black suit, white shirt, and black tie. His blond hair was parted and styled, not even looking like he had run his fingers through it yet. He looked professional, not to mention incredibly sexy.

Holy shiitake! I doubted Theo would approve of me stealing the phrase in reaction to his brother's hotness, but I couldn't help myself. *Is it warm in here?* I was seriously tempted to start fanning myself.

"Ready?" Liam asked.

What? I snapped my attention back to my spectacularly dashing date. *How am I going to survive this evening?* These guys were a major distraction on the best of days, let alone when they were prancing around looking like freakin' James Bond and a knight in shining armor.

"Yep," I chirped before cringing inwardly.

"Oh wait, we need a picture first." Liam handed his cell phone to Knox before grinning at me and wrapping his arm around my back. I could feel Knox's green eyes watching me, smoldering.

After a quick picture, Knox and I followed Liam out to the hall. As I brushed by Knox on my way through the door, he gently placed a hand on my lower back to usher me out. He leaned over, his voice low and gravelly in my ear. "You are stunning."

I bowed my head, attempting to hide the bashful smile that automatically appeared at Knox's unexpected compliment.

"You have the room key and your phone, right?" Knox asked as the elevator descended to the lobby.

"Yep." I held up my purse.

"Good. If you feel at all uncomfortable or unsafe, return to the room. Chase will be there all night."

I smiled and shook my head. Knox was back in protective mode. I stole one more glance at him as we exited the elevator, admiring how ridiculously good he looked. Not that I could think of a time when he didn't look good. Casual, business casual, professional, athletic, shirtless—nope, every version of Knox was amazing.

When the elevator doors opened, we were greeted by the sound of voices and music. Knox marched off in one direction while Liam offered me his arm and I gladly accepted, bracing myself for the crowd ahead. We walked past reception and toward the main entrance where a red carpet led up the stairs and into the foyer. Guests were photographed as they arrived, many exiting from limousines before heading up the stairs.

The costumes were all over the place. I was certainly impressed with the effort some people put in, while others shocked me with their lack of costume. I particularly enjoyed the period costumes and some of the more glittery, over-the-top outfits.

I had visited the hotel with Jackson for dinner, but I was totally unprepared for the complete transformation before me. Large round tables covered the back half of the ballroom, draped with black tablecloths, flower arrangements in rich reds and purples, and candles. The large chandeliers were dimmed, creating an atmosphere that was romantic and inviting. A band was already on stage providing background music, and space had been cleared for a dance floor.

"Want to check out the silent auction? See if anything strikes your fancy."

"Sounds good." I smiled, hoping Liam couldn't tell how nervous I was, or that I had no clue what a silent auction was.

Liam snagged a glass of champagne from a passing waiter as we walked toward a room off the side of the main ballroom.

"Aren't you on the clock, so to speak?" I whispered to

Liam.

He chuckled lightly and said, "Yes, but it's my job to blend in," before sipping the champagne.

Most of the people in The Phoenix Room were lined up at the bar or scattered around the room looking intently at items on the tables that lined the perimeter. In front of each item was a piece of paper with names in one column and a dollar amount in the other one. The first table had sports tickets, signed jerseys, and other memorabilia. Even with just a few bids, many of the dollar amounts were already at several hundred dollars and a few hovered closer to one thousand dollars. *What the . . .?*

"How about tickets to the U.S. Open?"

I glanced at the sheet. "You can't be serious? The current highest bid is $1,500."

"Is that a no then?" Liam smiled as he walked further down the table, pulling me with him. *Was he joking?*

"I would bid on the tennis lessons for you, but I'd rather continue to teach you myself." Liam glanced down at me, his look mischievous and seductive.

"Well you are *the best.*" I said, making air quotes as I emphasized "the best."

"And you deserve nothing less than the best, gorgeous."

"You're too sweet," I said in a sickly-sweet tone, but his charm was irresistible.

Liam pulled me more quickly to the next item. "Ohh, darling. I'm sure you couldn't resist a romantic getaway to a cabin in Aspen."

I snickered. "I think I'm good on cabin getaways, but thanks." Liam gave me a knowing smile.

"Actually, *darling,* if there's a tropical island escape, we should bid on that." If Liam was aiming to blend in, I could play along.

Liam raised an eyebrow. "I like the way you think. If we see one, I will win it for you." He lowered his voice, his lips hovering near my ear. "And don't worry—no bikinis necessary." I rolled my eyes.

When Liam bid on season tickets to the San Jose Opera, I had to say something. "I think you're taking this blending in thing a little too far. Are you trying to start a bidding war?"

"No, I want those tickets. If you play your cards right, I might even take you with me if I win." He winked.

I couldn't help myself, I snuck a glance at his bid before we moved on. *Seriously? I hope Liam has a lot of money.*

Another waiter passed by with appetizers and I snagged a few. I was starving and thankful we were headed for our table. Most of the tables were filling up like ours, and I hoped it wouldn't be long until dinner was served.

We passed a couple dressed as Scarlett and Rhett, an adorable Holly Golightly, and a Cat in the Hat. There were even a few more Gatsbys, but none looked half as good as Theo. Toward the perimeter of the room, I noticed two guys in black suits and realized it was Hunter and Logan from Team Falcon. I had yet to see Ethan, Jackson, or Tyler, although I was guessing Jackson would be in the control room all evening with Scott.

As we neared the table, I saw Theo hold a chair out for Kara while he waited for her to be seated. She looked fabulous. Her blonde wig was cropped into a short bob and accessorized with a beautiful diamond headpiece. And her silky dress with sequins looked perfect on her petite, athletic body. She smiled at me, and I returned it as Liam pulled out my own chair. I had no idea what the rest of the night held, but I was already enjoying myself.

24

HOLDING COURT

An older gentleman in a floppy hat, rumpled button-down shirt, and rolled-up pants held up by red suspenders pulled out the chair next to mine, setting his canvas bag on the floor. His costume was boyish and endearing, and once he was seated, he offered a hand.

"Good evening. I'm Reginald Drake." He spoke the words with a slight accent, the sounds of his vowels drawn out. His smile was warm and friendly.

"Are you sure about that?" I smiled. "Because you look more like Huckleberry Finn."

"Pretty and smart; your date is a lucky man."

Liam turned our way and stretched out his hand toward Mr. Drake. "Yes, I am. I'm Liam Carlyle, and this is Haley Jones."

"Pleasure to meet you both," said Mr. Drake. "Let me guess . . . Lancelot and Lady Guinevere. Am I right?"

I nodded, glad that it was apparent, especially compared to many of the other costumes. I had read a lot of books, but some of the costumes were completely indecipherable.

An older woman with beautiful gray hair pulled back in an enormous pink silk bow took the seat next to him. It took me a minute to process what her costume was as I assessed the white summer dress that covered her from neck to ankle, large silk bow tied at her waist, and basket full of flowers.

Reginald gave her a quick kiss on the cheek before introducing us. "Haley, this is my wife, Mary Drake."

"Pleased to meet you. Your costume is delightful."

She smiled. "Thank you. I always loved *The Secret Garden* as a young girl."

Meanwhile, Liam introduced himself to the girl seated on his other side, but all chatter quieted as a woman walked across the stage to a microphone. She was dressed as a very impressive, very scary Miss Havisham from *Great Expectations*. From the tattered Victorian-era lace wedding dress to the pale skin and white hair, I was almost scared of her.

"Ladies and gentlemen," she said into the microphone, and the room grew quiet apart from the movement of servers entering and exiting the ballroom with trays of covered dishes.

"Good evening. My name is Charlotte Waterhouse, and I am the Executive Director of Golden Gate Literacy. Our organization has been making a difference in the lives of Bay Area children for the past twenty years. Much of our success is thanks to people like you who support our mission of children's literacy."

She paused for a round of applause and beamed at the audience. While she continued speaking, I scanned the room, appreciating the variety of costumes. I sneaked a glance at Liam, still rather in awe of my handsome date. *Date? Not date?* The verdict was still out on that one. Not that it truly mattered, but for some reason I really wanted to know.

Lost in my observations, my ears immediately perked up when Charlotte mentioned the name Gerald Douglas. I had yet to see him and could feel my anxiety mounting.

"As I was saying," Charlotte continued, "we are incredibly grateful for the support of our many donors and volunteers. And tonight, I'd like to say a special thank you to our co-host and guest of honor, Gerald Douglas. Mr. Douglas, please stand so we can properly recognize you."

I held my breath and tried to remain calm as I watched Gerald Douglas rise. Despite his costume—a black suit with tails, white shirt, and black cravat—he looked exactly as he had on his website. It wasn't until I took note of the dark mustache and black raven on his shoulder that I realized he was paying homage to "The Raven" by Edgar Allan Poe. From across the room, he smiled and wave at the crowd before taking his seat once more.

The remainder of Charlotte's speech was a blur, and it wasn't long before a round of applause signaled the end. The room filled with chatter as the waiters circulated with dinner.

Liam was the perfect date, charming and attentive; at least when the girl on his other side wasn't vying for his attention, which was pretty much the entire meal. Dressed as Tinkerbell, her short green dress was covered in glitter, just like her wings and much of her skin.

I enjoyed listening to the Drakes travel adventures, but my attention was drawn by Tinkerbell's voice addressing Liam.

"So, Liam," she said, "Where did you go to college?" I sensed that she was bored with her date and found Liam attractive; not that I blamed her.

Based on Knox's comments, I figured Liam would jump

at the chance to discuss his so-called "glory days," but he simply answered, "Stanford."

"I'm in my second year of law school at Stanford," she said with an air of entitlement.

Out of the corner of my eye, I saw Liam merely nod, but despite his polite indifference, Tinkerbell continued. Referring to the man dressed as Captain Hook seated several seats away from her, she said, "Daddy is a supporter of Mr. Douglas, as is most of this table, it seems. Are you?"

"My uncle is, and Gerald used to sail with us occasionally." I wondered if that was true or just part of Liam's cover story for the evening. Jackson and Patrick had only ever referred to Douglas as a client, so I was leaning toward the latter.

"Oh, I love sailing." She gestured enthusiastically, her Tinkerbell costume sparkling with the movement. "Daddy has a Catalina 315 that we take out on the weekends."

"Yeah," Liam said, looking at me and winking. "I've been meaning to take Haley out on the water."

I had to give him credit; he kept trying to talk to me or at least include me in the conversation. He had introduced us, but Tinkerbell clearly preferred to pretend that I didn't exist. She finally shifted her attention to me at Liam's latest statement; fortunately, Peter Pan asked her something, forcing her to turn away from me and Liam.

The wait staff started collecting dishes while the band took to the stage. Several of the guests at our table had already gotten up when Liam stood and offered me his hand.

"What would you like to do now, my lady?" A silly smile played across his lips as I stood from the chair.

I shrugged my shoulders and leaned toward him. "Is interrogation an option?" Just knowing Douglas was in the room was making me antsy. I was more than ready to confront him, though I knew Liam was unlikely to let that happen.

"Sorry, gorgeous. Unfortunately, that's not on the table."

"And here I thought you were my knight in shining armor," I said playfully. "Have any other ideas?"

"Oh, I have plenty of ideas," Liam said, accompanied by a mischievous smirk.

With his hand on my lower back, Liam steered me away from the table, distracting me with his hilarious commentary on costumes. We had seen everything from the characters of *Alice in Wonderland,* a myriad of fairy tales, and even children's books like *Curious George.* Liam gestured to a couple in Regency-era costumes, clearly Darcy and Elizabeth from *Pride and Prejudice.*

"Alas," Liam sighed somewhat dramatically, "that could have been us."

"Frankly, I think Rhett Butler is a closer fit for you; you talk way too much to make a good Mr. Darcy."

Liam quickly turned his head toward me, surprise flashing across his face before his mouth curved into a grin. "Ouch. I wondered where my cheeky girl was hiding."

I elbowed his side. "You seem to provoke me."

Out of the corner of my eye, I saw a woman's hand swipe across the slope of Liam's shoulders in an intimate gesture. "Where have you been?" She purred. "It's been too long."

Liam looked at her, his jaw clenched. "Kat. This is my date, Haley."

I shook her hand, feeling extremely awkward, and wondered if she was a former girlfriend, fling, friend. One could never be sure with Liam.

"It's a pleasure," she said, openly assessing me while she

spoke. Kat returned her gaze to Liam, giving him a flirty smile. "I'm off to the bar. Come find me if you want to . . . catch up." She sashayed off, her hips swinging in her Katniss Everdeen costume.

Before I could inquire about Kat/Katniss, we were drawn into a conversation with other guests. I listened absently as Liam discussed jazz music with several characters from *The Chronicles of Narnia*. All the while, I was subtly scanning the room for Gerald Douglas, simultaneously craving and dreading the chance to see him up close and maybe even talk to him.

Between the staff, guests, and Zenith members, the space was full of people in constant motion, and the costumes were not helping my search. Considering the fact that I had a known target, I realized how well-trained the Zenith teams must be to effectively scan such a large crowd for unknown security issues. I still had yet to see Tyler or Ethan; I didn't expect to see Jackson unless there was an issue.

I straightened at the sight of Douglas not far away. Liam's arm curved around me and pulled me toward him, his hand resting almost possessively on my hip. Not long after, Liam excused us to check on several items at the silent auction.

When we were alone and not at risk of being overheard, Liam spoke in a low voice. "Haley, do you need to go back to the room?"

"No, I'm fine."

"You know it's always an option if being here is too much." He gently brushed my hair over my shoulder, his hand resting lightly on my collarbone.

"It's not. I'm just so close to him and I want answers."

Liam's face softened, his gray eyes staring into mine. "I know, but we have to do this a certain way. Okay?"

I nodded and he released me.

The crowd parted just enough that I finally caught a glimpse of Ethan standing against the wall, his gaze zeroed in on me. Dressed in his black suit, he looked imposing and, of course, incredibly handsome. But, the scowl on his face was what really caught my eye. I furtively glanced around in case I was mistaken and he was actually focused on someone else. *No, he's definitely glaring at me.*

When I gave him a tremulous smile, his expression remained unchanged, and my confusion increased. He wasn't usually quick to smile, but I expected at least a knowing smirk from him. *Maybe he is just concentrating on the job?* Somehow, that didn't seem right. *What is his problem?*

Liam clasped my hand, and I looked up at him, breaking eye contact with Ethan. Liam asked me to dance, and I agreed, following him to the dance floor. When I glanced back once more to where Ethan had been standing, he was gone.

Liam took me in his arms, and I felt surprisingly relaxed. I'd never admit it to him, but Theo did me a favor by coercing me into joining him at the jazz club. If I hadn't danced with Liam and even Devin that night, my nerves would have been exponentially greater among all of tonight's glamorous guests.

When Liam's left hand drifted up my back and his fingers began to slowly caress my bare shoulder, my steps faltered, and I forced my body to refrain from shivering at his unexpected touch. Unable to stop myself, I angled my head up just enough to find his lips pressed into a smug grin. Not wanting to make eye contact while he continued stroking my exposed skin, I found myself fixated on his mouth and how the fullness of his lower lip gave him a natural pout.

"Haley," he whispered, breaking through my fog. "You really are the most enchantingly beautiful woman in the room."

His enticing voice compelled my eyes to travel all the way up to meet his. Expecting to find his usual flirtatious expression, I was surprised to see only earnestness instead. I looked away and gave a small laugh. "Thank you, Liam, but you can stop with the flattery. It's not like this is a real date."

Liam pulled me even closer, completely eliminating the space between us. "It's as real as you want it to be, gorgeous."

Stunned, I fought the heat threatening to inch up from my chest to my cheeks. Knowing that I couldn't take Liam's words at face value, I tried not to read too much into them. Even if Liam did consider our evening a date, he went on dates all the time. It didn't mean anything. It couldn't.

When I felt a tap on my shoulder, I turned to see Theo standing behind me with a wide grin. "Hey, butterfly. May I cut in?"

Sighing in relief at the chance to get a break from Liam's intensity, I moved out of Liam's arms and into Theo's. "Of course."

If Liam was disappointed, he hid it well and pointed to The Phoenix Room before heading that direction.

"So," Theo's voice was impish. "Is our noble Lancelot behaving himself?"

I laughed, "Does he ever?"

"No, it's not in his nature to be good when in the presence of a beautiful maiden."

"Yeah, I've noticed." My eyes unconsciously sought Liam, now surrounded by at least three women on the edge of the dance floor. "He's just a little *too* charming."

"Yes, he is," Theo agreed. "You know, if his behavior ever bothers you, all you have to do is threaten to tell Knox. Liam knows Knox will go medieval on his butt, especially when it comes to you."

Choosing not to dwell on why Knox was so protective of me, I said, "I think I can handle myself, but I'll keep it in mind." Hoping to change the subject from Liam and Knox, I asked, "How are things going with Kara?"

"Great, actually. I've never spent much time with her, but she's a fun date. You two would probably get along smashingly, now that I think about it."

As the music changed, Theo groaned. "Haley, I hate to dance and run, but I can probably only get away with one dance with you tonight. I owe you a night of dancing at the jazz club," he said with a wink.

He led me from the dance floor and searched the room before saying, "It seems that Liam has disappeared for the moment. Do you want me to help you look for him?"

"No, I'm fine. I'll just go back to the table for a few minutes. I'm sure he'll find me."

As I made my way toward our table, I kept an eye out for Liam, but had yet to see him. Thankful for a momentary respite from conversation, I sank into my chair. The event was still going strong, and it seemed like the noise from the dance floor had only increased as the evening wore on.

"Hi, Haley. Are you having a good time?" Tyler asked, slipping into the empty seat next to me. Like the other Zenith guys, he was in a black suit, but his was a more stylish version with a subtle pinstripe vest and black bow tie.

Happy to see him, I smiled. "Yes, I am. As much fun as it is to dress up, I think my favorite part is the people-watching. Some of these costumes are incredible."

"Like that one," he said in a dry tone, pointing to a woman dressed as Moaning Myrtle from *Harry Potter,* complete with the toilet seat around her neck.

I laughed. "Okay, well some are a little on the crazy side, but mostly they're pretty great."

Tyler swept his eyes from my hair down to the shoe peeking out of my skirt. "I have to say that your costume is definitely my favorite. You look absolutely exquisite, Haley."

Not surprisingly, my face flushed at the compliment. "Thank you, Tyler. You look very handsome this evening."

"So . . ." Tyler stretched out the word. "You and Liam."

I shook my head and looked down. "It's not really like that. He needed a date and we're friends."

Tyler chuckled, "Right. Liam Carlyle is *friends* . . . with you."

"Is that so difficult to believe?"

Standing, he said, "A little bit, yeah. Anyway, I would love to chat with you for the rest of the evening, but I'm on the clock. Can I get you a drink before I get back to my post?"

"Thanks, but I'm good," I said before he nodded. Once Tyler was gone, I headed toward the restrooms.

Kara entered the bathroom as I was drying my hands on a towel. When I smiled at her, she paused; I got the feeling she wanted to say something.

"I love your costume, Haley. You and Liam make quite the pair."

I laughed. "Thanks. You and Theo are very glamorous—hands down, the best Gatsby couple here."

"Theo always seemed nice, but I've definitely had more fun tonight than I anticipated."

I laughed. "That's Theo; he can make anything fun."

"Theo and Hunter would really like each other if they could all see past this stupid rivalry."

I huffed out a breath and rolled my eyes. "Boys!"

She laughed. "Tell me about it."

When she walked toward a stall, I called, "See you out there."

After exiting the restroom, I saw two men in black suits stalking down the hall away from me. Even from behind, I recognized that it was Knox and Ethan, and they appeared to be on a mission. While it could have been related to event security, my stomach clenched at the thought that it might be something else.

Knox and Ethan quickly turned a corner, and I hesitated for only a second longer before deciding to follow them. If it wasn't related to my dad, I would return to the gala and leave them to their business. But if it did have something to do with my dad . . .

With no time to lose, I strode quickly down the hallway. I needed to reach the end in time to see where Knox and Ethan had gone and avoid being spotted by Kara as she exited the bathroom. But when I peeked my head around the corner, Knox and Ethan had vanished again. Fortunately, there were no other entrances or exits before the next turn in the hallway.

I approached the second corner and stopped to peer around it. Still no sign of Knox or Ethan, but there was only one place they could have gone—a glass door ahead of me that led to the courtyard. As I approached, I was thankful that the door was mostly blocked from view by trees and other plants. My heart clamored at the thought of what I might find on the other side. But I knew I had to get out there no matter the cost, so I quickly removed my shoes and slipped through the door as quietly as possible.

2 5

GUARDED

HOPING the tree I hid behind provided sufficient cover, I peeked through its branches to see Knox and Ethan speaking to Clive, one of Douglas's personal security guards.

Straining to hear Knox's deep voice clearly, I made out only the end of his sentence. ". . . us the truth about your involvement in Brian Taylor's disappearance."

Clive scoffed. "I have no idea what you're talking about. And even if I did, it wouldn't be any of your business. You did your job and found Taylor. You got paid. It's over." He turned away and started walking for the door on the opposite end of the courtyard from where I was standing.

Ethan moved so swiftly, I barely saw his long arms reach out and pin Clive's arms behind his back. "I don't think so," Ethan said, his voice dripping with amusement.

Knox continued, speaking louder this time. "You must have misunderstood me. We're not giving you a choice here. You will tell us everything you know about Taylor; we know you and your associate pursued Taylor after the explosion,

271

so there's no use denying it." His stance was relaxed, at odds with his harsh words and tone.

"Why do you even care?"

"We've known there was something suspect about this situation from the beginning, so we continued our investigation, and now we need to see it through." Knox paused before redirecting the conversation. "Why don't you start by telling me why you broke into Taylor's office in Coleville?"

Clive struggled unsuccessfully against Ethan's hold. "Why don't you fucking make me?"

Knox lost his relaxed demeanor, growling, "Do you honestly think you still have a choice here?"

"Fine," Clive practically spat at him. "But you're dealing with the fallout when Douglas finds out about your little interrogation. You boys are in way over your head."

"Why did you break into Taylor's office?"

"We didn't have anything to do with that."

"I don't believe you."

"I swear. I don't know anything about a break-in." His voice became slightly whiny toward the end; no doubt Ethan was putting some pressure on him.

"Fine. Then tell me where Taylor is now."

Clive stood there glaring at Knox, refusing to respond.

Knox moved back a few steps and lazily place his hands in his pockets as if he had all the time in the world. "I'm sure the press would *love* to hear about the skeletons in Douglas's closet. And, if you think I won't find every single one, you're out of your mind. Where. Is. Taylor?"

Clive laughed humorlessly. "Whatever, your funeral. We spotted Taylor in El Segundo about twenty-four hours ago."

I forced my hand over my mouth to stifle a gasp. I was

anxious to hear the rest but needed to stay hidden if I was going to have any chance of doing so.

"That's a start."

"We believe he was staying at the Seahorse Inn, but whether he's still there or even in the area, I have no idea."

My ears started buzzing, and I couldn't concentrate on the conversation playing out in front of me. *Oh my god. My dad is alive. I know where he is.* I was bombarded with a surge of thoughts and emotions. Elation. Anxiety. Hope. Uncertainty. Then, I felt a sense of calm. I knew what I had to do.

Glancing toward Knox and the others, I confirmed that they were still preoccupied and quietly slipped back through the door and down the hall. Skirting around corners, I hurried to the elevators, praying I wouldn't be seen by any of the guys. Considering the amount of noise drifting from the ballroom, the event was still going strong, so hopefully they were too busy to notice my absence. *Ha, keep dreaming.*

In the elevator, all I could think about was Chase's presence in the hotel room. Why couldn't he have been downstairs with the rest of the guys? If he spotted me, I'd just have to wing it.

Thankful they had given me a room key, I slid the card into the slot and cringed at the beep that seemed to reverberate in the silent hallway. I peeked into the room and released a deep breath when I didn't find Chase in the main room. Tiptoeing down the hall toward my bedroom, I held the voluminous skirt of my dress to keep it from swishing. When I made it past Chase's closed door and into my bedroom, I practically collapsed in relief.

Knowing I didn't have even a second to spare, I frantically stripped off my dress, leaving my bustier on. I quickly pulled on a pair of shorts and a chambray shirt, not taking the time to button it up. Hurriedly slipping on sneakers then grabbing my phone and purse, I waited at the door for only a second, hoping not to hear any evidence that Chase had left his room.

When I didn't hear anything, I softly headed out of the suite then immediately started sprinting toward the stairs. I couldn't believe I made it in and out of the suite without getting caught. It seemed almost too easy.

My shirt flapped around my torso as I ran down flight after flight of stairs. I was feeling so close to freedom I could taste it. It's not even that I wanted to leave the guys, but I somehow knew that if I didn't get away now and make it to my dad, I would lose my chance to find him. I could not, would not, let this opportunity pass me by. Not when I knew his location for the first time in six weeks.

Finally reaching the first level, I slowly opened the door to the stairwell and peeked out. When I saw that the coast was clear, I exited the stairwell and turned away from the lobby to a side exit I had noticed earlier. So far I had successfully evaded the guys; I tried not to get too excited with each step closer to the door. I avoided eye contact with a few partygoers that I passed and kept my sight focused on the exit.

Only a few feet from the door, a man dressed in black suddenly appeared from a connecting hallway and stepped out in front of me, blocking my way. Halting in my steps, I looked up, inexplicably shocked to find Jackson glaring back at me. *No. No. No. Was my timing seriously that bad or . . .? How did he do that?*

I marched forward, attempting to edge past his imposing form. "Just let me go, Jackson." My heart was pounding.

He shot his arm out, cutting me off. "Not going to happen, Haley."

"You don't understand." My voice took on a pleading note. "We're wasting time just standing here. I have to go after my dad."

Jackson crossed his arms, his stance unyielding. "You're not going anywh—"

"You can't stop me this time," I interrupted. "I refuse to let you order me around for one more second. Now move," I said forcefully, hoping my tone would be enough to remove him from my path. If it wasn't, I seriously debated actually shoving him out of the way.

"Haley, stop being irrational." His voice was cold, ruthless even, cutting off my immediate instinct to protest. "First of all, it's not safe for you to go waltzing off to freaking El Segundo on your own. And we're not wasting time. Knox and Ethan are already on their way there."

"What?" My voice sounded strangled, and I couldn't tell if I was more relieved or annoyed. "Why didn't they take me with them?"

"We don't even know if the intel is correct. Clive could have lied. Or maybe Douglas's people found someone who just happens to resemble your dad. Who the hell knows."

I remained silent, breathing heavily as I tried to sort through the information overload. I wanted to see my dad so badly, or even just confirm that he was alive and okay. And I had been so caught up in wanting it to be true that I hadn't stopped to think it might not be.

Jackson watched me, his expression transforming from frosty to agitated. "Look, Haley. I hope that Knox and Ethan are able to track down your father. You know that they will do absolutely everything they can, and the rest of us will pursue leads from here. But there's nothing you can do right now. You're staying; it's not negotiable." Each word was distinctly punctuated as if to emphasize the point.

I could tell that he wasn't going to budge, but I had to give it one last try. "I'm not helpless, Jackson. And I *need* to go. What if Ethan and Knox find my dad? He'll probably just run unless I'm there with them, unless he actually sees me. Please."

Jackson settled his hands on my shoulders, his indigo eyes boring into mine. "I understand where you're coming from, but you're not giving the guys enough credit. If they locate him, they'll find a way to get word to him that you're with us. I promise."

Frustrated, but trying not to cry, I shook his arms off my shoulders and looked away. "Your promise really doesn't mean much right now, Jackson."

His voice finally soft, he replied, "Be mad at me all you want, but at least you're safe. Come on, I'll take you back to the suite."

Realizing that relenting was my only feasible option, I straightened and said, "On one condition."

He merely raised an eyebrow, waiting.

"You keep me in the loop on every step of the process from now on. Every lead. Every phone call or text from Knox and Ethan. Every team meeting. If it has to do with my dad, I want to know."

Jackson stared at me for several long moments before nodding. "Agreed."

I started walking back to the lobby, tamping down the urge to make a run for it. I knew it was pointless; Jackson would stop me. But there was still a part of me that wanted to try, just to see what would happen. Perhaps it would help release some of the anger and frustration threatening to consume me.

"Haley! Jax!" I looked up to find Liam heading toward us, his chainmail jingling and his cape flowing behind him. Looking back and forth between me and Jackson, he said, "Is everything okay?"

Jackson ignored his question. "Will you escort Haley up to the suite? I have to get back to the control room and wrap things up."

Liam smiled, likely trying to defuse the tension radiating between me and Jackson. "Of course. I'd be delighted."

Jackson stalked off without another word, and Liam gently took my hand, leading me to the elevators. Now that the adrenaline of my almost-escape had dissipated, I was drained of energy, moving on autopilot.

Uncharacteristically quiet, Liam intertwined our fingers and softly brushed his thumb back and forth on the top of my hand. If I wasn't so distracted, I might have been more shocked by this new side to Liam; I'd definitely never considered him the comforting type.

When the elevator reached our floor, he tugged me down the hall, stopping in front of the suite. He leaned against the door and reached for my other hand, using both to pull me in close.

"Why are you so upset? This is the best lead we've had so far; it's a good thing."

Sighing, I replied, "I don't really want to talk about it right now."

Liam drew me a few inches closer. "That's okay. I don't mind not talking." His whisper turned seductive. "There are other things we can do." He pointedly looked down to my chest where my bustier was on full display under my open shirt. "That's a good look for you, by the way."

I didn't know if it was the stress of the last hour or

277

Liam's less-than-subtle lines, but I started laughing, almost unable to stop. *Never mind. Same old Liam.*

"Does that really work on girls? Maybe you're not the suave playboy I thought you were."

He scowled at me playfully. "I feel like I should be offended. You laughing at me like that. Surely it wasn't that bad." When I kept giggling, he finally laughed. "Okay, I admit, it wasn't my best work. But you can't blame me for trying. It's a shame that Lancelot can't even get a goodnight kiss from his lady love."

"Well, we can't have that, can we?" I lifted to my toes and placed a lingering kiss on his cheek. "Thank you for the lovely evening, kind sir."

Surprise then genuine affection crossed his face. "Anything for you, gorgeous."

EPILOGUE

THE CORINTHIAN, LATER THAT EVENING

JACKSON LOOKED up from his chair as Liam crossed the room toward him. "Any luck?"

Liam shot him a smug grin. "What do you think?"

"Good. What did he say?"

"We are scheduled to meet with Douglas early next week. He agreed to cooperate with the Taylor situation."

"Perfect."

"Are you going to tell Haley or do you want me to?"

"We can tell her *after* the meeting with Douglas."

"Seriously, Jackson? You promised to include her on everything."

Jackson paused. "I know, but I don't want to get her hopes up. And you saw how she reacted tonight—we can't risk her running off and doing something reckless."

Liam twirled his signet ring between his fingers, visibly agitated.

"What?" Jackson barked, the frustration evident in his tone.

"You need to tell her; she deserves to know."

"What is your deal with Haley? First you ask her to the gala without running it by me, or the group, and now this?"

"Bloody hell. Are you seriously still pissed about the gala?"

"Yes. You shouldn't have invited her." The tension was growing.

"Jackson, when are you going to learn that you can't control everything?"

"I know I can't. I just thought it would be better to remove her from the situation; instead, you'd have her waltz right through the fucking door."

"Oh please. There was nothing dodgy about the gala and you know it. We were lucky to have caught the break on Haley's dad when we did, but it was purely coincidence."

"Whatever," Jackson sighed.

"You know I'm right." Liam glared at Jackson.

"No. I think you're distracted by a beautiful girl, and you're not thinking clearly."

"*I'm* not thinking clearly? At least I admit my interest. You think I can't tell how much she's affecting you, mate? I'm your oldest friend."

"Why are we even talking about this? She's off limits."

There was a pause before Liam spoke again, his tone softer. "Jackson, you can't let what happened with Emily influence the rest of your life."

"Enough. This conversation is over. It's been a long night and we need to get back to the suite."

ABOUT THE AUTHORS

Autumn and Julia met at work and bonded over their mutual love of historic homes, photography, and good books. While they didn't plan on co-authoring a novel, what started as daydreaming transformed into brainstorming and then actual writing.

Together, Autumn and Julia make the perfect pair, balancing impulsive with indecisive and attention to detail with an eye for the big picture. Despite their different personalities, Autumn and Julia share a common vision in their writing and love bouncing ideas off each other. They see the creative process as a challenge, a game, and delight in living in a world of their own creation.